some sort of
HAPPY

A HAPPY CRAZY LOVE NOVEL

Melanie Harlow

ISBN: 978-1517284640

Someone I loved once gave me
a box full of darkness.

It took me years to understand
that this, too, was a gift.

~ Mary Oliver

chapter one

Skylar

I'm not an awful person, I swear I'm not, but you wouldn't know that if you saw me on Save a Horse (Ride a Cowboy).

Oh, you've never heard of it?

Good.

It's a ridiculous reality show where thirty beautiful girls compete for the love of a hot cattle rancher. To show their devotion, they do super meaningful things like wear red cowboy boots with tiny denim shorts, squeal for him at the local rodeo, and, of course, take their turn on a mechanical bull. This last activity will later be edited into a hilarious #FAIL reel since none of the women ever lasts more than ten seconds, and some not even two.

(If you must know, seven. And it wasn't pretty.)

"It's back on!" My younger sister Natalie bolted from the bathroom to the couch, jostling my arm when she flopped down next to me.

I frowned. "Nat, making me watch myself on Save a Horse is possibly forgivable, depending on how they edit this last segment. Spilling my margarita while I watch it is not." I'd hoped a tequila buzz would numb the shame of watching myself be an obnoxious twat on TV, but so far, it hadn't happened.

In my defense, producers told me to be an obnoxious twat. As soon I got to Montana, they took me aside and said, "We like you, but we want you to be the crazy one people will love to hate, and we'll make sure you stay on the show longer if you're good at it." After thinking it over for a minute, I agreed. After all, the whole reason I was doing the show was to get noticed. If I was just another nice girl who got cut after the first episode, where would that leave me?

Had I known that clever editing would make me look even worse than I'd acted—a feat I'd have sworn wasn't possible—I might have given that decision more than sixty seconds.

"Oh, come on." Always able to see a bright side, Natalie patted my head. "Every show needs someone to hate on, and that person is always the most memorable, right?"

Noisily I slurped up more margarita. "Is that supposed to make me feel better?"

"Yes! Can you name one nice person from a reality show? No," she went on before I could answer. "That's because nice people are not fun on TV."

Sinking deeper into the couch, I watched myself trash someone's outfit on the screen. "They're not making me look fun. They're making me look like a hideous bitch." I picked up my phone and checked Twitter, even though I knew it would be painful. "Yep. Just like I thought. Hashtag skylarsucks is trending. Oh here's a nice one: 'Skylar Nixon is not even pretty. Her mouth looks like my asshole.'"

Natalie took my phone out of my hands and threw it down between us on the couch. "Screw that, people are stupid and just like to hear themselves talk. Listen, you did this show to get your name out there. And it worked! A month ago, you were just a beauty queen from Michigan. Last week, you were in US Magazine! I'd call that a success, wouldn't you?"

"No. They took a picture of me pumping gas, and I looked fat." I shut one eye and cringed watching myself sidle up to poor, hapless Cowboy Dex and flirt shamelessly. "Jesus, I'm even more horrible than I remember. I don't think I can keep watching this train wreck." Tossing back the rest of my drink, I got off the couch.

"You're gonna miss the lasso ceremony!"

"Good." I stomped over to the kitchen counter, which, unfortunately, was still in earshot of the television. For the last month I'd been living in a small, repurposed barn on my parents' farm, and everything was in one long room, kitchen at one end, bedroom on the other. Actually, it wasn't even really a bedroom, just a bed separated from the main area by thick ivory curtains that pooled on the floor. I'd added that touch myself. In fact, one of the reasons my parents let me move in to one of their new guest houses rent-free was to help my mother decorate them. Not that I had a degree in interior decorating—or anything at all. But I did like the challenge of taking a raw space and making it beautiful. *I should have gone to college for design.*

Or taxidermy.

Or underwater basket-weaving.

Or fucking anything that would have given me a real career to fall back on when the whole I'm Gonna Be a Star thing went tits up.

Heaving a sigh, I took my time in the kitchen, plunking a few more ice cubes into my glass and pouring generously from the oversized jug of margarita mix. But I returned to the couch in plenty of time to watch Cowboy Dex give out lassoes to the girls who'd roped his heart that week. Rolling my eyes so hard it hurt, I marveled that I'd managed to keep a straight face during this nonsense. No, even better than straight—my expression was sweet and grateful as Dex handed me that rope. Poor guy. He was cute, but dull as ditchwater. We actually had no chemistry whatsoever, but I'm sure the producers told him he had to keep me around for a while.

Oh, you didn't know producers manipulate things on reality TV to get the conflicts and tension they want for ratings? They do. All the time.

Here are some other secrets I can tell you, although you didn't hear them from me:

Those shows are cheap as hell. All the contestants "volunteer" their time, and the only things that are paid for are travel, lodging, meals, and drinks. For the two months I spent filming, I've got nothing to show but more credit card debt because of all the money I spent on clothes and shoes and hair and makeup.

Speaking of drinks, contestants can have, and are encouraged to have, as much alcohol as they want at the ranch, because a bunch of tipsy women are always more fun to watch than a bunch of sober ones. The showrunners made it a point to ask about favorite drinks during the interview process, and always kept the bars stocked.

Which leads me to my final point. Producers are the masterminds of the show—the contestants are more like puppets. The show might not be scripted, but if you're not saying the things they want you to say, if you're not having the conversations they want you to have, they'll stop the cameras and tell you, "Talk about this." And they edit so shrewdly, snipping out what they don't want or stringing together words said on completely different occasions to create a sentence never uttered by anyone—there's even a name for it: frankenbiting.

Like that—right there. "I never said that," I said, lowering myself onto the couch and wincing when I heard myself remarking snidely, "People from small towns are all small-minded and stupid."

Natalie sucked air through her teeth. "Wow. That was pretty harsh. You didn't say it?"

"No! You can totally tell it's edited—see the way it cut away from my interview to a voiceover? My voice doesn't even sound the same! Those fucking producers were so slimy."

The shot went back to me during the interview, and God, I hated my face. And my stupid girly voice. And who told me that color yellow looked good with my skin tone? "I'm actually from a small town," I was saying. "I grew up on a farm in Northern Michigan, but I couldn't wait to get out of there."

Wait a minute. Had I said that? I bit my lip. I honestly couldn't remember. And seeing as I'd recently moved back to said small town in Northern Michigan, it was particularly embarrassing.

And then it got worse.

"It's nothing but a bunch of drunks, rednecks and religious gun nuts," I heard my voice saying as footage of some unfamiliar, old-timey main street flashed on the screen, complete with a farmer riding a tractor through town. "I'd never go back."

"What?" Furious, I got to my feet. "I *know* I never said that! That footage wasn't even taken here!"

"Can they do that?" Natalie wondered, finally sounding a little outraged on my behalf. "I mean, just take any words you say and mix and match like that? Seems wrong."

"Of course it's wrong, but yes, they can," I said bitterly. "They can do anything they want because it's their show." As I poured margarita down my throat, my cell phone dinged. I grabbed it off the couch and looked at the screen.

A text from our oldest sister, Jillian. She was a doctor and usually too busy for television, but lucky me, she must have found time tonight.

What the hell was that???

But before I could reply, another text came in, this one from my mother.

I thought you said last week was the worst. The thing with the mechanical bull.

My head started to pound. I opened my mother's message and wrote back, **I thought it was! I told you not to watch this show, Mom. They manipulate things. I never said that stuff.** But I knew she wouldn't get it. No matter how often or how well I explained the way editing worked, she still didn't understand. My phone vibrated in my hand. "Oh, Jesus. Now she's calling me," I complained.

"Who?"

"Mom. She's watching the show, even though I told her not to. Do I have to answer this?"

My sister shrugged. "No. But you live on her property. She can probably see in the windows."

I ducked, then sank onto the couch again. Generally, I didn't ignore my mother, but right now I really didn't feel like defending myself or lecturing her *again* on the how-and-why of editing for ratings. I tapped ignore and tossed my phone on the table. "Can we please stop watching this now?" Picking up the remote, I turned the television off without waiting for her answer.

"It's not that bad, Sky." Natalie got off the couch and went to the kitchen to refill her glass.

"Yes it is, and you know it. I just insulted everyone we know here."

"Maybe no one is watching," she said, ever the optimist.

"I seriously hope not." I hugged my legs into my body, tucking my knees under my chin. Glancing out the big picture window, I saw darkness falling over the hilly orchard where I'd grown up. Memories flooded my mind...running through rows of fragrant blossoming cherry trees in the spring, picking the fruit in the summer, rustling through crunchy brown leaves in the fall, throwing snowballs at my sisters in the winter. Maybe I hadn't appreciated it enough when I was younger, but I loved it here. For all its glitz, New York had never felt like home to me. I'd even liked Montana better than Manhattan.

Natalie returned to the couch and leaned back against the opposite end, stretching her legs out toward me. "All right, silver lining. You did exactly what you set out to do—draw attention to yourself. You've always been good at that."

Had she intended to be snide? Natalie wasn't the cryptic remark type, and neither was I. If we had something to say to one another, we said it.

I eyeballed her. "What do you mean by that, exactly?"

"Don't get prickly." She nudged me with one bare foot. "I'm just saying that you know how to work a room. You obviously charmed the producers into wanting you to stay on."

"But not so much that they thought I'd win the cowboy's heart on my own," I pointed out.

She shrugged. "You said yourself you guys had no chemistry."

"We didn't. But why me?" I whined. "Why couldn't they've asked someone else to play the villain?"

"Because they didn't trust anyone else to play it right. They needed someone to act devious and manipulative but who was also beautiful and appealing enough for it to be realistic that he'd keep you on so long. I think it was a compliment!"

I held up one hand. "Please. Everyone there was beautiful. And haven't you heard? My mouth looks like someone's asshole."

She kicked me. "Stop it. You have that something extra—you light up a room, you always have." She slumped like a hunchback and contorted her pretty features. "The rest of us just linger in the shadows, waiting to feed on your scraps."

I rolled my eyes. Natalie was perfectly lovely, and she knew it. She just had no desire to play it up. While I adored cosmetics, she usually went bare-faced. I was a hair-product and hot roller junkie; she let her natural waves air dry. I could easily—and happily—blow a paycheck on a pair of Louboutins; she saved every penny she could and always had.

And that's why she owns her own business at age twenty-five and you're still scrambling to get by at twenty-seven. You might be the big sister, but she's got a shop, a boyfriend, and a condo. What do you have?

I propped my elbow on the back of the couch and tipped my head into my hand. "God, Nat. I really fucked this up. It didn't lead to Scorsese knocking at my door, and I probably just alienated everyone we know."

"Quit being such a drama queen. They'll forgive you once you flash that Cherry Queen smile at them."

"Ha. Maybe I should dig out my crown and start wearing it around town. Remind them they liked me once upon a time."

"Does that mean you're staying here for good?"

Picking up my drink, I took a slow sip. "I guess so, although I promised Mom I'd be out of this guest house by the end of the month. That gives me about three weeks to figure out where to live, or else move in with them." I grimaced into the glass. "I'm such a loser. Moving in with my parents at twenty-seven."

"You're not, Sky. But if you still want to be an actress, why not go back to New York and try again? A lot of people don't break out right away."

How many times had I heard that over the last few years?

I swirled the ice around in the glass. Could I take the New York audition scene again? All the rejection was so disheartening. Then there was living in the city itself. New York had such frantic energy, at every time of day during every day of the week. Once upon a time I couldn't wait to be a part of that. Of course, I'd romanticized it entirely—the life I'd imagined included actually *getting* the jobs I auditioned for, and being able to pay my rent with plenty left over for shoes, blowouts, and trendy nightclubs, where I'd clink glasses with elite theater people who called each other darling and invited me to summer with them in the Hamptons.

Needless to say, that's not how it went.

I spent four full years in New York, and the last year I paid my rent solely by bartending, lying to my parents, my sisters, and anybody else who asked about going out on auditions.

How pathetic is that? I mean, plenty of people lie on their resumes about their successes, but there I was lying about my *failures*, making up jobs I *didn't* get.

That beer commercial? They went younger.

That legal drama? Turns out they wanted a brunette.

That web series about vampire nannies? Never heard back.

So after spending my entire childhood dreaming of being an actress and being voted Most Likely to See Her Name in Lights, turns out I wasn't cut out for it. Or maybe I just wasn't good enough.

Either way, it was really depressing.

I was debating calling it quits when the opportunity to do Save a Horse came up, and since I hated the thought of coming back a failure, I figured I'd give it one last-ditch effort to find success.

In hindsight, I probably should have just crawled out of the ditch and held up the white flag. Or better yet, told someone to shoot.

"I don't know, Nat. I...didn't really love living in New York." Admitting how homesick I'd been seemed like another failure.

"Well, what about going back on the cruise ships?"

I made a face. "Nah. Two years was enough for me—I only did it for the experience. And the money."

"Then stay here," she said firmly. "Your roots are here. Your family is here. You've got a new job you like, and you can easily find a place to live."

"I do like my job." I looked over her head out the window again. "And I did miss it here," I admitted. "But won't everyone think I'm a big fat failure?"

"Fuck everyone!" Natalie said in a rare outburst. "What do you care what people think of you anyway?"

I shrugged, wishing I didn't care. But I did. So much it hurt. My ten year high school reunion was three weeks away, and as it stood now, I'd walk in there with a pretty dull story—Failed Actress with No Plan B.

I wanted to be able to say I'd achieved something in the last ten years. But the problem was, I hadn't. I had no career, no husband or children, no home of my own. Everybody else there would have pictures of their beautiful families to show and stories of their successes to tell. And what did I have?

Seven seconds on the mechanical bull.

And some really nice shoes.

chapter two

Skylar

The next day, I showed up for work at Chateau Rivard praying no one at the winery had seen the previous night's show.

"Morning, John," I called to the tasting room manager.

"Morning, Skylar." He was inspecting wine glasses behind the long, curved wooden tasting counter. In his fifties, he was thin on top and thick through the middle and way, way too serious about wine, but I liked him well enough. He'd taught me a lot in the last month.

"Just give me a sec and I'll help you." I went to the employees' room in the back and stowed my purse and keys in a locker before joining him again. "Hey, I wanted to ask you about doing some videos this month. I had an idea for a series of tasting clips, just short ones for our website and the YouTube channel, that would teach people about tasting different kinds of wines but not be snooty or overly preachy, you know? Just something fun and approachable, and we could highlight our riesling for summer."

"YouTube?" John squinted at me. "Do we have a YouTube channel?"

"We will. I hope." I smiled at him as I unrolled the sleeves of my white blouse. It was a warm day for May, so I'd cuffed them this morning, but the cavelike tasting room always stayed cool with its stone floors and walls. To me, it was a little dark and dungeony, and the fancy French furniture was definitely tired and uncomfortable, but the Rivard family was all about tradition, and resistant to change. Even though I was technically just the assistant tasting room manager, I thought I could help to modernize the place a little bit—not only the look of the tasting room but in other ways as well. After all, if I was going to work up the nerve to ask for a raise so I could afford an apartment, I'd better prove my worth. "I also have some ideas for additional summer events. I'm going to talk about it all with Mrs. Rivard as soon as possible."

"Actually, she does want to see you." John set one glass down and picked up another, holding it up in the dim light thrown by the ugly old brass chandelier overhead. "She said to send you to her office when you arrived."

"Oh." That was a little odd. I usually didn't meet with her in the mornings because we did vineyard tours then. "Do I have time? Isn't it like quarter to ten

14

already? We've got two groups booked this morning."

"I'll cover for you here. Go ahead."

An uneasy feeling weaseled its way under my skin. "Did she say what it was about?"

He shook his head. "Nope. Just said to send you."

I tried a joke. "Should I be worried?"

"No idea. But you should probably go now. She doesn't like to wait around."

No, she didn't. Miranda Rivard was a stickler for many things—punctuality, manners, tradition. She was the family's third generation winemaker, although the Rivards had farmed this area long before that, and she was entirely dedicated to preserving its history. That devotion was nice when it came to saving the lighthouse or securing historical landmark status for an old home, but difficult to work around when it came to convincing her to update her tasting room or embrace technology.

As I took the steps up to the winery's large, ornate lobby—also outdated, I wondered why I was being summoned like this. Could it be something positive? Why couldn't I shake the feeling it was something bad?

At the far end of the lobby, I opened the heavy wooden door labeled Offices. Mrs. Rivard's—I didn't dare call her Miranda—was at the end of the long hall, but that morning I wished it were longer. I walked as leisurely as I could, my gaze on the frayed teal carpet runner. When I reached her door, I stood with my hand poised to knock and gave myself a little pep talk.

Relax. There's no way Miranda Rivard watches Save a Horse. It's probably something about the social media accounts you suggested setting up.

Right. That had to be it. Smoothing my skirt and squaring my shoulders, I knocked twice and waited.

"Yes?"

I opened the door and poked my head in. "John said you wanted to see me?"

"Yes, Skylar. I do. Come in." She gestured to the chairs in front of her desk and my stomach lurched.

Stop it. This is where you interviewed, so it's probably where she conducts all her employee meetings. I'll just leave the door open. No one gets fired with the office door open.

"Shut the door. Have a seat."

Fuck. I'm so fired.

I approached the chairs and stared at them, like maybe if I chose the right one this would go better for me.

"Sit, sit," Mrs. Rivard said a mite impatiently. She looked exactly the way you imagine a witch would look in real life—sharp features, shrewd eyes, long skinny fingers—but without the bedraggled hair. Her silver bob was perfectly even and hung in one shiny sheet to her chin. She wore very little makeup but her skin was actually pretty good for a woman her age, and I briefly considered opening with a compliment. I reconsidered when I saw the critical look in her eye, the firm set of her mouth.

Slowly, I lowered myself to the edge of one brown leather chair, desperately trying to think of a way to change the tone of this meeting. *Speak before she does! Open with something positive!*

"I'm glad you wanted to meet with me this morning, Mrs. Rivard, because I had an idea I wanted to run by you for a video series." I tried the beauty queen smile on her.

Fail.

"Skylar," she said firmly, linking her fingers together beneath her chin, "I'm afraid I had to make a difficult decision."

I kept a ghoulish smile frozen in place. "Oh?"

"Yes. It's about your position here at Chateau Rivard. You see, our brand projects a certain image, and—"

"Mrs. Rivard," I broke in. "If I could just—"

"Don't interrupt," she said sharply.

Fail.

"As I was saying, Chateau Rivard is very serious about its reputation. We are the oldest winery in this area and have always been dedicated to quality, professionalism, and tradition. We stand out in the market because we are more upscale, and we cater to discerning wine drinkers who expect our wines— and our staff—to be beyond reproach. Do you understand?"

I sighed. "Am I here to be reproached?"

"When you interviewed, I was pleased with your appearance, your family's history in the area, your role as former Cherry Queen, and your enthusiasm for our wines."

"And now?"

"Now, I regret to say that I'm afraid those initial impressions have been eclipsed by your recent behavior on television and the subsequent media attention to it. Specifically, this morning's article in the Peninsula Press."

"What article?" I asked, gripping the arms of the chair. My Froot Loops churned in my stomach.

"You've not seen it?" She raised one thin brow and glanced meaningfully at the newspaper on her desk.

"No." Panicking, I jumped up and grabbed the paper. My eyes scanned the headlines—and there it was.

FORMER CHERRY QUEEN MORE TART THAN SWEET.

Oh God.

I read the article quickly, my heart sinking with every snarky comment and embarrassing rehash of my misdeeds on the show. The writer mentioned how proud everyone had been to see a "hometown honey" on television but how that pride had withered as the weeks went on. *Who'd have thought we'd ever see our sweet Cherry Queen drunk on vodka and suggestively riding a mechanical bull?* he asked.

"What? That's not even right! It was tequila, not vodka!" I blurted.

"I hardly think that detail makes a difference." Mrs. Rivard's tone was arch.

Maybe not, but I was hoping for more erroneous statements in the article, things I could point to and say, That wasn't me! I never did that! I never said that! But unfortunately, everything he'd written about was something shown on screen. He ended the article by condemning me for the terrible things I'd said about where I came from, where my family still lived and worked, and scorned me for insulting good people with my catty, callow words, the same people who'd crowned me Cherry Queen and happily allowed me to represent them all over the country.

The country! The farthest I ever went as Cherry Queen was an Elks Lodge in Flint!

But it wouldn't serve me now to be defensive. If I wanted to keep this job, I needed to apologize and agree that my behavior was not appropriate.

"Mrs. Rivard, I'm very sorry about the show. I agree, the way they are portraying me is not very…appealing."

"The way they are portraying you? You don't think your own actions were…unappealing?" She mocked my use of the word.

"Well, yes and no. I mean, I did do and say some things I shouldn't have, but the editing makes it look much worse. People have to realize that."

She tilted her head. "Perception is reality, Skylar. I'm surprised you haven't learned that yet."

Fail.

I didn't know what to say. She was right. My entire body felt as if it were shrinking.

"And I'm afraid that the way you're perceived now isn't the image I want in a front-of-house employee."

I said nothing as the heavy shame of being fired settled over me like thick gray fog.

"I'll mail you a check for your last week. Good luck." She stood, and I took it to mean I was dismissed.

"Thank you," I said morosely.

"I'm sure you'll find another job," she added when I was at the door. "You were a good salesperson, and many comment cards specifically mentioned your name as a positive aspect of our tasting room experience. But I might suggest moving. People have long memories in small towns."

I nodded and slipped out without meeting her eyes, desperate to stem the tidal wave of tears I felt gathering momentum inside me. She didn't deserve to see me cry.

Skirting the crowd in the tasting room, I quickly ducked into the employees' room and grabbed my purse and keys, then rushed out again without even saying goodbye to John. I was sure he knew I'd been fired. How humiliating to think about our earlier conversation—he'd known I was going upstairs to get canned, but let me chirp away about YouTube videos!

Choking back sobs, I got into my mother's battered old SUV and drove away, allowing anyone who watched to perceive the reality of my middle finger out the driver's side window.

At first I was just going to go back to the guest house and crawl back under the covers, but I found myself passing the road that led to my parents' farm, unwilling to explain the situation to my mother yet. Without consciously thinking about it, I kept going north, straight to Lighthouse Park at the tip of the peninsula. I'd been back for weeks but hadn't yet visited this spot, a favorite of mine as a child. My dad used to take my sisters and me for walks on the paths there, pointing out the "Indian Trees" with their trunks bent at extreme angles by Native Americans hundreds of years ago to mark the trails. We'd hunt on the beach for fossils and tour the lighthouse, and he'd tell us about the ghost of Mable Day—a lovelorn sixteen-year-old girl from New York whose wealthy parents refused to let her marry a sailor she met while summering here. When he sailed again without marrying her and his ship was lost at sea, she drowned herself in the bay. I could still hear my dad's hushed, eerie tone as he delivered the final line: *And if you listen carefully at night, you can hear her crying in the wind.*

Those were the kinds of stories I'd shared with guests in the tasting room, thinking that local color always helped to make a sale—it gave them an emotional investment in the product, something to talk about when they uncorked the bottle back home.

I parked in the near-empty lot and walked past the lighthouse and down the dozen wooden steps to the beach, where I slipped off my heels. The breeze off the water was cool, as was the sand beneath my bare soles.

Glad to have the beach to myself, I moved a little closer to the water and plunked down in the sand, tucking my flared striped skirt around my legs. Leaning back on my hands, I closed my eyes and tilted my face up to the sun.

Come on, think. Refocus. So no acting jobs materialized from Save a Horse, but did you ever really think they would? No. And instead of considering the consequences of acting like an evil twunt on national television, you jumped in and did it just to please those producers and stay in the limelight. The problem with you is that you never think ahead—you just grab on to opportunities here and there without ever thinking about what will happen if things don't turn out perfectly.

I frowned. This was not peppy.

But I had to face it—many things in my life could be summed up with the phrase, *It seemed like a good idea at the time.*

Rollerskating down that slide in fifth grade. (Lost my balance.)

Waterskiing in a bikini at the sophomore class picnic. (Lost my top.)

Shooting whiskey with Tommy Parker before climbing in the bed of his pickup at the senior class bonfire. (Lost my virginity.)

Actually, it wasn't a terrible first time, from what I can recall, although that's not saying much—the memory is a bit fuzzy to this day. But Tommy was sweet to me afterward and we hung out all summer before he left for college in the fall. Three years later, when I was in contention for Cherry Queen, I was a little nervous he'd show up telling everybody about the time I'd "displayed poor conduct" in the back of his truck, which would make me ineligible. But he didn't—he was a good guy, just like most of the people I knew around here. I felt awful that I'd said such nasty things about them.

And the shitstorm was only getting bigger. When I thought about the article about me in the paper, I wanted to make like Mable Day and disappear under the water. My reputation was shot. Tearing up, I lay back on the sand, covering my face with my hands. God, I'd made such a mess of things. Once upon a time, I'd been admired and respected around here. Played the starring role in every production. Waved from floats and pedestals. People had asked for my autograph. Taken pictures with me.

Now I was reviled.

But what could I do to show everyone I wasn't that bitch from the show? That I was still the same girl they'd always known, just a little older and wiser—OK maybe not wiser, but at least trying to learn from my mistakes? I'd signed a contract forbidding me to talk about my time on Save a Horse, so it's not like I could come totally clean. There had to be another way to remind them I was still the girl they were proud to call their own.

Wait a second—that was it! I'd go back to my roots by reaching out to the Cherry Pageant people! All the festivities were coming up in July, and maybe there would be a role for me as a former queen.

I sat up with renewed energy. Yes—this was perfect. I'd repair my reputation by embracing my community, getting involved, doing good deeds. I'd donate my time and energy to needy organizations. I'd work any event at the festival they wanted me to. I'd visit schools, cut ribbons, kiss babies, pick cherries. They probably wouldn't pay me, but that was OK. My parents would let me move in with them for the summer, and after the festival, my reputation would be repaired, my confidence would be restored, I'd find a new job somewhere, and start saving up for my own place.

I took a deep breath, and the cool, damp air revitalized me. It smelled both earthy and clean, like the woods and the water, like the springs of my childhood. A rebirth. Getting to my feet, I brushed the sand off my skirt and turned around, proud of myself for coming up with a solution, like a real grownup.

To my surprise, I was no longer alone on the

beach.

A man sat about twenty feet away, forearms draped over his widespread knees, hands clasped between them. He knew I was there, he must have seen me when he arrived, but he said nothing as I made my way to the steps and never looked away from the water. He had a nice profile, actually. Short dark hair, strong jaw covered with neatly trimmed scruff, nice ears. Sounds weird, I know, but I got the Nixon ears that stick way out, which is why I rarely wear my hair back and always notice ears on other people.

He wore aviator sunglasses, jeans, and a light brown jacket, and when I got closer I noticed he had a thick notebook next to him on the sand, the old fashioned spiral kind with a bright red cover. Intrigued, I nearly said hello, but something about the utter stillness in his pose told me he didn't want to be bothered, and the greeting stuck in my throat.

Maybe he watches the show, I thought glumly. Maybe he knows exactly who I am and just doesn't want to talk to me.

My spirits withered a little as I reached the wooden steps, where I realized I hadn't picked up my heels from where I'd been sitting. I pivoted sharply, but somehow my ankle didn't get the message and I went down hard on my hands and knees in the sand. A little squeak escaped me as I hit the ground.

Oh God. Please don't let him be watching me.

A few seconds later I heard his voice.

chapter three

Sebastian

I saw her. Of course I saw her.

I thought she was crying at first, because she was lying on her back, hands over her face. Although I was disappointed not to have the beach to myself, I felt a tug of sympathy and thought about asking if she was OK. But when I got closer and realized it was Skylar Nixon, I hesitated.

Skylar Nixon.

I hadn't seen her in ten years, but I knew it was her. That hair—so light blonde it was almost silver against the sand. Her fingers covered her eyes, but I knew they were blue. Not a bright or sharp blue, like a gemstone, but sweeter, softer, like faded denim. I didn't know this because of any extended time spent gazing into them directly, but from staring at her senior yearbook photo every night for a year while feverishly jerking off to the fantasy of her straddling my body in the dark.

But I'd bet every guy in our graduating class had that fantasy. She was just so beautiful.

We didn't run with the same crowd back then—mostly because she had a crowd and I did not, which was fine with me. In those days, I preferred solitude. I sought it. Much easier to be alone with my anxiety than have to explain it to anyone.

It was still easier.

But I wasn't that kid anymore, and here was a chance to prove it. Maybe this was serendipity.

I started walking toward her, and suddenly the voice in my head spoke up. *Don't do it. She's too lovely, too fragile. You'll hurt her.*

Suddenly the disturbing image of Skylar gasping for air, my hands around her neck, lodged in my brain, along with the question, *What if I choked her?*

I stood there, paralyzed, desperately trying to push the thought from my head, and then I remembered I wasn't supposed to do that. I had to talk back.

Stop it. Those fears aren't rational. I've never choked anyone.

I hadn't, had I? My mind suddenly went into overdrive, sifting through years of memories, trying to find the one where I must have choked someone. That's why I was thinking about it now, wasn't it?

Rational thought tried again. *No! This is fucking ridiculous. You've never fucking choked a person!*

But already that gut-gripping unease had me reconsidering my intent to speak to her. Even if I'd never choked anyone in the past, I must want to.

The other voice refused to quiet.

You know what will happen if you go over there and speak to her. So maybe you won't choke her, but you'll make a mess of things. Go ahead, start a conversation. If you're lucky, she'll remember you as the class freak and run off like a scared rabbit. If she likes you, you're in even bigger trouble, because that's how it all starts. And it ends with you ruining her life, just like you ruined Diana's. You're poison.

By this time, my heart was pounding furiously and my hair stood on end. The voice was right, he was totally right.

Distressed, I moved away from her, being certain to take an even number of steps, and sat down quietly in the sand, waiting for my heart to quiet down.

But it didn't, because a moment later, she stood up, brushed herself off, and saw me.

Did she recognize me? I hoped not. I knew I looked different than I did back then, but I still didn't want to take any chances.

Don't look at her.

I said it eight times in my head.

Out of the corner of my eye, I saw her walk toward the steps and then hesitate, like she might say hello. I held my breath. Counted to eight.

Suddenly she turned and went down hard in the sand, letting out a little shriek of surprise. Before I could stop myself, I was on my feet, rushing toward her.

"Are you all right?" I asked, taking her by the elbow to help her up.

"Yes," she said quickly, her cheeks going adorably scarlet. "Just a little sandy and a lot embarrassed. Thank you."

Once she was on her feet, I dropped her arm and stepped back as the horrible fear of harming her popped back into my mind and stuck there. She looked up at me curiously, like maybe she was trying to place me. If it was possible, she was even more beautiful than I remembered.

"I'm Skylar."

"I know who you are." It came out colder than intended. I hadn't meant it in a bad way, but I was trying so hard not to think about hurting her that my voice was strained, my tone sullen. *Fuck, I'm an asshole.*

She must have taken offense, because her face fell, her complexion darkening further. "Right. Well, OK then." Without any kind of goodbye, she brushed past me, scooped up a pair of shoes from the sand and stomped back over to the steps. She quickly slipped her feet into her heels and thumped up each stair with angry clacks.

Part of me wished I would have at least told her my name, reminded her that we'd once known each other, but another part just felt relief that she was gone and I hadn't harmed her. The thought of choking her stubbornly refused to leave my head, and I walked back over to where I'd been sitting and dropped down onto the sand, hating myself.

Fucking hell. I'd made so much progress in the last year, and I'd let the sight of an unrequited ten-year-old crush undo it all. I was a fucking disaster and I always would be. Grabbing the notebook next to me, I hurled it into the water.

Two seconds after I heard the splat, I regretted it. "Fuck!" I jumped to my feet and trudged into the water to get the damn thing, which hadn't gone very far. The water was frigid but shallow, and I rescued the journal before it was submerged, although I soaked my sneakers and the bottoms of my jeans in the process.

Reaching the sand again, I dropped down and fanned open the dripping notebook, its pages covered in neat, small, identical lettering. In the beginning, the pages all looked the same.

Eight words per line.

Every line.

Ken, my therapist, never actually read my journal, it was just for me, so at first I'd reverted to the old habit, even though the whole point of the journal was to help me stop engaging my compulsive behaviors. But eventually, I'd stopped writing in it that way. I'd stopped doing a lot of things I used to do. In fact, I couldn't remember the last time I'd had a setback like I'd had today. Then again, it was the first time I'd approached a woman I was attracted to since everything with Diana fell apart. Add to that it was a girl I'd crushed hard on back in high school, and maybe it was no wonder.

Frustrated, I dropped the notebook into the sand. Maybe it was just too soon. Maybe it was just the wrong woman. Or maybe I was just doomed to be alone for the rest of my life. My own misery was enough—why should I make someone else unhappy too?

Ken was always encouraging me to be more social, but I hadn't come back here to make friends or reconnect with anyone. I'd come here for peace and quiet, to start over, to forget about New York and everything that happened there.

Forget that I'd lost my mind.

Forget that I'd lost my job.

Forget that I'd lost the only woman willing to love me.

No, that was wrong—I hadn't lost her. I'd driven her away.

I deserved to be alone.

chapter four

Skylar

   Inside my mom's car, I pulled the door shut and let my forehead drop onto the steering wheel.

Forget him. He doesn't matter.

But the way the handsome stranger on the beach had looked at me with such blatant contempt, the scornful way he'd said *I know who you are*, truly bothered me. How long would I have to be ashamed of myself?

Don't think about that. Think about the plan you have to make things better. Taking a deep breath, I sat up tall and turned the key in the ignition.

When I got back to the guest house, I made a peanut butter and jelly sandwich and poured a glass of iced tea. With my sandwich in one hand, I opened up my laptop with the other. I found contact information for pageant marketing director Joan

Klein easily enough, and as soon as I finished my lunch, I dialed her number.

She didn't answer but I left her a message explaining who I was and volunteering my time for the festival and related activities. I told her I was free anytime and eager to get started, and I gave her my cell phone number.

After that, I changed from my work clothes into jeans and a tank and grabbed my bucket of cleaning supplies from the pantry. I'd give the place a good dusting and scrubbing, and then later I'd invite my mom over for a glass of wine and give her some more decorating ideas. *I'll show her the Pinterest board I made, run some paint colors by her for the bathrooms, and offer to do the painting myself—if I'm not too busy with my new job.*

I smiled as I filled the bucket. Through the open window I could hear an old Hank Williams tune, which meant my father was probably working in the nearby pole barn with his radio on. It lifted my mood further, and I hummed along to *You Win Again* as I dusted, the melody taking me back to grade school summers, when Jilly, Nat, and I would all pile in the front seat of his truck and go for ice cream after dinner, my mother howling from the driveway about seat belts. Those summers always went by so fast—you blinked and it was September again. I'd blinked and a decade had gone by! I couldn't believe it had been ten years since I'd graduated from high school. Where had they gone? And what about the next ten years...would they fly by just as fast?

For a moment, I tried to imagine myself ten years from now, age thirty-seven. Where was I? What was

I doing? Did I have a career of some kind? A husband and family? I had no clue, which was kind of distressing, so I shoved that thought out of my mind and focused on my housework.

About fifteen minutes later, my cell phone rang. I set down my dust rag and looked at the screen.

Yes! It was Joan Klein.

"Hello?"

"Hello, is this Skylar Nixon?"

"Yes, it is," I sing-songed.

"Hello, this is Joan Klein from pageant corporate.

"Hel*lo*," I gushed like she was my long-lost best friend. "How *are* you?"

"I'm fine, thank you. I'm glad you called, Skylar. We'd like to meet with you."

"Fantastic!" I bounced around a little. "I can meet any time."

"Could you come down to the office this afternoon?"

"Of course, no problem."

"Around three?"

"I'll be there."

"Thank you. We have some paperwork for you to sign. Oh, and if you could just bring your crown with you, we'd really appreciate that."

"Certainly I can. I know just where it is." Wow, they wanted a photo already! I'd put my work clothes back on—I hoped I hadn't gotten my new skirt too sandy.

"See you then."

"See you then!"

I ended the call and hugged my phone to my chest, thanking my lucky stars that something had gone right today. Deciding to forego the floor mopping for now, I left the guest house and walked over to my parents' house to fetch my crown.

No one was there, but the door was unlocked as usual, so I let myself in and hurried over to the mantle above the fireplace. There was my crown, right next to a photo of me at the coronation. I picked up the frame and studied the picture—I looked so happy. So hopeful. So confident that every dream I had would come true if I just wished hard enough, worked hard enough, wanted it hard enough.

My smile faded as I set the frame down and looked at the other items displayed on the parental Mantle of Pride. There was Jillian in her cap and gown, graduating from medical school. There was Natalie cutting the ribbon the day she opened the coffee shop. Moving back a few steps, I tried to look at everything as a stranger might. What did these things say about us? For a moment, I imagined my mom showing our photos to a new friend.

This is Jillian, the smart one. She's a doctor now, isn't that something?

This is Natalie. She's our little entrepreneur!

And this is Skylar. Isn't she pretty?

Frowning, I grabbed the crown off the mantle and left the house before my mother got home and asked me why I needed it.

• • •

"I'm sorry. What did you say?" I was seated in front of Joan Klein's desk, staring at her in disbelief. "Maybe I misunderstood."

Joan, a former beauty queen herself, had a blonde beehive hairdo that might have been shellacked in 1975 and eyebrows penciled in way too dark. She cleared her throat. "Corporate feels, Ms. Nixon, that your current reputation is at odds with the qualities we look for in a Cherry Queen. We do not believe you would be an asset to the pageant at this time, and in fact we feel you have violated your contract."

"Violated my contract? Are you joking?" I blinked a few times, but her pursed mouth did not ease into a smile.

"No. I am quite serious. If you look at your contract, which I have a copy of here, you will see that you agreed to refrain from engaging in any public behaviors that would discredit the Queen or the pageant."

"But—but that was seven years ago!" I sputtered.

"The contract has no end date. Once a queen, always a queen," she said dramatically.

"Oh my God. So now what?"

"Your crown and title are being revoked, and we'd like you to sign right here." She set another contract in front of me, the page full of tiny black print. "This says that you understand your title is being forfeited due to breach of contract and you will no longer refer to yourself as a former Queen, advertise yourself as such, or appear at any functions claiming to be such."

"Seriously? I made a mistake! Don't we all make mistakes sometimes?"

"Yours were very public, Ms. Nixon. Too public."

"It was just a TV show!" But in my head I heard Miranda Rivard's voice: *Perception is reality, Skylar.*

"It was a reality show. You played yourself," Joan pointed out. "We would appreciate it if you did not speak to the press about this or mention it on any social media. We'll handle it."

"Speak to the press? Are you kidding? Why would I want to call attention to this?" I scribbled my name on the contract without even reading it. Didn't matter what it said, I no longer cared.

"Leave the crown, please. It's pageant property."

My jaw dropped and I hugged the crown to my stomach. "You can't have my crown."

"Yes, I can." She tapped my signature with the pen. "You just agreed to return it."

I wanted to throw it at her, but I mustered my pride and managed to set it down gently on the desk—right after I bent that stupid fucking rhinestone-studded piece of shit in half with my bare hands.

chapter five

Sebastian

After the episode at the beach, I went straight to the gym. In college I'd learned that working out helped me stay mindful of the present moment and stop "fearcasting" about the future. When I was running or lifting or hitting the heavy bag, all I thought about was my body getting stronger, my muscles working harder, my heart pumping faster. It forced me to stay in the moment, helped me work off the tension and anger I carried, and had results I could see, a clear cause and effect.

However, even running an extra mile and adding extra reps hadn't been enough to banish Skylar Nixon from my mind.

But actually, it was kind of nice.

Because rather than the disturbing thoughts I'd had at the beach, my head was filled with other images of her—pleasant images. As I pushed myself to the limits of exertion, I thought of her body beneath mine, her hands on my back, her lips falling open. I thought of those blue eyes closing as I slid inside her, slow and deep. I thought of the soft sigh of pleasure I'd hear before she whispered my name and pulled me in deeper.

At home in the shower, I invited those thoughts back in, welcomed them as I let the water run down my body and took my dick in my hand.

Oh yeah, jerking off was another activity in which I stayed mindful of the moment. Sex was too, although I hadn't had sex in almost a year. Fuck, I missed it. But sex with strangers had never been my thing—although I might have to make it my thing unless I wanted to spend my life celibate.

Or maybe sex with a friend...

I tightened my fingers around my shaft and stroked myself with long, hard pulls as the steam billowed up around me.

God, what would it feel like to get inside Skylar? To smell her skin, taste her lips, watch her arch beneath me?

Could I make her come?

Was she quiet or loud?

Did she like it on top?

Would she let me tie her up? Pull her hair?

Bury my tongue in her pussy?

My hand worked faster, harder. "Fuck," I whispered, over and over again as my cock went rock solid and then throbbed in my hand. I groaned as the tension inside me released in thick hot spurts, my leg muscles tight and trembling.

For a solo flight, it was a pretty fucking good orgasm, and it made me wonder if maybe I should try talking to her again.

Immediately, the voice was back.

Don't be fucking dense. You think jerking off to some adolescent fantasy means you can handle being alone with her?

I wouldn't have to be alone with her. I could just talk to her. Reintroduce myself. Be her friend.

No. You can't trust yourself. You want her too much.

I wanted to argue, fight back.

But I had no weapons to battle with, no words to hurl at this fucking ghost that refused to stop haunting me, shadowing my every thought, my every intention.

After getting dried and dressed, I scrubbed my shower tiles and called my therapist to see if he could fit me in this afternoon.

• • •

"I had a setback today." I wasn't much for small talk.

"Oh?" Ken, a soft-spoken man with glasses and a thick blond beard, crossed his legs and regarded me patiently. "What do you think triggered it?"

I shifted uncomfortably on the couch in his office. "I saw someone from my past, a girl I went to school with."

"A friend?"

"Not exactly…I didn't really have friends in high school, partly because of my erratic behavior in years prior, but also because I kept to myself. People really didn't know what to make of me. But this girl. She was just…nice. We were assigned as lab partners in chemistry a few times. I used to get so nervous before school if I knew we had to work together."

"Did you have thoughts about her back then?"

Fuck yes I did. I still do. "Not obsessive thoughts. Just average teenage boy thoughts and average teenage boy nerves around a pretty girl. But mine were compounded by the fact that I knew everyone thought I was crazy. I thought I was crazy."

Those years had been such a fucking nightmare— my father dragging me to doctor after doctor to figure out why I was so obsessed with germs, why I was always counting things like leaves on trees or blades of grass or lines on the highway, why I was convinced that terrible things were going to happen to people I loved because of me. They did everything from dismissing the shit I did as adolescent quirks to diagnosing me with depression.

Several therapists were convinced I secretly blamed myself for my mother's death from a car accident when I was eight (she was coming to pick me up from a friend's house) and believed the fear of doing harm stemmed from that, but they couldn't tell my dad why I had to flip a light switch on and off eight times before leaving a room or explain to my teachers why I had to click my ballpoint pen eight times before answering every test question or clue my middle school gym classmates in as to why I would play second base but not first or third. I could still recall the what-the-fuck looks on their faces when I tried explaining that two was a good number because it was even, and even better, a factor of eight, but one and three were bad numbers because they were odd.

Ken pushed his glasses further up his nose. "You once mentioned things were better by the time you finished high school."

"They were," I conceded. By junior year, we'd found a doctor familiar with OCD and I was put on medication, and started seeing a therapist regularly. "By then, I had more good days than bad, but the social damage had been done, and I just figured, fuck it, I'll start over in college."

Ken flipped back a few pages in the notepad on his lap. "You said your undergraduate years were fairly normal, but we haven't talked much about them. You had friends? Dates?"

"Yeah. Starting over in a new place felt good. The thoughts and the compulsions never entirely went away, but I learned to cope. I felt I had control over them." I thought about Skylar and the back of my neck grew hot. "As opposed to fucking today."

"But we've talked about how having *control* over your thoughts isn't the answer. It isn't possible for anyone, really. One of your main goals at this point is to let go of that excessive need for control and learn to live with risk and uncertainty. Learn to let the obsessive thoughts be."

"Yeah, I know that, and when I'm sitting here or when I'm alone or out among strangers, I'm fine with it," I snapped. "But today was different."

"OK, so what happened today?"

I told him what had transpired on the beach this morning, the image of Skylar's blonde hair against the sand, her slender legs extending from her skirt still fresh in my mind. "And yes, I tried talking back and reasoning with myself and being an observer and all that, but nothing was working. I couldn't deal with it the usual ways." I shrugged angrily. "So I counted. Ran away from her."

Ken nodded slowly. "And afterward?"

"I felt like shit. I was furious. I wanted to punch someone. Myself, I guess."

"What did you do?"

"I went to the gym." *And then I went home and jerked off while thinking about her just like I used to when I was seventeen. I'll probably do it again tonight because two is a better number than one.*

"Did that help?"

I almost smiled. "Yeah. Sort of."

Ken rubbed his beard and thought for a moment. "Do you think, if you saw her again, you might try speaking to her?"

I linked my fingers in my lap and stared at them, trying to imagine shaking her hand without fear. "I don't know. Part of me wants to. Another part says why invite trouble? I'm doing OK these days, you know? At least, I was. Working on the cabin, handling a couple cases for my dad's firm, writing every day, staying active... Until I saw her this afternoon, I felt stronger than I have in a long time. I think that's why I'm so fucking angry about the relapse."

"One setback doesn't mean relapse. And it doesn't undo all the progress you've made, Sebastian. It could just be a bad day." Ken uncrossed his legs and leaned forward, elbows on his knees. "I'm not going to force you to do it, but we both know that avoidance is never a successful strategy when it comes to obsessive thoughts. It always backfires, which leads to more anxiety and distress. If you really want to move forward, you should talk to her. Is this someone you think might be just a friend…or something more?"

"Just a friend," I said quickly. "I'm done with relationships."

"Give yourself time. You're only twenty-eight, Sebastian. One bad breakup doesn't mean you won't find happiness with someone else eventually."

Happiness. What the fuck was that, anyway? "It wasn't just a bad breakup—I've fucked up every chance at a relationship I've ever had. This was just the first time I actually wrecked someone's life too."

"You didn't wreck her life."

"She said I did." Agitated, I ran a hand over my hair. "Diana had a wedding dress, Ken. Invitations had been ordered. Deposits paid. Honeymoon cruise booked—not her dream honeymoon, of course, which was my fault because I refuse to get on a plane, but a honeymoon nonetheless. I'm never doing all that shit again, because it will all have to be undone when I panic and relapse and she realizes she can't be married to a fuck-up like me who has—wait, let me see if I can get this right—no fucking clue what it means to love someone because I can't get out of my head long enough to put someone else's needs first unless I'm fucking her." I spat Diana's words at Ken as if he'd spoken them.

"Sebastian, stop." Ken sighed and straightened up. "We're not talking about proposing to this woman. Or sleeping with her. We're talking about a conversation. And if the obsessive thought returns, don't try to banish it and don't run away. You've got tools to work with. Try magnifying, or the watching/waiting we've talked about. Do the writing exercise where you imagine the worst. That's worked for you in the past."

I was quiet for a moment. Flexed my fingers a few times. "I'll think about it."

After the session was over, I left Ken's office building and walked down the street to Coffee Darling. When I first started going there last year, I had to bring my own cup from home because I was so worried about contamination. But exposure therapy had helped me work through it, and now I felt a lot more comfortable walking into a bar or restaurant and using whatever was given to me. Did I love it? No, and a little doubt always lingered about how clean the utensils were, not to mention the kitchen, but usually I managed to cope without embarrassing myself or anyone with me.

The long, narrow shop was empty, and the owner, Natalie, was wiping down the counter, but she looked up and smiled at me when I came in. "Hey, stranger. Haven't seen you in a while. How's it going?"

"Good, thanks." I liked Natalie, partly because she talked so much I never felt like I had to say anything, and also because she understood when I shamefacedly explained why I brought my own coffee cup to her shop. She never launched into any defensive explanation about how clean her place was—and it was clean, I never even hesitated before using the bathroom, and public restrooms were a huge trigger for me—she just poured coffee and chatted away. When I was finished, she'd always rinse and dry the cup for me, too. Best of all, she seemed to know when I didn't want to be bothered, and she'd leave me alone with my caffeine and my notebook.

"Come on in. The kitchen's closed, but since you're just a coffee drinker, have a seat and I'll pour you a cup."

"Are you sure? If you're closed, I can—"

"No, no, come sit down. You can keep me company while I go through the closing routine."

Removing my sunglasses, I set them and my keys on the counter and sat down. After Natalie poured me some coffee and disappeared into the kitchen, I opened up my journal, frowning at the damp pages, and turned to what Ken called my Exposure Hierarchy. The idea was to list things that make me anxious and then rate them with subjective units of distress, or SUDS, based on how uncomfortable or scared they made me. Then I had to tackle them, and I wasn't allowed to count while I did them, or numb myself, or repeat any mantras.

I thumbed through the list, page after page of things I'd forced myself to do over the last year. Some were related to my fears about germs and contamination, some were related to my ordering and number compulsions, and some were related to frightening "what if" thoughts that tortured me for no good reason, like thinking I'd go batfuck crazy and stab someone if I held a kitchen knife in my hands.

After a sip of coffee, I pulled my pencil from my jacket pocket and turned to the end of the list. Taking a deep breath, I added another item.

Talk to Skylar Nixon.

I stared at the words and tried to think about rating the task—how anxious did the thought of talking to her make me? But before I could decide on a number, I got the uneasy feeling that someone was watching me. I looked over my left shoulder, and there she was. Standing just inside the door, so pretty she took my breath away, and staring right at me.

chapter six

Skylar

Our eyes met, and a shiver moved through my body.

Holy shit. It's him again.

And he's really hot.

After leaving the pageant offices in a huff, I'd marched down the street to Coffee Darling, Natalie's adorable little bakery and coffee shop. When she opened it two years ago, it was only coffee and the muffins or donuts she made herself at the asscrack of dawn, but she'd since hired another pastry chef and also offered light salads and sandwiches at lunchtime too.

It closed after the last of the lunch crowd left, usually by three each day, so I'd been surprised to see someone still seated at the counter when I walked in.

He looked over his shoulder at me, and now that he'd taken off his sunglasses, I could better appreciate his good looks—the light green eyes, the angled cheekbones, the full mouth. When he frowned, I felt the embarrassment of face planting in the sand all over again, which was dwarfed only by the shame I'd experienced when he'd said *I know who you are* that way and I realized he'd seen me on Save a Horse.

And he probably read the paper this morning. He hates you, just like everyone else in this town.

Fine, I could handle it.

I scowled right back.

Just then Natalie came through the door from the kitchen and grabbed the coffeepot behind the counter. "How about a warmup?" she asked him.

He kept staring at me without answering her question, and the tension was too much for me to bear. "For fuck's sake, just say it!" I exploded. "Yes, I'm who you think I am. Yes, I'm that bitch on TV. Yes, I said shitty things about nice people, so just stop staring at me and tell me flat out that I deserve all the crap that's happening to me today, including falling on my face!"

"Skylar!" Natalie glanced frantically back and forth from me to the guy. "I'm sorry, Sebastian. This is my sister, Skylar, and apparently she's having a *very bad day*," she said with a murderous look at me. "Otherwise I cannot imagine why she would come in here and scream obscenities at my customer."

I looked at the guy again, but he was no longer focused on me. He was frantically closing his notebook and tucking it out of sight in his jacket.

Instantly I felt guilty. "Hey, don't go. I'm sorry about that."

"It's all right," he said quietly. "I'm done anyway." He pulled out his wallet and threw a few bills on the counter.

"No, please stay. You just got here." Natalie filled his cup with coffee and set down the pot. "And put your money away. Coffee's on me."

"Keep it as a tip then. See you around." He picked up his keys from the counter, put his sunglasses back on, and moved toward the door.

I raced ahead of him, unable to bear the thought he would leave still thinking I was a horrible person, even though I felt like one. "Hey, don't leave on my account. I really am sorry." Leaning back against the glass door, I smiled. "Can I try again?"

Slowly, he lifted his head and met my eyes. Stared directly into them, so hard my breath caught in my chest, and I felt desire stir low in my belly. With the short hair and the aviator glasses, he looked like a fighter pilot or something. Even the stubborn set of his jaw turned me on. Rawr.

"I'm Skylar," I said, extending my hand. Then I wrinkled my nose. "But I guess you already know that from the Save a Horse, right?"

His brow furrowed. "Save a what?"

"Save a Horse. The reality show." The fact that his expression remained perplexed gave me hope. "You mean you haven't seen it?"

"No. I don't watch much TV." He paused. "You don't remember me."

"I don't think we've met." I tilted my head coquettishly. "I'd remember you. Definitely."

Although, wait a second—there *was* something familiar there. Had we met? Why couldn't I place him? Was he an actor I'd been introduced to in New York? And why wouldn't he shake my hand, which was still extended between us?

It took him forever, but finally he reached for it.

"And you are?" I prompted. Man, this guy was gorgeous but a bit lacking in social niceties.

"Sebastian Pryce."

"Nice to meet you," I said, enjoying the cozy fit of my hand inside his. "Are you—"

And then it hit me.

I did know him.

At least, I'd known a Sebastian Pryce. We'd gone to school together for years. But this couldn't be *that* Sebastian…could it? I looked down at our hands. The Sebastian I'd known wouldn't have shaken hands because he was always so paranoid about germs. Kids used to tease him by touching his shoulders and saying, *Better go wash your hands, Sebastian. I gave you cooties.* And even though it was ridiculous and we all knew there was no such thing as cooties, he always asked to go wash his hands after that. Once, in fifth grade, our teacher had said no because we were getting ready to take a test, and he'd completely flipped out and started tapping on his head and counting out loud. It was awful.

He let go of my hand and I continued to stare at him. Now I saw it, but talk about duckling to swan. I swallowed. "Wow. Sebastian. You look…different."

"You look exactly the same."

Was that a compliment? Hard to tell from the way he said it. "Thanks," I said uncertainly.

"You're welcome."

Wow, this was awkward. Like trying to flirt with a tree. I wasn't usually tongue-tied around men but I had no idea what to say to Sebastian Pryce after all these years. And why did he seem so angry? Was it because of the way he'd been treated in school? I'd never teased him myself—wait, I'd actually been kind to him, hadn't I? Although he'd probably been bullied a lot, and I hadn't exactly stood up for him. Was it possible he held a grudge?

"Could I get by please?" he asked tersely. "You're blocking the door."

"Oh. Right, sorry." Flustered, I watched him push it open and bolt out like the building was on fire.

Off kilter, I turned to Natalie and put my fingtertips to my temples. "That was weird."

"It was, kind of." She shrugged. "But he's not your average guy."

I looked out the door again, recalling the punch-in-the-gut feeling I'd had when he'd turned to look at me. Then I noticed the notebook on the sidewalk—the red spiral one I'd seen earlier at the beach. "Hey, he dropped something."

Hurrying out the door to pick it up, I looked down the street in the direction he'd gone. There was no sign of him, so I took it back into the shop.

"He'll probably be back for it in a minute," Natalie said. "He's always carrying that thing around."

"It's soggy," I said, holding it by one corner. "What the hell does he do with it?"

"Writes in it, I assume."

I slapped the thing onto the counter next to the dollar bills he'd left and sat down, eyeing it curiously. "I wonder what he writes about."

"No clue. Now tell me how you two know each other. Was it school?" Natalie picked up a rag and began wiping the counter, moving the notebook aside. "He's not much of a talker but he did say he grew up around here."

"Yes, you don't remember him? He was in my class, so a few years ahead of you, but he looked totally different back then."

"What did he look like?"

"He had this long shaggy hair he used to hide behind and he wore really baggy clothing all the time." I thought for a second. "Or at least it seemed baggy. Maybe he was just really skinny."

Natalie's eyebrows shot up. "Not anymore. One time he took off his jacket and he was wearing this really fitted t-shirt. That guy is ripped now—his arms and chest are amazing."

"Seriously?" Spinning on the stool, I glanced out the door again, wondering where he'd rushed off to. "Does he ever come in with anyone else? I don't remember him having friends in school."

"That's sad."

I frowned. "Yeah, but he was a pretty odd duck. He used to be obsessed with germs, like total OCD. People used to tease him about it."

She nodded. "That makes sense. The first time he came in here, he brought his own cup."

My jaw dropped. "He did? That's weird."

"It *was* weird," she admitted, "but also kind of pitiful. And at first he just said he preferred to use his own cup, but after he came here a few times, he told me about the germ fear and said he was working on it. And then one day, he didn't bring it."

"Did you, like, congratulate him?"

"Nope, I didn't even mention it. I just poured his coffee and went about my business. Like I said, he's not really a talker, and I didn't want to embarrass him. And I think..." Her voice trailed off and she caught her bottom lip between her teeth.

"What?" I asked, suddenly eager for any scrap of information on him.

"Nothing. I shouldn't spread gossip." She focused extra hard on her cleaning rag.

I rolled my eyes and put a hand over her wrist, stopping her frantic motion. "Nat, please. Who the hell would I tell? No one is even speaking to me around here!"

She sighed and stopped wiping. "Well, after he left here one day, I heard these women talking about him, something about his having a nervous breakdown last year and moving back home to recover. One of them might have been a relative of his."

"A nervous breakdown? Really?" My heart ached a little for the lonely, frustrated kid he'd been and the awkward man he'd become. Memories long forgotten surfaced—the way he'd arrived mid-year in the fourth grade and struggled to make friends. The way he'd stayed in at recess once to help me in math. The way he'd struggled to meet my eyes the few times we'd been lab partners. The way he'd eaten lunch alone. *I should have been nicer. Then and now. I'm a horrible person.* As if I needed another reminder.

"That's what I heard. Apparently he was a lawyer in New York City, and engaged to be married."

Intrigued, I reached for a chocolate chip cookie from under the glass lid of a cake stand and took a bite. "Wow. I wonder what happened to the girl."

She shrugged and resumed her cleaning. "I don't know, but he comes in here a lot and there's no wife or girlfriend that I've seen."

I took another bite, trying to recall one real conversation we'd had in all the years we knew each other, and failed. "That's sad. I remember him being, like, super smart. He helped me in math sometimes. And chemistry. His family still around here? If I recall, he had some older brothers. Maybe one of the women was a sister-in-law."

"I think they're still around, based on the limited conversations we've had, but he still seems lonely to me. Like he might need a friend, you know?"

Depressed, I stuck the rest of the cookie in my mouth. "Well, he doesn't want to be my friend," I mumbled. "He made that pretty clear."

"I think he's just shy."

"I think he hates me," I said, swallowing the last of the cookie and eyeing another one. "Just like the rest of the world."

"So what happened to you today, anyway? Why were you so mad when you walked in?"

While she swept up, I told her about being fired, about my brilliant idea to work for the festival, and about the humiliating meeting with Joan Klein. Then I reached for a second cookie.

"They took your crown away?"

"Yes!" The outrage hit me all over again. "So I smashed it!" I took a giant chomp out of the cookie as Natalie burst out laughing. "It's not funny!" I yelled, crumbs flying from my mouth.

"I'm sorry, I know I shouldn't laugh, but it's just so silly. Who cares who was queen all those years ago? It's ridiculous."

"I care!" I thumped my chest. "It was the one thing I had, the one great achievement in my life, my mantle picture! And now it's gone and I have nothing! My life is a complete mess and I'm a total failure at everything I do!" I threw the cookie down, put my face in my hands, and finally gave in to the urge to cry like a baby, which made me feel even worse about myself.

Natalie came over to sit beside me, leaning the broom against the counter. "Hey," she said, rubbing my shoulder. "Don't say that. You're not a failure. You've had plenty of great achievements. Look at all the starring roles you had around here growing up. Mom has entire albums full of your pictures on stage."

I picked up my head, tears leaking from my eyes. "Yes, I was a big fish in this little pond. But I wasn't good enough to make it for real, Nat. I didn't even like trying. You know what I liked best about acting?"

"What?"

"The curtain call. The applause when it was over." I sat up straight and sniffed. "Let's face it. I'm shallow and vain."

She slapped my shoulder gently. "Come on. Everyone likes to hear praise sometimes. And OK, maybe you're a little vain, but you're a hard worker too—you just need to find what it is you like to do. If it's not acting, it's something else."

"But I'm not good at anything," I fretted. "I'm not smart and ambitious like you and Jillian."

"Stop it, yes you are. And you could be good at anything." She slung her arm around my neck and squeezed. "You'll figure it out, Sky. Things will work out."

"How? The entire town, possibly the entire country, hates me, I have to go home and ask Mom and Dad if I can move in with them because I was canned, and a really cute guy just gave me the brush off."

"Mom and Dad will support you no matter what, and so will I, and so will Jillian. That's what family does."

I swiped at my nose. "I'm just so fucked up compared to you guys."

"What?" She leaned away from me. "What are you talking about?"

"You and Jilly did everything right. Your lives are perfect."

"Now you're just talking crazy. No one's life is perfect. Jillian was just complaining to me the other day that she wants to date but can't meet anyone worth her time, and she's buried in student loans. Running this business is exhausting and I've got a bunch of debt from it, and if you want to know the truth, I think Dan's cheating on me."

I gasped. "What? No way. You guys have been together forever."

She shrugged. "That doesn't mean anything. I saw some text messages on his phone from a girl at his office that have me wondering."

Dan was like a brother to me, since he and Natalie had been together since high school, but I'd kill him if he hurt her. "You need to talk to him. Right now."

"I will. Maybe it's nothing." Her expression said otherwise. "Anyway, we were talking about you. Are you going to be OK?"

"Yeah." I sniffed. "I need a tissue."

Natalie reached for the napkin dispenser and slid it over to me. "You still have plenty of old friends here. Why don't you look them up? You work all day and spend all your downtime working on those guest houses. You should get out a little."

Plucking a napkin from the dispenser, I blew my nose. "I don't know. I only stayed in touch with a few people after I left. And everyone who stayed around here is either married and pregnant or married with kids. It's hard to relate."

"Well, then, I think you should make a new friend." She flashed a meaningful look out the door.

I considered it. He was cute, and smart, if a bit socially awkward. Maybe I could draw him out. That was one thing I was good at, talking to people. "I could ask him if he's going to the reunion, I guess."

"There you go." She stood and picked up the broom again, resumed her sweeping.

"How can I find him?"

"He'll probably be back in here first thing tomorrow looking for that notebook. I'm surprised he's not here already."

I thought for a second. "I do need a job. Want to hire me?"

"You know what?" She stopped sweeping and looked at me, resting her chin on the top of the broom. "I *was* planning to hire someone part time since the tourist season is picking up. I can't pay you what Rivard paid you, and you won't like the hours, but the job's yours if you want it."

"I'll take it. At this point, I don't even care what it pays, I just need something to do while I figure my life out." I picked up my half-eaten cookie. "These are amazing. I'm going to get fluffy working here."

Natalie groaned. "They are, and I've eaten way too many today so I'm heading to the gym after this. Want to go for a swim with me?"

Natalie had been a champion swimmer in high school. Her definition of "go for a swim" was not the same as mine, which involved more floating than laps, preferably on a raft with a cupholder for my frozen daiquiri.

"No way," I said. "I'm too out of shape to swim with you. But I'll get on a bike or a treadmill or something."

"Great. You can come for dinner if you want too. We're grilling kebabs."

"The chicken wrapped in bacon?" I asked hopefully.

"Yep."

"Sold." I felt a little better. Nothing makes a bad day better like bacon. "What can I do to help you close?"

"Why don't you sweep, and I'll do kitchen duty?" She held the broom out to me, and I saluted before taking it from her.

But after she'd gone into the kitchen, I remained on the stool with the broom in my hand, staring at the notebook on the counter.

Sebastian Pryce. After all these years, he was a hot, mysterious lawyer with a firm handshake and a tragic past. Was his standoffish demeanor just a defense mechanism? He'd jumped up to help me at the beach this morning in a heartbeat, so I knew he had manners somewhere under the icy exterior. And those eyes. When he'd taken his glasses off and looked at me, there was something other than anger in them. Was it fear? Sadness? Was he still afraid of being rejected? I flattened one hand on the notebook's front cover. What was in here?

For a moment, Sebastian's right to privacy warred with my insane curiosity about him...

How wrong would it be to take a peek?

Totally wrong.

But maybe there was an address or phone number in it? I could justify it that way, right?

You just want to get up in his business.

I ignored that and opened up the front cover. Blank. I flipped to the back cover. Blank.

Well, damn, I thought, randomly flipping to a page in the middle. *Guess you'll have to find me, then.*

And speaking of me.

There was my name.

My mouth fell open as I took in all the words on the page, which really didn't make much sense to me.

Refrain from spacing hangers in closet just so. 50
Write less than eight words on a line. 30
Eat a mint after it falls on floor. 80
Zip up my fly less than eight times. 50
Turn off the television on an odd channel. 60
Lock the front door less than eight times. 70
Sit in a restaurant chair that feels "wrong." 75
Eat at a restaurant without bringing own dishes. 80
Go to a hospital and sit in lobby. 80
Handle a kitchen knife while others are present. 90
Talk to Skylar Nixon.

What the hell was this?

I read the list again but felt no closer to understanding it. Some of the items seemed like maybe they were things that made him nervous, and others were just odd behaviors. Zipping his fly eight times? A chair that feels "wrong"? Why couldn't he handle a kitchen knife in front of other people? Was he scared of knives? And hospital lobbies? Maybe that was the germ thing? And what was with the numbers? I felt sorry for him, but boy...this was pretty odd.

If he wanted to have a conversation with me, why hadn't he done it today? He'd had plenty of

Some Sort of Happy

chances. Was he just too shy? Biting my lip, I turned
the page.
    And saw my name again.

    Skylar
    I think I loved you
    is not the best introduction
    after we've just met
    I realize this. And maybe you will
    never know
    never know
    never know
    never know
    never know
    never know
    never know
    never know

    Maybe it is too soon (or too late?)
    to tell you about the dream I had
    your laugh was a butterfly

    Today when I touched you
    I felt a familiar chill down my arms. I think it
    came from the future (or the past?)
    With your hand in mine I saw the
    tragedy of us
    unfold quite clearly

    I have no choice but to
    keep my distance
    but your beauty is gravity
    and terrestrial bodies will always fall

I read it again and again and again, gooseflesh rippling down my arms. He wrote poetry? Had he written this for me today? Did he really feel this way about me? My heart was pounding. I stared at the words, trying to memorize them, scared Natalie was going to catch me snooping but needing desperately to take something beautiful from this day, even if it was sad too.

A few seconds later, someone pounded so hard on the door that I gasped.

Spinning around, I slapped my hand over my heart when I saw Sebastian through the glass. I slammed the notebook shut. *Act natural. You saw nothing. You know nothing.*

But suddenly I wanted to know everything.

chapter seven

Sebastian

Fuck, I scared her.

I watched Skylar whirl around and put a hand over her heart. When she saw it was me, she picked up the notebook from the counter and walked toward the door. The moment she unlocked it, I yanked it open and snatched the notebook rudely from her hands. I'd been in a complete state of panic since realizing it wasn't in my jacket, but I felt only mild relief to have it back in my possession. Had she looked inside it?

Fucking hell. I'd die. Die.

"Hi," she said brightly, coming outside. The door swung closed behind her. "I wondered if you'd come back for that."

"Yeah. Sorry." I couldn't bring myself to look her in the eye, so I stared at her feet. They were small and narrow, and even though she wore high heels, she was still a good six inches shorter than me.

"No problem, we're still here closing up."

I nodded, the tension in my gut uncoiling a little. She wasn't acting as if she'd seen anything crazy. I risked a glance at her, and those blue eyes cranked my adrenaline right up again.

"I'm sorry I didn't recognize you earlier. Do you live nearby?" Her tone was light and friendly and she leaned against the door, hands behind her back. It made her breasts stick out a little, and I looked at them before I could help myself. The thought of accidentally choking her jumped unbidden into my mind, and I took a step back.

Shit. Just get the fuck out of here.

"I gotta go." Without meeting her eyes, I turned and counted off my paces in sets of eight as I hurried away from her.

Hating myself, I went home and cleaned my house from top to bottom, took another shower (during which I jerked off to her again, which only made me feel more loathsome), ate dinner staring at a stupid cable news show that reaffirmed my belief that the world was a fucked-up place full of greed and cruelty, and went to bed.

Staring at the empty space beside me, I counted myself to exhaustion, and fell asleep.

• • •

The next day was better, although I was angry with myself for being such a dick to Skylar.

To work it off, I went to the gym in the morning and spent the early afternoon working outside at my cabin. The piece of property on Old Mission Peninsula I'd inherited from my mother was small, but it was well off the main road and had about twenty waterfront feet, although no beach. The land had been in her family for a hundred years or so, and when she died, it was divided into three parcels and willed to my two brothers and me. They'd sold their plots to a developer, but I'd held on to mine and built a cabin on it. A contractor had done the construction last summer, and I'd spent my winter working on the interior, installing reclaimed wood floors and kitchen cabinets, stained concrete counters, new appliances, a stone and tile bathroom downstairs. The whole place wasn't even eight hundred square feet, but it was plenty of room for me.

My latest project was an outdoor shower. With the water line prepped and in place, I began working on installing the solar water heater, so that showers out here would be refreshing rather than dick-shrinking cold. Of course, the entire time I worked I pictured Skylar underneath the shower heard, warm water running down her body, dripping off her curves, clinging to her skin. Oh fuck. Now I was hard. Frowning, I adjusted my jeans and kept working.

Damn it, why did I panic around her? Why couldn't I manage a simple conversation? I'd been battling obsessive thoughts for the majority of my life, and Ken was right—I had plenty of strategies in place for dealing with them. So what the fuck was it?

Was it her looks? Was it because I felt guilty for the way I used to think about her? The way I still thought about her? Or was yesterday just a bad day? It was almost like I'd had too many good days, and the asshole in me needed to speak up and remind me I wasn't OK. I'd never be OK. No matter how many good days there would be in my life, I'd always have to battle the fucked up circuitry in my brain.

I wondered what she was thinking. Would she even talk to me again if I approached her? Once something was on my list, I couldn't give up on it—and if I didn't work through my issue with her, it would continue to haunt me. This wasn't a huge town, so I was bound to run into her from time to time, and I couldn't run away whenever that happened. Ken was right about that too—avoidance never works, not for me.

I might be an asshole, but I wasn't a goddamn coward. Not anymore.

Next time I saw her, I'd do better.

chapter eight

Skylar

I started working for Natalie the next day, and by three o'clock, my feet were killing me, my lower back ached, and I was exhausted. My sisters were both early risers, as were my mom and dad, but waking before six AM felt like medieval torture to me, and the weather wasn't helping. It had been cloudy and gray all day, and the rain had just started to fall. Nap weather.

"Is it over?" I asked, when the final lunch customers had left, opening their umbrellas before heading out. "If it isn't, I think I have to quit."

"It's over." Natalie grinned at me over her shoulder as she piled dishes from their table on a tray. "We can close up."

"Thank God." Wincing with every step on my sore feet, I went to the door to lock it and flip the sign to CLOSED. Then I collapsed on the nearest stool, flopping forward over the counter. "I'll help you in a second. I need a rest."

"Don't close your eyes," she warned. "You'll fall asleep, I know you."

I did have a knack for falling asleep pretty much anywhere when I was tired. My eyes were already drifting shut as I settled my cheek on one arm. "Shush. Just need a minute."

"I'm taking these dishes to the kitchen, and once they're loaded in the dishwasher, your rest is over."

"Mmkay." Drowsy and warm and lulled by the sound of the rain, I'd just started to doze off when a few sharp raps on the glass jarred me awake. "Go 'way. Closed," I mumbled without picking up my head.

The knocking continued, growing even louder. What the hell, could this person not read?

"OK, OK." Reluctantly, I slid off the stool and turned to see a drenched Sebastian Pryce through the glass, rain coming down in sheets behind him.

My stomach jumped, and I rushed over to the door, fumbling with the lock before pushing it open. "Come on in," I said, a little breathless. All I could think of were his words about me. I could still see them on the page...

I have no choice but to
keep my distance

"My God, you're soaked." I looked him up and down, taking in the dark jeans and the light brown jacket, although it was dripping wet, as was his hair. "Can I get you a towel or something?"

"No, that's OK."

"How about a cup of coffee then?" I glanced behind me to make sure we still had some in the pot.

"No, thanks. I didn't come for coffee. I was just running an errand downtown and saw you through the window. I didn't realize you worked here."

I smiled. So talkative today—almost friendly. "It's my first day." Lowering my voice to a whisper, I leaned toward him and spoke behind one hand. "But you just caught me napping on the job."

He smiled at me, a slow, sly grin that made my knees go weak. "I won't tell."

"Thanks." I waited for him to tell me why he was there but he said nothing for a moment, his eyes running over my hair and face, lingering on my mouth.

but your beauty is gravity

I licked my lips. "Are you sure I can't get you anything to drink? The kitchen just closed, or I'd offer you something to eat."

"I'm sure. I'm not hungry. I just came in to talk to you."

and terrestrial bodies will always fall

"You did?" I rocked forward onto the balls of my feet.

"Yes. I owe you an apology."

A blush warmed my cheeks. "It's OK."

"No, it isn't. I shouldn't have rushed off yesterday. I feel bad about it."

"Well, I shouldn't have come in here screaming like a banshee either."

He shrugged. "It's all right."

God, he was so damn cute, all wet and sheepish. "Sure I can't get you some coffee? I hate to send you back out into the rain so fast. I'll sit with you." *Come on, let's get you out of those wet clothes.*

His lips tipped up again, and my heart ka-banged like a sixth grader's with her first crush. I loved how one of his eyebrows sort of cocked up higher than the other when he smiled. "No, thank you. I should go." He turned and pushed the door open, then looked back over his shoulder. "But it's good to see you again."

When he was gone, I stood there staring out the window at the rain for a solid five minutes, suddenly wide awake and more curious about him than ever.

• • •

Coffee Darling was only open until mid-afternoon, so I had plenty of time left over in the following weeks to help my mother finish the guest houses. I'd get up at five, work at the shop until the lunch crowd left, and then head back home to paint, put up window treatments and light fixtures, and make up beds with beautiful linens in soft, neutral colors. On my days off, I'd go hunting at antique shops for old chairs I could recover, tables my dad could help me refinish, or just pretty things that would look nice hanging on the walls or sitting on a shelf.

In the evenings, I helped my mother tweak their website, which was dated and busy. I also convinced her to hire a photographer to take some professional photos of the houses and grounds, and found a graphic designer to work on a new logo.

I can't say I was any closer to figuring what to do with *my* life, but I felt good about helping out my family, and staying busy made it easy to put off worrying about the future. My most immediate concern was that damn reunion—could I show my humiliated face? My final episode of Save a Horse had aired, (no, I did not watch) but I still felt the disgusted stares and heard the angry whispers of locals here and there. Perhaps if I hadn't thrown that cosmo in fan favorite Whiney Whitney's face, I'd have come off a bit more sympathetic, but I just couldn't take one more of her tearful meltdowns. Besides, I let her push me in the ranch's pool in an evening gown and stilettos. Ratings for that episode were sky high!

If only I had someone to go to the reunion *with*. But my two closest girlfriends from school lived out of town and weren't attending, and Natalie said showing up with her as my date would be worse than going alone. If Sebastian had come into the shop again, I would've asked him about it, but he never did. I asked Natalie about him once, and she said he was kind of like that—he might come in every day for a week and then not at all for two. Then she teased me about the crestfallen look on my face so much that I didn't ask again.

I was starting to think I'd imagined his poetic words about me when I ran into him at the hardware store one night in late May.

I was in aisle four looking for screws for these cool cast iron bin pulls I'd just bought at an old barn-turned-antiques store, and I was having trouble finding the right size. Frowning again at the vast selection in front of me, I was thinking of asking for help when I heard a voice behind me.

"Skylar?"

I turned, and there he was. "Oh! Hi." Suddenly I remembered my hair was in a ponytail and quickly tugged the elastic out before he could notice my Nixon ears. Slipping it over one wrist, I tried to shake out my hair, fluff it a little.

"Hi." He smiled and my heart thumped hard at the slow stretch of those full lips and the arched brow. Why on earth had he hidden that face for so long? "How are you?"

"Good. I'm just looking for a screw." My eyes went panicky wide as I realized what I said. "For some screws, I mean. Not *a* screw."

He laughed then, a warm, genuine chuckle that sent joy spiraling up inside me. "Do you need some help?"

"I do, actually." I held up one bin pull. "I bought this antique hardware but I can't find the right fit for the hole."

Oh, for fuck's sake.

"I hate when the fit is wrong for the hole." With an easy grin on his face, Sebastian took the pull from me and examined it. "Hmm. Let's see." He hunted around for a moment, during which I covertly studied him from the corner of my eye. He was tall and trim, with a nice round ass which I may or may not have leaned backward to check out while he tested a few different size screws. "Aha." He faced me and held one out. "This should work."

"Great. If they have eight of them, I can get this job done tonight."

"You need eight screws to get the job done?" That brow cocked even higher. "That happens to be my favorite number."

Now *this* guy I could flirt with.

I rolled my eyes and pushed gently on his chest, which was broad and thick. He wore a dark gray track-style jacket which fit his upper body much better than the old baggy sweatshirts he used to wear in high school. "Very funny. So you're talking to me today, huh?"

The smile slid off his face, and immediately I was sorry I'd mentioned anything about our previous meeting. "Yeah. Sorry again about… that one day. I was just…" He closed his eyes for a moment and took a deep breath, his muscular chest rising and falling. "I don't know. I was having a bad day."

"Me too. God." My shoulders shuddered at the memory. "An awful day."

He looked at me sideways. "Yeah?"

"Yeah. I got fired. And then I fell on my face in front of you at the beach. And then the Cherry Pageant people took my crown away." At the time, it had seemed like such a serious personal insult—now it just sounded silly, like I was a child whose favorite toy had been taken away.

"Why?"

I sighed, closing my eyes. "It's a long and embarrassing story."

He shoved his hands in his pockets. "We all have those."

I thought about what Natalie had said about his recent past. *What do you know, Sebastian Pryce and I have something in common.* It gave me an idea. "Hey. Want to trade long and embarrassing stories over a drink?"

His expression immediately went from sympathetic to scared, and I wondered if I'd gone too far.

"I'm sorry." I glanced around. "You came here for something, and the store's about to close. I shouldn't keep you. It was just a thought. Maybe some other time."

"No, no. It's OK." He paused. "Actually, I think I'd like that."

I cocked my head. "You don't sound too sure about it."

"I'm sure." He tapped my nose, an affectionate gesture that surprised me. "Listen. It's not every day that *the* Skylar Nixon asks me for a drink. You have to give me a minute." Lifting an arm in between us, he pinched the skin on his wrist.

"Oh, stop." Flustered, I pushed his hand down. "Don't be silly."

He grinned. "I need to grab some chairs, though. Should we meet out front?"

"Chairs? You're shopping for furniture at the hardware store?"

"For my patio. They've got some on sale here this week."

"Where do you live?"

"On Old Mission. I built a cabin."

"Really? I live on Old Mission too. I mean, my parents do, and I'm—" I shook my head. "Never mind. That's another embarrassing story. Anyway, that's awesome about the cabin. I love cabins. So much charm."

He shrugged. "I'm not sure you'd call it charming yet, but it's working for me."

"I'd love to see it. Maybe I can help." He looked at me sort of oddly, and again I wondered if I was being too forward. "Sorry—it was just a thought. I tend to say anything that comes into my head. I should really learn to think before speaking."

"No, it was a nice thought. I just—haven't had many visitors."

I decided to drop it. "Well, I'm going to pay for my screws"—I sighed, squeezing my eyes shut. "Don't even make a joke, please—and then I will meet you out front. Sound good?"

He nodded, a smile tugging at his lips. I liked the way the bottom one was fuller than the top. "Sounds good."

He brushed by me, and I pretended to occupy myself counting out eight screws, but really I watched him as he walked away, enjoying the fluttery feeling in my stomach. I admired the round ass, the trim waist, the V of his torso to his shoulders. I imagined what he'd look naked, and the flutter moved lower.

Whoa, there, Skylar. Just calm down. Yes, it's been a while since you were in the saddle, but that is no mechanical bull you're looking at. And if what Natalie said was true, he probably needs a friend.

Still.

I tilted my head to get a better view.

I could go seven seconds on that body. I could go seven seconds on that body all. night. long.

chapter nine

Sebastian

The fact that I ran into Skylar again on a good day was the most mercy I'd been granted in a long time. It's not that the obsessive thoughts weren't there, but they didn't feel so huge or compelling. I was able to consciously file them in a compartment of my brain I thought of as the Fuck You I Don't Care folder and be myself. On my good days, I could do that.

It felt so easy to talk to her, and she was so sweetly embarrassed about her unintentionally dirty remarks.

But I'd had an unintentional twitch in my pants when she put her hands on my chest, and I'd faltered when she mentioned my behavior from two weeks ago. I had no decent explanation. The truth was, not a day had gone by that I hadn't thought about her.

And then there she was. Chatting me up. Asking me for a drink. Expressing interest in where I lived. Wanting to come over and see it.

And I'd handled myself just fine.

I could have said no to the drink. I could have gone home, crossed off Talk to Skylar Nixon off my list, called today one of my best days yet, and allowed myself a celebratory beer on the deck in one of my new chairs, most likely followed by celebratory jerking off to the memory of her ass in those yoga pants. (Twice, of course.)

But the truth was, I didn't want to be alone.

Was it wrong to take her up on her offer just for a little company? Would it be too misleading? She was pretty and sweet, but dating was out of the question. She deserved better than me. And I couldn't see her as a fuck friend, either. She was too good for that.

Keep it in your pants asshole. She said a drink, that's all.

So while I selected and paid for my Adirondack chairs, I made up my mind to get to know her the way I wished I would have in school, and not to let either my attraction for her or my irrational fear of hurting her get in the way. I'd keep my compulsions in check, and stay in the moment.

For a guy like me, it was a pretty fucking tall order.

But today was a good day.

• • •

She pulled up next to me as I slid the heavy boxes containing the chairs into the back of my truck. "What do you think?" she asked through the open windows of an old Ford Explorer. It surprised me—I'd pictured a girl like her driving a much flashier car. Although her clothing today had surprised me too. I couldn't ever recall seeing Skylar Nixon in sweats before. They looked good on her, though. She was small but curvy, not waif thin like a lot of the beautiful women were in New York. Skylar looked like the kind of girl you could go hiking with, but then you could take her out for ice cream afterward, and maybe she'd order a double scoop.

It gave me an idea.

"Hey, have you had dinner yet?" It was close to six, and I hadn't eaten. A restaurant was always a trigger risk, but if ever I was going to take one, it should be on a day like today.

"No." She glanced at the plastic bag on the passenger seat. "I was trying to get this last chore done first, but I don't care about it now."

"Would you maybe want to grab a bite?"

She smiled. "Sure. Place?"

"What do you feel like?"

She thought for a second. "I wouldn't say no to a cheeseburger."

"How about Sleder's?" I suggested. "Meet there?"

"OK. Or we could drive together," she said with a shrug. "I'll ride with you and you can drop me here afterward."

"All right." I said it, but the hair on the back of my neck stood on end as I moved around to the passenger side to open the door for her.

"Thanks." She hopped up into the cab and I shut the door, my heart pumping a little too quickly for comfort.

And then the voice spoke up.

Maybe this was a mistake. Now you'll be alone with her in your car, and—

No. No. This is a good day. Please don't ruin it, I begged the voice. Please let me enjoy her company without complications. One evening. It's all I ask. One normal evening with a friend, the first one in a year.

I slid behind the wheel and shut the door, feeling the tension in my shoulders, my arms, my jaw. Sticking the key in the ignition, I put both hands on the wheel and gripped tight. *Fuck.*

"Hey." She put her hand on my arm, and I couldn't even look at it. "Hey. Look at me."

Reluctantly, I met her eyes. Their color looked even sweeter in the soft pink light of the sunset. I flexed my fingers on the wheel. My composure was slipping, and she knew it. *You're going to scare her. Fucking quit it.* But how could I explain my erratic behavior to her *without* scaring her? Before I could get a handle on what to say, she spoke up again.

"I don't know you at all, Sebastian. And maybe girls shouldn't jump into trucks with strange men who could be serial killers. But you know what? I need a nice night out with a friend. And for whatever reason, I trust you. Somehow I get the feeling that it's *me* making *you* uncomfortable."

Damn, she was intuitive. And a chatterbox, just like her sister. For a second, I felt like smiling—how did those two ever have a conversation without talking over each other? I cleared my throat. "Yeah."

"Would it be better if I drove myself to Sleder's?" She took her hand from my arm and put it on the door handle. "I really don't mind. I shouldn't have just assumed I could jump in with you."

"No," I said, too quickly and loudly. After a deep breath, I turned my upper body to face her. *Better to tell her on a good day. It'll come out clearer.* "Please stay. I'm just going to be upfront about this, Skylar. And if you want to drive yourself after I tell you, or if you want to forget dinner altogether and just go home alone, I'll understand." *I'll die a little, but I'll understand.*

"OK." She put her hands in her lap and looked at me expectantly. Her trust in me was so endearing, suddenly I couldn't resist a little joke.

"I'm really a serial killer."

For a second, her face blanched, but she recovered quickly, slapping me on the arm. "You big jerk! Come on. Talk to me. I know we weren't friends in school or anything, but we've at least known each other for a long time. Fourth grade, right? You came in the middle of the year."

She was right. We'd moved up here from Chicago after my mom died to live closer to my dad's family. "You remember that?"

"Yes. And I remember that you were really good at math and once stayed in at recess to help me with lattice multiplication."

"I did?" Holy shit, how could I have forgotten that? I was touched that she remembered something about me—something positive and not odd. The tension between my shoulders eased a little. "OK,

I'm not a serial killer. But the problem is that sometimes I think I could be."

"What?" She looked at me strangely, then glanced behind her out the window, like she was considering making a run for it. Not that I blamed her. I hesitated...was telling her the right thing? If she bolted, wouldn't I feel even worse?

Stop fucking second guessing yourself. Just tell her.

"It's this glitch in my brain," I finally said. "A fear of doing harm lodges there and refuses to leave. I've read that other people have these thoughts occasionally, a fleeting image of doing something completely out of character, something violent and horrible, but then it passes as quickly as it comes. Not for me. When that kind of thought enters my brain, it takes up permanent real estate, and nothing I do or say can evict it."

"Like what kind of harm?" she asked cautiously.

I couldn't tell her about choking her—I just couldn't. "It's usually something specific," I said, rubbing the back of my neck. "For example, I used to refuse to pick up knives in the kitchen at home if anyone else was around because I was scared I'd lose my mind and stab someone. In fact, I made my father hide the sharp knives, and I'd only use plastic."

Her jaw dropped. "What? But you know you wouldn't stab anyone."

"Doesn't matter. I feel like since the thought is there, that must mean I really want to do it and I'm not the person I thought I was." I braced myself, waited for her to say *You're not the person I thought you were either, so I'm getting the fuck out of here.*

"That's awful," she said softly. "Have you always felt like that?"

"It started when I was about eight, but I didn't really get diagnosed until my mid-teens. And all the stuff I used to do, that I still sometimes do, the counting and all that, the obsessions with certain numbers—somehow my brain thinks that helps. It relieves the anxiety for the time being and makes me feel safe, makes me feel other people are safe."

She nodded slowly, taking it all in. "And the...germ thing? The hand washing?"

So she does remember that. "That's related too. Those are visible, compulsive aspects of OCD, the ones people tend to focus on, but for me, at least at this point in my life, the worst are the obsessive thoughts. I'm usually able to manage the other stuff."

"Can't you just..." She flipped a hand in the air. "Shove them out of your mind? Like, think about something else? That's what I do."

I shook my head. "I wish I could, but not only is that impossible for me, the more I try to do that, the worse it gets."

"God, Sebastian, I had no idea. That must be so hard to live with."

"It is." It felt surprisingly easy to open up to her. The only other person I'd talked to like this in the last few years were therapists. I sure as hell hadn't ever talked to a woman on a date this way. But it felt good. "You know that voice in your head that knows all your deepest fears and apprehensions, the one that knows exactly how to make you doubt yourself, the one that refuses to leave you alone until you feel so on edge that you can't even function?"

"Yeah," she said quietly. "I hate that voice."

I regarded her a moment. "What does yours say?"

She sighed. "That I'm stupid. That I'm a failure. That I'm never going to be as successful as my sisters and I should just stop trying."

Her candor surprised me, as did her doubts about herself. On the outside, Skylar Nixon appeared to have everything going for her. But I knew better than anyone that you can never tell what demons someone is fighting. "And you know that's not true. But it's hard to ignore, isn't it? For me, it's impossible. I have to learn to accept it as part of me without being its victim, without sacrificing my entire life to it." *Or worse, someone else's*, I thought, hearing the sound of Diana's anguished sobs behind a locked bedroom door.

She tilted her head, her expression curious. "How do you do it? Medication?"

I refocused on the woman in front of me. "That's part of it, but the meds don't cure it. I think the bigger help, for me anyway, is the therapy." I took a deep breath and exhaled. "I have good days and bad. Today is good."

She smiled. "I think so too."

• • •

It might have been a good day, but walking into a restaurant with Skylar still made me edgy. We were seated at a four-top table, and she sat adjacent to me, which put her closer than if she'd sat in the chair across from mine. People were staring at us, and they were probably wondering what a girl like her was doing with an eccentric like me. I wasn't stupid—I knew rumors had gone around after I'd returned from New York, especially since one of my sisters-in-law has a big mouth, but I was used to not caring what people thought. Skylar, though, kept her head down, her hair hanging in her face. Was she ashamed to be seen with me? If so, then why had she suggested a drink? This was a mistake.

"Are you OK?" she asked, her eyes concerned. "I'm sorry people are staring at us," she said. "It's my fault, and it's probably making you feel weird."

"Your fault? I think it's my fault."

Her eyes went wide. "Your fault? Why would it be your fault? I'm the one who made an ass of myself on national TV. My God, I drunk-rode a mechanical bull for seven seconds."

"Fuck," I said with a straight face. "That's a horrible number."

She looked confused, and then it registered. "Oh, ha ha ha." She slapped my arm. "I'm glad my humiliation is so amusing."

Laughing a little at her red face, I assured her I had never heard of the show and couldn't care less about it, nor did I care what other people in here might be whispering about her.

"Thank you. I wish more people cared less. I keep getting the evil eye from all corners of the room." We sat back as our server set two plates in front of us and warned us they were hot.

"You know who you are," I said once we were alone again. "Fuck them."

She smiled ruefully. "I wish I could have that attitude. I know I shouldn't care about what people think, but easier said than done."

"Yeah. I know that feeling."

She gave me a sympathetic half-smile and picked up her cheeseburger. "So you had a good day today. Tell me about it."

While we ate, I told her about how I'd hung a hammock between two birches that morning and took a nap in it this afternoon.

"I love naps," she enthused, munching a french fry. "Any day with a nap in it is automatically better."

"Agreed." For a moment, I indulged in a fantasy of the two of us in my hammock, Skylar lying on top of me, head on my chest, her bare feet tangled with mine, the leaves shading us from the afternoon sun. I'd play with her hair and she'd sigh softly, and I'd feel her body melt into mine. We could fall asleep to the sounds of the birds and and the wind, and the water, and—

Fuck. I wish things were different.

I picked up my beer and took a long pull. No sense in thinking like that. I was who I was. "So did you have a good day?"

"I guess so. I worked this morning, and then I went shopping for something to wear to the reunion."

"What reunion?"

"Ours. Our ten-year high school. It's this Saturday. I was going to ask you if you were going." She picked up her wine glass.

85

"Uh, no. No fucking way." I took another drink and shook my head as I set the bottle down. "There's no one there I'd want to see."

"Oh." Her face fell, which she tried to hide by taking a long sip of wine. Several long sips.

"Let me rephrase that," I said, sorry I'd hurt her feelings. "I'm looking at the only person I'd want to see."

Her eyes lit up, her cheeks blooming pink. "Thank you."

"But there's no one there who'd care about seeing me."

"That's not true," she said, setting down her empty glass. "I'd care."

"Thanks, but I'd rather fucking shoot myself than go to that thing."

She sighed. "That's kind of how I feel about it now too. I know everyone there will just be talking shit about me, being pretend-nice to my face."

"Then don't go."

"I have to."

"Why?"

"Because if I don't, everyone will talk shit about me."

My forehead wrinkled. "Wait, you just said they'd talk shit about you if you did go."

"Yeah, but it would be worse shit talk if I wasn't there," she said with some sort of baffling female logic. "So I have to go, and you should go too. In fact, we should go together."

I almost choked. "What?"

"We should go together." She braced her elbows on the table and leaned toward me, her eyes twinkling with mischief. "Then we could give them something new to talk about."

I leaned in too. I couldn't resist. "Yeah? Like what?"

"Like this."

And without any warning whatsoever, she kissed me. Put those soft pink rose petal lips right over mine and left them there for a second, during which I was too stunned to move. My cock jumped, and I pulled away.

Then she sat back, her expression horrified. "Oh God. I'm so sorry."

chapter ten

Skylar

Holy shit. What did I just do?

I kissed him. I kissed him.

I kissed Sebastian Pryce.

I tried to read his expression, but I couldn't. Best I could tell, it was somewhere between *Jesus Christ, why the hell did she do that?* and *Goddamn, let's flip this table out of the way and go at it.*

An eternity passed. Several species of birds went extinct. Continents drifted.

"Say something," I begged. "I feel horrible right now. I shouldn't have done that. Can I blame the wine?" Yes. That was it. Pin the kiss on the Pinot.

But had it been the wine? Maybe it was something else. I was no math expert, but this was an intoxicating equation: Hot Guy with Mysterious Past + Way With Pretty Words x Chivalry at Beach / His

Aloofness at Coffee Shop (Immunity to My Face & Flirty Efforts) + Innuendo at Hardware Store x Honest Confession about OCD Struggles —> Curiosity + Arousal (Belly Flutters + Pulse Quickening)=ATTACKISS.

Right?

Or was I overthinking it? Maybe the plain, crazy truth was just that I was really attracted to Sebastian Pryce. But he was probably one of those quiet, tortured geniuses that didn't go for girls like me. He went to law school, for heaven's sake! He wrote poetry!

His lips tipped up slightly, those warm lips that had felt so good against mine. "Ah. Sure. It's fine. Don't feel horrible, really. You just surprised me." He shifted in his chair.

"I can tell." I reached for my wine glass but it was empty. Frantically, I looked around for our server. *Waiter! This is an emergency!*

"Hey." He put his fingers over my wrist. "It's OK."

"Are you sure?"

His sea glass green eyes were clear and his voice gentle. "I'm sure. I don't want you to feel bad."

"OK." Since he'd been pretty forthcoming about everything tonight, I was sort of hoping he'd elaborate on his feelings, but that's all he said.

For the rest of the night.

I mean he totally shut down.

Not in an angry way or anything, but he just stopped talking. No more jokes, no more smiles, no more stories. Was he anxious? Angry? Confused? Scared? In any case, I was so embarrassed and flustered I talked about anything and everything just to fill the silence.

We finished our meals—I decided against the second glass of wine, especially since he just had the one beer—and he drove me back to my car. I chirped like a bird on crank about random nonsense the entire ride back, and as we pulled into the hardware store lot, I looked over and saw him laughing a little.

"What?" I asked.

"You. Do you ever stop talking?"

I slapped my hands over my face. "No. I mean yes, but no. Not when I'm nervous." Beneath my palms, my face was hot.

"Why are you nervous?"

"Because! I made an ass of myself by kissing you in the restaurant! And you're all smart and silent and mysterious and I'm just…" I threw my hands in the air. "Obvious and silly."

"Is that what you think?" He put the truck in park and shifted on the seat to face me.

"Yes." I turned toward him. "Because before I did that, everything seemed fine. And then afterward, you kind of just…shut down."

Nodding slowly, he rubbed the back of his neck. "Yeah. I guess I did."

"Why? Are you mad?"

He looked at me strangely. "Why would I be mad?"

"I don't know! I can usually read people pretty well but your face was like totally impassive. Fucking stonehenge. And you weren't *talking* either, so I felt crazy awkward and tried to talk for the both of us."

He cracked a smile. "You did it well."

I stared helplessly at him, finally out of words.

"OK, look." He put an elbow on the back of the seat and propped his head on his fingers. His expression was more relaxed, amused even. "I'm sorry I shut down. I was trying to process some things."

"Like what?"

"Like why you did it."

"I did it because I felt like it. How'd you feel about it? Be honest."

He smiled lazily, and I had the insane desire to trace his lips with my tongue. "Good."

I gaped at him. "That's it? Good? You've been silent for an entire hour and a half and that's all I get? Good?"

"Uh huh." His eyes glittered in the dark, and I hoped he was undressing me with them.

"Oh, that is so mean."

"Sorry. I'm a man of few words."

"How can a lawyer be a man of a few words?"

A beat went by. "Did I tell you I was a lawyer?"

Oh fuck. Fuck fuck fuck. "Um, you must have, right?"

"I don't think I did."

He didn't seem angry, exactly, but there was an edge to his tone that hadn't been there before, a wariness, maybe. I decided to come clean. If we were going to be friends, I felt like I owed him the truth about what I'd heard. After all, he'd been more than honest with me tonight.

Plus the silence was killing me.

"OK, don't be mad. Natalie mentioned that she'd

heard some women talking in the shop about you. She told me she overheard you were a lawyer in New York."

"Anything else?" His voice was tight.

I took a breath. "Yes. There was something about you having some sort of...mental breakdown last year." I decided to skip the fiancée part.

He nodded slowly, a reaction I was starting to recognize as his *I need to take this in so don't ask right now* gesture. But I was me, so I asked.

"Want to talk about it?"

"No."

"Oh. OK." At a loss for what to say and worried I'd pushed too far, I slung my bag over my shoulder and reached for the door handle. "I should get going anyway. Thanks for dinner. I had fun." I opened the door, and he grabbed my arm.

"Hey."

I looked back at him.

"Come here." He tugged me toward him, and I shut the door. "I'm sorry. I just don't want to talk about that stuff right now."

"It's fine," I said with a shrug. "Your past is none of my business. I shouldn't have asked about it."

"Skylar." Taking my hand in his, he gently rubbed his thumb across the tops of my fingers. "I've said more to you tonight than I've said to anyone but my therapist in the last year. And I don't even remember the last time someone kissed me by surprise."

My heart raced with pleasure—not desire or lust or sympathy, just pleasure. It meant something to me that he'd opened up a little tonight, especially since he'd built such protective walls around himself. Not that I blamed him. The more I thought about what school must have been like for him, the worse I felt. How horrible to live like that, to be so alone.

"I'm glad you did," I said softly. "I like listening to you, and talking to you. And kissing you." I lifted my shoulders. "I like you, Sebastian. I want to know you better."

His eyes dropped to our hands. "I'm not an easy person to get to know."

I tipped his chin up, forcing him to look me in the eye. "I'm willing to try."

chapter eleven

Sebastian

She got out of the truck and shut the door without another word. I watched her open up her car, get in, and drive off, wishing I'd have had the nerve to kiss her.

Of the two of us, she's the brave one. Brave enough to ask me for a drink, brave enough to trust me alone with her, brave enough to kiss me just because she felt like it. That actually made me smile. *I did it because I felt like it.* I could still hear her voice, guileless and sweet. And I could still see the look in her eye as she leaned toward me, daring and sexy. Then her lips on mine... I groaned aloud and put the truck in drive.

She had no idea what she did to me. Of course I couldn't talk after that. I was too busy trying to adjust my boxers and not think about my dick. But of course, since I was trying not to think about it, it was all I could think about. Couldn't she tell?

Maybe not, since she thought I might be mad that she'd kissed me. Mad, for fuck's sake. The only thing that made me mad about it was that I hadn't kissed her back. I hadn't told her how much I liked it, how much I'd wanted to do it again before she got out of the truck, how many times I'd imagined kissing her back when she barely knew I existed—and how much better the real thing was. It had taken some serious fortitude not to yell "CHECK, PLEASE," grab her by the hand, and run out of there so I could take her back to the cabin and kiss her properly. Lavishly. Thoroughly.

How long had it been since I'd had a woman stretched out beneath me, moaning with pleasure while I devoured every inch of her skin? And Skylar's skin looked so delicious. I bet it would feel like satin under my tongue. Taste like cherries and vanilla ice cream.

Fuck, I was hard again.

And she knew things about me. She knew about New York, or at least the bare bones of it, and she'd still asked me out.

As I drove the long, dark highway up the center of the peninsula, her SUV ahead of me, I found myself wishing again that things were different. No, that I was different. That I had something to offer her. Sure, there would be good days, like this one. And for a while, maybe the good days would outweigh the bad, or maybe she'd find the good days worth the bad. But that wouldn't last.

So when Skylar turned off 37 onto the road leading to her parents' farm, I didn't follow her like I wanted to. I didn't pull up next to her in the dark, get out of the truck and wait for her to ask me what I was doing there. I didn't grab her and crush my mouth to hers without saying a word. I didn't hold her body close to mine and fiercely whisper how much it meant that she was willing to try.

But I wanted to.

So badly it hurt.

• • •

When I got home, the cabin seemed particularly dark and empty. I didn't feel like mindless television, and the internet would only depress me, so I picked up a book my dad had given me recently, sat on the couch and tried to read. But I couldn't focus on the story—the silence was smothering me tonight. Throwing my jacket on, I walked outside and unloaded the Adirondack chairs from the back of my truck. But once I'd lugged the boxes over to the patio, I didn't feel like putting them together. Instead, I left them there and wandered down to the dock, grateful for the nighttime noise of the crickets and owls, the water lapping softly against the rocky shore.

What was Skylar doing right now? Sleeping? Watching TV? Or did she like to read at night like I did? Maybe she'd felt industrious when she got home and was attaching her bin pulls to the kitchen cupboards. I wish I was there to help her. I should have offered. I didn't even have her number to call her again. Why hadn't I asked her for it?

After a few minutes, I went back inside and sank onto the couch, feeling so lonely and sad I did something I hadn't done in months. I picked up my phone and called Diana.

As always, it went to voicemail.

"This is Diana. Leave a message, and I'll get back to you as soon as possible."

"Hey...it's me." I closed my eyes. "I know it's been a while. But I was thinking about you and thought I'd try to reach out. I guess you're still not ready to talk to me, and that's OK. I just wanted to let you know that you were on my mind and I hope you're doing well. And...I'm sorry. I know I've said that a million times, but I am. I wish I could go back and do it all differently. Anyway. Goodnight."

I ended the call, feeling, as I always did after calling Diana, a mixture of guilt and disgust with myself. I should delete her number and quit bothering her.

I was about to do just that when it vibrated in my hand.

It was Diana's number.

Fuck. She'd never actually returned a call. Now what? Grimacing, I pressed Accept. I owed her at least that much.

"Diana?"

A long pause. "Hi."

"How are you?"

"Fine. I...heard your message just now."

I closed my eyes. "Yeah. Sorry about that. I shouldn't call you."

"No, you shouldn't." She sighed. "But I guess if I really wanted it to stop, I'd have changed my number by now."

"I've often wondered why you haven't."

"I don't know. I must like the reminders you're

doing OK." She paused. "Are you?"

I answered semi-truthfully. "Mostly. What about you?"

"I'm OK."

"Still in New York?"

"Yes." She was silent again, and I worried she was crying. Fucking hell, had I not caused this woman enough pain? "Why did you call tonight?" she finally asked, and I heard the struggle in her voice.

To punish myself. "To apologize, I guess."

"You can stop doing that. I've gotten all your messages."

"Does that mean you forgive me?"

She didn't answer right away. "For what, Sebastian?"

Something twisted in my gut. *Proposing when I wasn't sure. Shutting you out. Refusing sex. Not making time for therapy. Not taking the meds. Overdoing alcohol. Being late for everything. Lying to you. Calling off the wedding. Breaking your heart.*

The list was so endless I couldn't even begin.

"Does my forgiveness even matter anymore?"

I swallowed. "Yes."

"Why?"

"Why?" I parroted, although it was a fair question. Diana and I were over, after all. But I hated the thought that she'd resent me for the rest of her life. I deserved it, but deep down inside, I felt like if she told me that she was able to let it go and move on, that she was happy again in spite of the pain I'd caused, then maybe it would mean that I deserved some happiness too. That I wouldn't have to punish myself forever. "I don't know. It just feels right to ask for it."

"God, Sebastian. That apology sucked."

I winced, but I also smiled a little. It reminded me of something Skylar would say. "Yeah. You know me. Not great with words."

"That's not true. You just don't trust yourself to say what's on your mind."

Again, I thought of Skylar. "I suppose you're right. Maybe I should work on that."

"Are you going to therapy?"

"Yes."

"Good. And you're back in Michigan?"

"Yes. I built a cabin on the property I own. Where I tried to make you go camping that time, remember?"

"Oh, God. That experience still haunts me."

I imagined her shuddering, the shake of her narrow shoulders. "Yes, city girl. You'd hate it."

"Well, that doesn't matter anymore. You can camp out in the woods all you want now. I'll be here in my apartment with my doorman out front. And if I feel like flying off to Rome or Paris for a romantic vacation with my boyfriend, I can do it."

There it was—the dig at me for being scared to fly. She never did miss an opportunity. "Sounds perfect for you."

"It is." She was quiet a moment. "Are you dating?"

I paused. "No."

"Why the hesitation?"

"I don't know. It feels weird to talk about it with you. And I'm not really dating anyone. I met someone recently, but—"

"Who is she?" she asked quickly.

"No one you'd know. Just someone I went to school with."

"Oh. She's from there?"

"Yeah." On the off chance that Diana knew Skylar from that reality show, I decided to change the subject. "Anyway, it's nothing. I barely know her." The conversation was starting to feel a little strange, so I decided to end it. "Well, thanks for calling me back. I appreciate it. And…it's good to talk to you." That was true. Her low, smoky voice didn't have the power over me it once had, but I felt relief that we were finally able to have a civil conversation. And I was glad she seemed well. Maybe I hadn't done irreparable harm.

But she didn't hang up. "Can I ask you a question, Sebastian?"

Oh shit. "OK."

"Why did you propose? We could have just broken up if you didn't love me enough."

I closed my eyes and pinched the bridge of my nose. *Fuck. I never should have said that to her.* "I told you. I was trying to be the person you wanted me to be."

"So it was my fault." A hard edge to her tone now.

"No. None of it was. I've told you that too. I'll take all the blame."

"I loved you. I was willing to put up with all your shit. And you gave up on me. On us. You humiliated me."

"I know." That thought haunted me. Diana had

loved me, even with all the strange quirks. What if I never had that again? Even if I hadn't been madly in love with her, maybe I should have tried harder to make it work. "You deserved better."

"Damn right I did," she said bitterly. "We had a perfect wedding planned, Sebastian. A perfect life."

No, we didn't. Not for me. That life in New York... The eighty hour work weeks, the all-nighters, the tedious grunt work, the insane deadlines, the constant pressure to bill, the competitive social scene, the pressure to constantly work more, earn more, have more. You loved all that. But it was tearing me apart.

"I should go." I ended the call without saying anything else and went to bed, upset that I'd made the call in the first place. What the hell did I expect? I'd called off the wedding with six months to go, told her she wasn't the one—why should she forgive me?

Sometimes I wondered if I'd made the wrong decision...maybe I had loved her enough and didn't know it. Maybe I should have tried harder to live with the doubt. Maybe I should be married to her right now.

But it wasn't Diana I missed when I got between the sheets that night. It wasn't her body I wanted next to mine as I slipped my hard, swollen flesh through my fist. It wasn't her smile or her voice or her laugh or her eyes or her mouth I thought about at the moment of agonizing, sublime relief.

It was Skylar's.

And even though I knew I was no good for her, I also knew I wanted her too much to stay away.

chapter twelve

Skylar

I had the following day off from Coffee Darling, and I went to bed relishing the thought of sleeping in. But, wouldn't you know it, my body clock was used to waking up early now, and my eyes opened at six and refused to stay closed again. *Oh well.* I swung my legs over the side of my bed. Maybe I'll get a nap in later. *Might as well get up and get some things done.*

By nine, I'd attached all the bin pulls to the kitchen cupboards—laughing to myself when I recalled all the screw jokes from last night—taped off and primed a bathroom, and thought about Sebastian approximately one million times. Despite the slightly awkward ending, the spontaneous date had been a lot of fun.

Besides being handsome, Sebastian was a great listener and he made me laugh. I loved how open he'd been about his OCD, how honestly and self-deprecatingly he'd told me what it was like. My heart ached for him and how tough it must have been all those years before getting treatment, especially without the support of friends. And every time I thought about the beautiful, sad words he'd written about me, I got chills.

He'd said he wasn't easy to get to know, and I'd meant it when I said I was willing to try.

Would he let me?

While the primer dried, I decided to get started refinishing an old bookshelf I'd found in my parents' attic. My mother helped me carry it out to the driveway, where I'd laid newspapers on the ground.

She ran a hand over the top, which had several gouges. "Cripes, this thing's pretty beat up. It was my grandfather's. It's called a lawyer's bookcase."

"Really?" I said, my ears perking up at the word lawyer. "I'm going to take off the varnish and paint it white."

"That'll be nice. He'd be pleased you're going to use it."

"I won't keep it, Mom. It's for a guest house." I picked up the can of paint and varnish remover I'd purchased and began reading the directions on the back.

"No, you should take it when you move out."

Was I imagining things, or did she emphasize the words *move out*? Was she dropping a hint? My eyes traveled over the words on the can without processing them.

"Where are you thinking of going?" she went on breezily.

"I haven't decided yet." I finally looked up. "I didn't know I was being thrown out quite so soon."

"Honey, I'm not throwing you out." Her tone was soothing but firm. "You're always welcome here."

"But?" I shook the can. Violently.

"Well, don't you think you should have a plan?"

"An exit strategy? I'm working on it." I pulled off the cap, hoping she'd leave me alone to work. When she didn't, I began spraying.

Out of the corner of my eye, I saw my mother cross her arms. She was petite and curvy, like Natalie and me, albeit with a few extra rolls around the middle. Only Jillian got our dad's long, lanky frame and dark hair.

"Are you going back to New York?"

"I don't know yet, Mom. I just said I don't have a plan." I tried not to sound as annoyed as I felt.

"Well, do you have a deadline in mind? For *having* a plan, I mean?" she pressed.

I stopped spraying and faced her. "Do I need one? If I'm not welcome at your house, just say it."

"Sky, don't be silly. I said you're welcome. My children are always welcome. I'm only trying to help you think ahead. You don't want to live with your parents forever."

I realized that she also meant *I don't want my adult daughter living at home with me forever.* She and my dad were probably used to their privacy and routine by now. As if that wasn't enough, she went on.

"And what about a job? It's nice you're working with your sister, but is that really what you want to do, work at a coffee shop?" She held up her hands. "If it is, that's fine, but—"

"I get it, Mom." I turned back to the bookcase. "I'll come up with a plan."

"OK." She turned her own dazzling beauty queen smile on me. "Dinner's at six thirty, don't forget. I'm making fried chicken," she said proudly. "Nat, Dan, and Jilly are coming too. Won't that be nice?" She patted my shoulder and headed back into the house.

Sure. Another family function where we can all compare the Nixon sisters. Which one of these is not like the others?

Usually I looked forward to family dinners, but my mother's words had cut deep. For the past couple weeks, I'd done a pretty good job avoiding the hard questions, but clearly I couldn't go on like this forever. If only I had some kind of calling, like Jillian's to be a doctor, or a dream that was achievable with hard work and dedication, like Natalie's shop.

As I scraped off the old varnish, I tried to think of jobs I'd enjoy going to every day, something I could get excited about. My mother was right in that coffee shop employee wasn't really on the list. And as much as I loved the farm, agriculture wasn't really my thing either. I'd enjoyed the job at Rivard, but there was no way I'd get that position back. I was too ashamed to even ask for it. But maybe something like that...something fun, something that allowed me to work with people, something that allowed for creativity and spontaneity.

Christ. That is the vaguest fucking job description ever. You suck.

I did. I did suck.

By the time I'd taken off the varnish, eaten a quick lunch, and plugged my dad's sander into the extension cord I'd run from the house, I was convinced I'd never be happy and I should just face the fact that I was a twenty-seven-year-old loser with a pretty face and not much else.

And even that wasn't going to last forever. Thirty was around the corner, and then forty, and then fifty, and then sixty...decades of wrinkling skin and cracking bones and sagging flesh. But would there even be anyone who cared? My romantic history was as crappy as my job history—I wasn't even sure I'd ever been in love.

I was still brooding about it when Sebastian's truck pulled into the driveway an hour later. Immediately my mood improved.

"Hey," I said, telling myself to walk, not run, toward him as he got out. It's not like he was offering a life preserver to my drowning ass. "What are you doing here?"

He shut the truck door and leaned back against it, hands in his pockets. The sunglasses on his face hid his eyes, but he was smiling. "I came to see you."

My insides danced a little. "How'd you find me?"

"I went to the shop. Your sister told me it was your day off and said you might be here." He glanced over to where I'd been working. "Am I interrupting?"

"Not at all. I need a distraction, actually." *The kind that happens without pants.*

"Want to show me what you're working on?"

"Sure." Trying to keep my thoughts clean, I led him over to the bookcase and explained what I was doing. "It was my grandfather's bookcase."

"Even better. You have a connection to it."

"Yes." I clasped my hands together and rocked back on my heels. "What are you up to today?"

He shrugged, dropping his eyes to the ground a moment. "I had to go into town for a few things, but it's such a nice day, I thought maybe I'd put together those chairs I bought last night and sit on the patio this afternoon."

"Sounds nice. It is beautiful today, supposed to hit seventy-five. Can you believe it? In May?" *Invite me. Invite me. Invite me.*

He ran a hand over his short hair. "You mentioned wanting to see the cabin. I thought maybe—"

"I'd love to! Just give me one minute, OK?" Turning around, I went to unplug the sander when I panicked. I faced him again, my lower lip caught between my teeth. "Wait. You were going to ask me to come over, right?"

He laughed, his face lighting up. He looked so different when he smiled! "Yes. I was."

"Whew. OK, good." I put away the tools, and Sebastian helped me move the bookcase into the guest house, where I snuck away to quickly run a brush through my hair and rinse with mouthwash.

Not that I was planning on attackissing him again. But maybe he'd take the lead—I'd just do my best to let him know I was interested without being too forward.

"I like your house," he said when I came out of the bathroom.

"Thanks. It's my parents' house, technically." Recalling the conversation with my mother, I frowned.

"You don't like living in it?"

"No, it's not that. I just don't...you know what?" I sighed, shaking my head. "Let's not talk about it."

His mouth fell open. "*You* don't want to talk about something?"

I slapped him lightly on the arm. "Ha ha. No, I don't. So let's go, I'm dying to see your place."

"Yours is much fancier," he said as we walked outside. "Mine's going to look very bare to your eye."

I'd like your ass bare to my eye, I thought as I followed him to his truck. "Hey, do you want me to drive myself? That way you won't have to bring me back."

He opened the passenger door for me. "I don't mind bringing you back."

"OK. Thanks." I climbed into the truck, feeling his hand brush my lower back. My entire body jittered with excitement, and I felt like a kid who just learned school is canceled for the day. There was some kind of new current between us—I couldn't put my finger on it exactly, but I thought it had to do with the difference in him...he was so much more relaxed than he'd been at the end of the date last night. Did this mean he was up for seeing where this might go?

I told him to take the long, winding drive around the orchard before heading back out on to the highway, and I pointed out all my favorite spots on the farm—the best trees to climb, my favorite shady spot for reading, the perfect hiding places for hide and seek or ducking chores.

"You must have missed all this when you moved away," he said, turning onto the main road. "Sounds like you really love it."

"Yeah, I do. And I did miss it."

"Think you'll stay here for good?"

"Probably," I said, staring out the window at the familiar landscape—the rolling hills, the orchards and vineyards, the old red barns with their peeling paint, the new faux chateaux of stone and brick. "What about you?"

"Staying. At least, that's the plan for now."

I asked him if he'd liked living in New York, and we both agreed it was great in some ways and difficult in others. He confided that the pace of big city life and the demands of his job probably contributed to his relapse. "I like the outdoors a lot," he said, a little wistfully. "Hiking, fishing, camping. And I didn't get the chance to do those kinds of things very often. Plus my ex-girlfriend wasn't into them."

I was surprised he mentioned her. "A city girl, huh?" I questioned, totally curious.

"Yeah." Out of the corner of my eye, I saw him rub one finger along the stubble beneath his lower lip. After a moment, he went on. "Actually, she was my fiancée."

I risked a sideways look at him. "Wow. It was pretty serious then, huh?

"Felt like it. For a while."

"What happened?"

He shrugged, his jaw stiffening. "I don't want to talk about it."

"Sorry." *You brought it up.* Feeling unfairly chastised, I turned my attention out the window again.

A minute or so later, I heard him sigh. "Sorry."

I looked at him but said nothing. A moment later, he spoke up.

"I lied to her."

"About what?"

"Losing my job. I got fired from the firm I was with for being late all the time, behaving erratically, and then there was the time I took a few punches at a senior partner for calling me a fuck-up when I missed an important deadline."

"Yikes." I had no idea what to say. I mean, I'd been fired too, but his experience sounded worse. "Was it...the OCD?"

"Yeah. I was really stressed out about basically everything in my life, the direction it had taken. It all felt really out of control." He shook his head. "Anyway, I didn't tell her about getting fired right away, and she found out a week later."

"Was she mad?"

He laughed bitterly. "Yeah. She told me she loved me but I'd better get my shit together before the wedding. Then I told her I wasn't sure she was the one, and she freaked the fuck out."

"Ouch." Although secretly I was pleased. Was that mean of me?

He frowned. "Actually, I said I wasn't even sure I believed in the *idea* of the one, but even if I did, I wasn't sure it was her."

"Double ouch. And the ring was still on her finger at this point?"

"Until she took it off and threw it at me."

"How's her aim?"

That actually brought half a smile. "Shitty."

"Guess it wasn't meant to be, then," I said, trying to look on the bright side.

"No, it wasn't. Sometimes I'm surprised she lasted as long as she did."

I wondered what he meant by that. "Because of the OCD, you mean?"

"Yeah." His tone had gone darker. "But there were other problems too. I've been told I don't communicate well. Also that I'm stubborn, unpredictable, and a real dick when I want to be."

My eyebrows shot up. "Wow. That's quite a list. And she still said yes when you proposed, huh?" Feeling this moment could use some levity, I leaned over and gave his leg a smack. "You must be dynamite in the sack."

His shoulders relaxed as he cracked a smile. "That list wasn't all from her," he said, turning onto a gravel drive that led through the woods. "But come to think of it, I've never had any complaints about my sexual prowess."

"Good to know." I wanted to keep flirting, but just then the cabin appeared through a clearing, and I gasped. "Sebastian, it's beautiful!"

"Thanks." He parked on a gravel drive that looped in front of the house, and I got out of the truck and shut the door behind me. It was so quiet, all I heard were birds and the breeze rustling the leaves on the birch trees.

"Oh my god!" I squealed, clasping my hands beneath my chin. "Look at your cute front porch!" Two wooden rocking chairs sat facing the woods. *Two*, I thought. Was he eventually thinking he'd share the place with someone? Or did he really just hate the number one?

"Yeah, I like to sit out there in the morning, watch the sun rise while I have coffee." He went up the steps and unlocked the front door.

"Sunrise?" I winced, following him inside. "I'm more of a sun*set* sort of girl. The sun rises too early for me."

He laughed. "Then you'll like the patio in the back. You could watch the sun set over the bay."

"Perfect. Show me."

He took me through the cabin first, apologizing for its lack of furniture and decoration. True, it was a bit sparse, but it had a rustic, masculine beauty about it that just needed a little touch of feminine texture and color. I loved everything he'd done so far, from the floors to the counters to the bathroom tile, and the whole place smelled amazing—like lemon and cedar and Tide. He probably cleaned it constantly because of his OCD. Was it wrong that it sort of turned me on?

"You've done a great job, Sebastian. You should be really proud. What's up there?" I gestured to the ladder leaning on the wall between the kitchen and bath. "Bedroom?"

"Just a loft. But it's nice. You've got to watch your head up there because of the sloping walls—well, I do," he teased, looking down at me. "But there is a nice big skylight."

I started to climb, looking over my shoulder. "Mind if I go up?"

chapter thirteen

Sebastian

Good fucking God.

She was climbing the ladder to my bedroom and her ass was right in front of my face. My cock began to stiffen.

Sweet Jesus, could I please go ten minutes without getting an erection around her?

I'd hardly slept last night because I couldn't stop thinking about her, and I'd woken up this morning (hard) with her still on my mind, and even though I'd told myself a million times not to go looking for her today, I hadn't been able to resist. *I just want to be around her,* I told the doomsayer in me before he could go on the offensive. *I won't touch her. I just like seeing her smile, hearing her chattering bird voice, making her laugh.*

"Go ahead," I told her. "I'll wait down here."

She looked down at me with playful eyes, making my heart pump harder. "You can come up too, silly. I don't think you're going to try anything."

Oh no? You should feel my dick right now. "It's pretty small up there."

"It's not small, it's cozy," she said, reaching the top. "Get up here." She moved deeper into the loft so I couldn't see her anymore, and I quickly adjusted myself before climbing up after her.

When I reached the top, she was standing in front of the huge, sloping window opposite my bed. "You have a family of cardinals," she said.

"I know. They're noisy in the morning." I stood next to her and looked out. Goddamn it, I could smell her. Mostly it was the varnish remover she'd been using, but there was a hint of something sweet and floral beneath it—I fucking loved that she was girlish and feminine but not afraid to work with her hands.

"I thought you were up before the sun, mister coffee-on-the-porch-before-dawn." She poked me in the ribs, sending a jolt through my veins that seemed to go straight to my cock, and that part of my anatomy didn't need any more encouragement right now. I moved away from her a little, and she giggled. "What, are you ticklish? Huh? Huh?" She started poking me over and over again, in the ribs, on my stomach, on my chest.

"Goddamit, Skylar, knock it off." I tried to back away but she followed me, poking at me everywhere. "Quit touching me."

"I know, I'm handsy, aren't I?" She stopped and held up her palms toward me. "But they're clean, I swear."

"That's not what I meant," I snapped. I knew she'd been joking but her comment was a good reminder that girls like her didn't belong with creeps like me. I didn't need the voice to tell me that.

"OK, OK. Relax." She dropped her hands to her sides, the light leaving her eyes. "Sorry. I was just playing with you. Friends do that, you know."

"I know what friends do," I said angrily. "I have had friends before, Skylar, I'm not a total fucking loser anymore, despite what you might remember." But my tone was anything but friendly, and I hated myself for it. It wasn't her I was mad at. Yet I went on. "Although you didn't even remember my face, so you probably don't recall anything else about me either. I didn't exist for people like you, did I?"

Shaking her head, she backed away from me. "Jeez, you can be an asshole out of nowhere."

"I'll add that to the list."

She climbed down the ladder without looking at me.

I let her go, sinking onto my bed. Knees splayed, I propped my elbows on my legs and took my head in my hands. Fuck. FUCK. I *was* an asshole out of nowhere. But she didn't understand what it felt like to want someone so badly and be terrified to touch her. How was I supposed to deal with my feelings for her when I couldn't even handle the thoughts in my own head? My heart was telling me to go after her, but my head wouldn't fucking let me.

But she didn't know any of that. She just knew that I was perfectly friendly one minute and a jerk-off the next.

I heard the front door open and close and thought I wouldn't blame her if she took off in the truck. Dragging my feet, I climbed down the ladder and went to find her.

She wasn't on the porch or in the truck, and I stood still for a second, rubbing my face with my hands, weighed down by guilt and regret. What had I done? Where had she gone? Had it been the back door I heard? I walked around the side of the cabin and looked around. She wasn't on the patio or back steps, and I didn't see her on the dock either. Frowning, I turned and looked back at the driveway, which snaked through the woods. I hoped she hadn't taken off on foot. *Oh God. What did I do?* I was just about to get in the truck and go find her when I heard her voice.

"I'm over here. In the hammock."

Relief washed over me. I looked over to my left and saw her sitting in the hammock, her feet dangling. Slowly, I made my way over to her. My chest hurt when I saw the downtrodden expression on her face. "Hey."

"Hey," she repeated tonelessly, staring at the patio.

I nudged one of her sneakers. "Room for two on there?"

"I'll get off." She started to get up, but I put a hand on her shoulder.

"No, don't. Can I sit with you?"

117

She shrugged, but she sat back and let me lower myself onto the thick woven ropes next to her. My heart beat quicker at her nearness, at the warmth of her leg against mine, at the scent of her hair. I wanted to touch her so badly, hold her close and apologize, ask for another chance. But I couldn't.

We sat in silence for a moment, and I waited for the voice in my head to start in with all the horrible calamities that could befall her from sharing a hammock with me. But I heard nothing but the birds and the water. *Apologize, asshole. You hurt her feelings.*

"I'm sorry, Skylar." I slid my hands up and down the tops of my own legs to keep them off hers. "I shouldn't have been short with you."

"Whatever. It's fine." Her voice was flat. She still wouldn't look at me.

"No, it's not." I decided right there to tell her the truth. It was either that or leave her alone forever, and I couldn't bear that thought. "I'm angry with myself and I took it out on you."

"What are you angry about?"

"Lots of things, but mostly that I don't trust myself around you." I curled my fingers into fists.

"What? That's silly." Her tone had lightened a little.

"But it's the truth. It's my truth, anyway. And it makes me push you away. "

"It doesn't matter that I trust you?"

"It's not that it doesn't matter, Skylar. It does, and I appreciate it." A warm breeze blew in off the water, and I closed my eyes a second. "What you did upstairs, make a joke…that's actually good for me."

"It is?"

"Yes. Ken, my therapist, would have taken your side and told me to lighten up."

She frowned. "That doesn't sound very nice. You can't help the way you are."

Now she was defending me. So fucking adorable. "No, I can't. But I wish I could. I wish I were different." I looked down at her, and those wide blue eyes pulled another truth from me. "Especially where you're concerned."

She shook her head. "I don't want you to be different, Sebastian. I like you, even though you're moody as fuck."

I laughed—that was as apt a description of me as I'd ever heard.

"And I understand that you need time to feel comfortable around me."

"Thank you." I braved putting my hand on the top of her thigh. Her skin was warm and smooth beneath my palm.

She looked at my hand on her leg, started to say something, and stopped herself.

"What?" I asked.

"I'm just wondering…" She fidgeted, looking up at me through her lashes. "I mean… God, this is so embarrassing. I guess I'm wondering if you're even attracted to me. Part of me says not to flirt with you because you just need a friend right now, and another part says I can't help it, because I really like you."

Christ, was she serious? She thought I didn't want her that way? "Well, part of *me* says I spent the entire second half of dinner last night trying not to think about fucking you. And failing. Does that answer your question?"

She gasped, her mouth hanging open. Her eyes danced with shocked delight, and I wished I could keep going, tell her all the things I wanted to do to her, just to keep that happy, stunned look on her face.

"But you were right—I do need time."

"OK," she finally managed.

We sat there for a few minutes in silence, and I gently rocked the hammock forward and back. Eventually, her head tilted toward me, and she rested it against my arm, making me smile. This I could handle. This was the sort of pure, peaceful moment I desperately needed to feel like myself. A sense of calm pervaded me, and I breathed deeply, allowing the woodsy air to fill my lungs. Skylar's breathing was deep and even too, and a moment later I realized she'd fallen asleep.

Testing myself, I lowered my lips to her head and gently pressed them to her hair.

No voice. Just stillness and peace.

Flooded with gratitude, I inhaled the sweet floral scent of her shampoo before closing my eyes.

It might not have been the nap fantasy I'd had last night, but it was a damn good start.

Maybe there was hope for me.

Hope for us.

chapter fourteen

Skylar

I woke up leisurely, completely comfortable. Next to me, Sebastian's breathing was slow and steady, so I figured he'd fallen asleep too. There was something so nice about falling asleep next to someone you liked—it was intimate without being sexual, which was exactly what we needed.

Well, it's what *he* needed. I was up for letting things get sexy right here in this hammock. My insides warmed when I thought of the way he'd said he wanted to let me in, and they went molten when I recalled him saying he'd thought about fucking me all night. He could go from one extreme to the other so quickly. What would he be like as a lover? Sweet and tender? Rough and demanding?

And that body. My God.

My belly flipped as I let my eyes sweep over his abs and crotch and legs, and heat tingled between my thighs. *I could stretch and brush my hand right there...*

Stop it. You just agreed to give him time, and it's probably been about twenty minutes.

Right. He probably meant more time than that.

Just then his hand twitched on my leg, and his breathing altered. "Mmm. Did I fall asleep?"

"Yes. But I don't blame you. It's so quiet and peaceful here, I fell asleep too. In fact, I could go back to sleep." I closed my eyes, not wanting him to move yet. He trailed one finger up my thigh, sending gooseflesh rippling across my skin. God, I wanted his hands on me so badly. How long would I have to wait?

He patted my knee and got up. "I'm going to put those chairs together."

Sighing, I watched him walk over to the two big boxes on the patio. Then I stretched out on my side in the hammock, tucking my hands beneath my face. Guess I'd have to wait a little longer, although I could think of worse ways to spend an afternoon than watching Sebastian perform manual labor outside in the heat, arm muscles flexing. I was dreamily watching him finish up the first chair when he asked if I was awake.

"Yes, just enjoying the view."

He flashed a quick grin at me as he set the drill aside. "You said something last night I'm curious about."

"What was it?"

"You mentioned how the voice in your head tells you you're a failure."

"Oh, that." I frowned. "Yeah, it does. All the time."

He started working on the second chair. "Why?"

Between short bursts of noise from the drill, I opened up about how I felt kind of lost at this point in my life, about how ashamed I was that I'd failed to make it as an actress, and about how my sisters' success only served to make me feel worse. "I feel horrible saying that," I admitted. "I'm so proud of them and I'm happy they're so good at what they do. It's not like I begrudge them their success. I just feel bad about my lack of it."

"But if Natalie's business hadn't done well, would you have called *her* a failure?"

"No, of course not."

"Well, then?"

I frowned. "That's different. That was a business. My failure feels more personal. And yet it was totally public. Add to that I got fired from the only job I've ever really liked and the fact that my mother told me to get a fucking life this morning!" Frustration tightened my throat, and I willed myself not to cry and spoil this nice afternoon.

"Your mother said that to you?" Sebastian stood up and looked at me with concern.

I squeezed my eyes shut against the tears. "She didn't say it like that. She just pressured me about getting a real job. She knows working for Natalie is only a short-term thing. But I'm not good enough at anything to make finding a new job easy, and I have no college degree and nothing interesting or unique to put on a resume."

"That's not true," he said firmly. "You could be good at anything. You just have to decide what you want."

"How am I supposed to do that?" I blustered, sitting up swiftly and nearly toppling backward out of the hammock. "I feel like I've been impersonating some version of myself for so long, I don't even know who I am anymore!" To my dismay, I burst into tears, and I was so embarrassed I jumped out of the hammock and ran down toward the dock, where I put my face into my hands and sobbed.

I heard footsteps behind me, and then felt Sebastian's hand on my shoulder as he turned me into his arms. "Hey, you. Come here."

His chest was warm and solid, and I collapsed against him, crying into my palms. He rubbed my back and trembling shoulders, shushing me gently.

"Here I thought it was *my* anxiety I'd struggle with today," he said after a few minutes. "But you're a mess."

I half-laughed, half-sobbed. "Thanks."

"How much of this is because of that stupid reunion on Saturday?"

"I don't know. Some of it, I guess." I took a few hitching breaths, trying to calm down.

"You should blow it off. I think it's making you feel worse."

"I know it is. But I have to go. I said I'd help with decorations." I looked up at him with tearful eyes. "Would you come with me? Please? Just as friends," I said quickly. "I won't try anything."

He smiled but shook his head. "I really can't, Skylar. It would serve no purpose and just dredge up painful memories. Nothing about high school was good for me."

Nodding sadly, I wiped my eyes and sniffed. "I understand."

"Need a tissue?"

"Yeah."

"Come on. Let's go find some in the house, and then after I finish the chairs, we'll go do something fun. How does that sound?"

"Good." I sniffed again, wondering what his idea of fun was. Algebra? Sudoku? "What'll we do?"

"I don't know. Want to go buy a canoe?

I couldn't help smiling a little, it was so random. "A canoe?"

"Yeah, I've been wanting one. Or maybe a rowboat. You can help me decide."

"All right."

"Then we'll bring it back here and take it out on the water if it's calm enough. How does that sound?"

"Good."

"Can you paddle a canoe?"

I nodded. "I'm good at it, actually."

He elbowed me as we walked toward the cabin. "And you said you've got nothing for your resume."

I laughed, my spirits lifting.

• • •

We compared prices of canoes and rowboats at the sporting goods store, but Sebastian seemed less worried about price than he was about buying the perfect boat. He ended up buying a beautiful wooden rowboat plus some oars and an anchor, and the total cost was so high it made me wonder where his money came from. He'd said he worked part-time for his dad, but was that enough to live on, build and furnish that cabin, *and* have money for luxuries like a boat? Once everything was loaded in the truck and we were on our way back to the cabin, I had to ask.

"So this might be none of my business, and you can tell me to piss off, but without a full-time job, how do you live?" I asked, sucking on the honey stick he'd bought me at the counter. I never could resist those things.

"I have some investment income." He ran a hand over the scruff on his jaw before going on. "My mother's family had money. Old money. My father had no interest in it, so after she died, he and her parents set aside an inheritance for each of her children. I used some for law school and some to rebuild the cabin, but the rest is invested. I don't like to touch it, but I *have* used some of the interest to live on over the last year."

"Oh." I wondered if his mother's death was too painful to talk about. "Were you close to your mom?"

He nodded before taking a deep breath. "I was only eight when she died. As painful as the last year of my life has been, it doesn't come close to that loss. Nothing ever will." His voice broke a little, and my heart did too.

"It's a good thing we're driving because I really want to hug you right now and I can't."

He gave me a threatening look. "You stay in that seatbelt."

I winked at him. "For now."

We drove in silence for a few minutes, and when we passed Chateau Rivard I couldn't resist flipping Miranda Rivard the bird again, even though she couldn't see it. Sebastian laughed.

"Sorry," I said, although I wasn't really.

"That's OK. I did a lot worse after I got fired."

"The worst thing was that I actually liked that job. Doing tastings, giving tours of the chateau and vineyard, talking to people about the wines and the area. I had some ideas for the place too."

He glanced at me. "What kind of ideas?"

"Design ideas. I wanted to modernize the place a little, but there was resistance, and I wasn't there long enough to convince them."

"Maybe you'd like something in marketing or PR, then."

"Maybe." A little hope bubbled up inside of me, although marketing and PR sounded like something I'd need a degree for. "But I don't have any real experience or skills. I just know what looks nice. Or at least what I think looks nice."

"Skylar, anyone who meets you knows you have good taste. I think you'd be great at a job like that. You just need to market yourself confidently and find the right one."

Pleasure swelled inside me at his compliments, at his confidence in me. I wished I had it in myself. "Thanks. I'll give it some thought."

When we reached the cabin, we hauled the boat down to the dock and put it in the water. It was late afternoon but the sun was still high in the sky, and air was hot and still, just a slight breeze off the bay. I wiped the sweat from my forehead with my arm while Sebastian tied the boat to the dock.

"I wish I'd have grabbed my bathing suit. The water looks good."

He looked up at me with a doubtful smile. "You'd swim? It's a warm day, but the water's still pretty cold."

I lifted my chin. "I'm a brave little toaster. Hey, do you have any sunscreen?"

He straightened up. "Yes. Bathroom drawer on the bottom right."

"Thanks." Inside, I fought the urge to rifle through Sebastian's entire bathroom cabinet to learn more about him. I opened only the bottom right drawer, which was very neat and contained sunscreen, shaving cream, razors, and bar soap. Using the mirror over the sink, I applied some SPF 30 to my face, arms, and legs, and brought it outside with me to offer some to Sebastian.

Oh fuck. He took off his shirt.

My belly backhandspringed repeatedly as I approached the dock, where he was loading the paddles into the boat. Natalie hadn't exaggerated; Sebastian *was* ripped. He was tall and slender, so it wasn't an obnoxious sort of ripped, but the curves and lines on his body made my breath come faster. His skin was as beautiful as his bone structure— golden and smooth.

"Want some of this?" I asked, holding up the sunscreen. *Or some of this?* I thought, refraining from patting my ass.

"Nah. I don't mind the sun."

"Sebastian! You have great skin. You should be nicer to it. Here, let me." Hahaha, fucking genius! Hiding a smile, I flipped the lid and squirted some into my hand. "Turn around."

He sighed, but did as I requested, and I put my hands on his upper back. Biting my lip, I slowly rubbed the sunscreen into his skin, sliding my palms across his broad shoulders and along the back of his neck. I stayed well away from the waistband of his faded red shorts, but I did notice his blue plaid boxers peeking out above it. My stomach contracted.

"OK. Front."

Slowly, he turned to face me, and I swear I was just going to offer him the tube to do it himself, but the combination of his face and those glasses and the stubbled jaw and the sculpted chest and the abs— THE ABS—overpowered me. I nearly moaned aloud, imagining how those muscles would flex as he moved above me.

Gahhhhhh, don't touch him, Skylar. He doesn't want it.

But...but *abs*.

Right. If he said no, he said no.

"Want me to do it?" I asked brightly.

He hesitated. "OK."

FAHK.

Trying to control my racing pulse, I squirted some more sunscreen into my palms and rubbed them together. Then I put them on his chest.

And left them there.

Awestruck, I stared at my hands on his sun-warmed chest. Bits and pieces of me tightened and tingled.

"I think you're supposed to rub it in." His tone was amused.

Honey, I'll rub anything you want me to.

Slowly I began to move my hands in lazy circles on his *pectacular* chest. When it was absorbed, I slid my hands lower without bothering to put more sunscreen on them. The hard ridges of his abdominal muscles rippled beneath my fingers, and I slid them back and forth along the furrows.

Yes. I fingered his furrows.

"Wow." My voice cracked, and I swallowed. "You must do a lot of crunches."

He chuckled, and the muscles twitched beneath my palms, shooting pure lust through my veins.

Oh, God. If it was any other guy, I'd have slipped a hand between his legs right then and there. But Sebastian was different, and I didn't want to ruin this by moving too fast. Last time I'd gotten touchy-feely with him, he'd panicked.

But he was still now. Too still, maybe.

I looked up at him. "Is this OK?"

chapter fifteen

Sebastian

Was this *OK?*

Your hands are inches away from my rising cock. Your nipples are hard—I can see them through your shirt. You're looking up at me with such sweet concern, but I can see the way you want me, too, and fuck, I want you that way too. But something inside me won't let me touch you.

I cleared my throat and took a step back. "It's fine. Should we go?"

Her face fell, but she nodded.

After jumping onto the boat, I took Skylar's hand and helped her on, but I noticed that she let go of me as soon as she had two feet on the bottom of the boat. She settled at the front, arms wrapped around her legs, sunglasses hiding her eyes.

After untying the rope, I pushed away from the dock and picked up the oars, angry with myself again. I knew she'd been hoping I'd be fucking normal for a few minutes and at least kiss her or something, but I couldn't. Not that I didn't want to—my God, I was lucky I didn't come in my pants the second she put her hands on me. Every male instinct in my body was screaming at me to throw her down right there in the boat and ravage that hot little body until she begged for mercy.

Was I crazy not to?

She wanted it, didn't she?

It had been so long…and I wanted her so fucking badly.

As I watched her tilt her head back, lifting her face to the sun and exposing the pale white skin of her neck, I waited for the voice to kick in.

But it didn't. Amazed, I allowed my gaze to travel from her neck down her arms to her hands, which were crossed in front of her shins. She'd taken off her sneakers and her toenails were painted bright blue. Her legs were folded up in front of her chest, but I remembered how her nipples had been hard a few minutes ago and wondered if they still were. What color were they? Pale pink? Or deeper, like a rose? What would they feel like beneath my fingertips, between my lips, against my tongue?

Fuck, I was so hard, and wanted so badly to touch her. I could be gentle, couldn't I?

It was worth a try. She was worth anything.

"Your toes match your eyes," I said, hoping to make her smile.

Her lips tipped up, but she said nothing.

"Skylar, you've been silent for five whole minutes. That's a record, I think."

"Ha ha."

I stopped rowing and let us drift. On a Wednesday afternoon, there weren't too many boats out on the bay, and none were heading in our direction. I dropped the light anchor into the water and made sure we were tethered. Skylar still hadn't said a word, but at least she'd opened her eyes and was looking at me.

"Everything OK?" I asked.

She lifted her shoulders. "I'm just embarrassed. I keep touching you, and it's the wrong thing."

"No. It's not."

"You get so jumpy."

"I know, but it's not because I don't like it. I do. It scares me how much I do."

She said nothing and tipped her head back again, then wiggled so she was lying on her back on the bottom of the boat.

Carefully I moved to her side and stretched out next to her, head propped in my hand. "Hey." I tapped her nose.

She ignored me, which made me smile.

"Still thinking about taking a swim?"

"Maybe. If I get hot enough." She folded her hands on her belly.

"That an invitation?"

She stuck out her tongue at me.

Smiling, I took her sunglasses off and studied her for another minute, appreciating the flawless symmetry of her face.

I fucking loved symmetry.

Her rosebud mouth pouted just a bit, and I set her glasses aside before tracing her lips with one fingertip. She was startled by my touch, her mouth opening slightly, her breaths warm and quick against my hand.

Pretty soon I couldn't resist—I leaned over and pressed my lips to hers.

She let me kiss her, but didn't really kiss me back, and her hands remained on her stomach. I lifted my head and looked down at her again. *Stubborn little butterfly. Give in to me.* I kissed each eyelid and the tip of her nose. Then I lowered my lips to her forehead and left them there. The voice returned.

You really think you should do this?

Yes. Shut the fuck up and go away. Or don't. But I want to know what it's like to kiss this woman, to touch her and feel her touch me. So you can either stick around and watch, or you can fuck right off.

Feeling proud of myself, I kissed her lips once more, and her eyes opened.

"Sebastian," she whispered. "What are you doing?"

"Ignoring the voice in my head telling me not to touch you."

She reached up and took my face in her hands. "Good."

My mouth closed over hers and she rolled to her side, putting her lower body flush to mine.

Easy, easy, I told myself as her lips opened wider and I slipped my tongue between them. She tasted sweet, like mint and honey, and I lazily stroked her tongue with mine. My hands itched to explore her body, slide beneath her clothes, feel her bare skin, but I didn't allow myself the pleasure yet. It had been so long, and my cock ached to get inside her, but I wanted to go slow, do this right.

She wasn't making it easy, though—not with the way she kissed, playful and light one moment, greedily sucking my tongue into her mouth the next, not with the way she raked her nails through my hair and held my head in her hands, not with the way she pressed her curvy little body closer to mine, throwing one leg over my hip. My erection bulged against my shorts, and I put my hand on her ass to pull her closer, rub my cock against the sweet spot between her legs.

She moaned as I kissed her throat, swirling my tongue on her skin. "Mmmm. That feels so good," she said softly, sliding a hand down my arm. "You surprised me."

I buried my face in her neck, breathing in her scent. "Yeah?"

"Yeah. In a good way." She took my jaw in her hands, bringing my mouth up to hers. As the kiss deepened, she slipped a hand between us and rubbed my cock through my shorts...sweet, soft, slow strokes that made me dig my fingers into her back and pant against her lips. I rocked my hips, thrusting against her palm, and slid my hand underneath her shirt.

Are you fucking crazy? You can't touch her like that. You won't be able to stop. You're already so hard it hurts. Another minute and you'll be totally out of control and she'll be helpless against you. And you're all alone out here on the water. No one would hear her scream.

"Skylar," I said, leaning my forehead against hers. "Maybe we should stop."

"You want to stop right now?" She pressed harder against my erection. "I can think of something more fun."

I groaned. "I know, but—just wait." I sat up, breathing hard.

"Okayyyy," she said, clearly confused.

I shoved my sunglasses on my face and moved to the opposite end of the boat from her to sit on the bench. But first I had to adjust myself.

She laughed. "I'd say I'm sorry, but you know I'm not."

"I know. And I'm not either. It's just…" I ran a hand over my hair and decided to be honest. I'd fucked up with Diana by trying to hide shit. "The voice is telling me I'll hurt you."

She looked surprised, her eyebrows rising. "It is? Right now? Tell it to fuck off." She leaned forward conspiringly and whispered, "I like it a little rough, anyway."

"For God's sake, Skylar. Don't say that stuff to me," I snapped. "You don't know me at all."

"I'm trying, Sebastian! What the hell?" she cried, throwing a hand up. "Listen, if we're going to be friends and I'm going to help you through whatever issue you have being close to me, then you should get used to the way I talk. I told you, I'm a very open person. I say what's on my mind. Now what the fuck is on yours?"

"I told you. I'll fucking hurt you."

"How?"

The words stuck in my throat, but finally I blurted the fucked-up truth. "I'll choke you."

Her jaw dropped, and her fingertips touched her throat. "Choke me?"

I nodded angrily. "Yes. I know it's irrational and stupid, and I know you can't understand, but it's real to me."

Rather than reassure me I was being ridiculous, she crawled over and knelt between my feet. "Sebastian," she said firmly. "Put your hands on me."

"What?"

"Around my neck. Do it."

"No!" I gripped the edge of the bench, and she grabbed at my wrists.

"Come on, grab me by the throat," she said, her voice growing louder as she grappled with me. "Choke me if you're going to!"

"Will you fucking stop it?" I yelled at her, putting my hands in the air. "Get away from me!"

"No!" She stood and kept grabbing at me, the boat rocking perilously, and finally I did as she asked and wrapped my hands around her neck or else she was going to tip us over. She dropped to her knees again at my feet, her fingers tight around my wrists, holding them to her.

I felt sick inside. "Is this what you want? For me to hurt you?"

"You won't hurt me." In contrast to my panicked yelling, she spoke quietly, if a little breathlessly, and in her eyes I saw no fear. "You won't hurt me."

We paused there a moment, both of us breathing hard. My heart pounded, my body coursed with adrenaline, and my hands shook. Desperately I battled the urge to count as I inhaled and exhaled slowly, trying to calm my overwrought nervous system. But as the seconds ticked by and I did nothing violent, I realized she was right—I wasn't going to harm her. My body relaxed, my breathing slowed.

"There," she said softly. "See?" She pulled my hands off her neck, and immediately I curled my fingers over the edge of the bench again. She scooted even closer to me, resting her arms on my thighs. "Now tell me what else to do so we can go back to what we were doing."

"There's nothing you can do," I said sourly. "It's just the way I am." I looked out across the water, unable to handle the hurt expression on her face. *You fucking coward.*

"I don't believe that."

"Well, it's true." I fucking hated myself, so I took it out on her, of course. "You think this is the first time this has happened to me? I know how this goes, Skylar." I forced myself to look at her. I wanted the asshole in my head to see exactly what he was giving up. "We have sex because we like each other and we're attracted to each to each other and we think that's enough but then who we are isn't really what the other person thinks we are, so nothing works out and six months later we end up disappointing each other and blaming ourselves for what we should have admitted in the first place—this shouldn't happen."

She sat back, her butt on the boat's bottom. "Holy shit, Sebastian."

"What?"

"You're killing me. I can't even think where I'm going to live next week and you're able to imagine exactly what would happen in six months if I give you a hand job in this boat."

She was going to give me a hand job. Fuck.

"Is that what happened with your ex?"

I exhaled. "Sort of." The wind picked up, and I listened to the waves lap against the side of the boat for a moment. The sound calmed me. "I'm sorry. I panic easily."

She nodded. "I'm beginning to see that."

Well, this was it. She was realizing how difficult I was, how frustrating it was to get close to me, and she'd abandon me because of it. It's nothing I didn't expect…it had happened plenty of times before with girls a lot less beautiful than Skylar. So her next words shocked me.

"You know what we need? Some fried chicken. You're coming to dinner at my parents' house."

Nausea hit me. Strangers. A dinner table. A new situation. "I don't think that's a good idea."

"Well, I do. And you're going to come along and make it up to me for being a jerk just now when all I'm trying to do is have some fun." She hugged her knees again, tilting her face to the sun. The light played with her hair, streaking it with silver and gold. It looked so soft and warm, and I wondered if I'd ever get another chance to run my hands through it.

"What time is it?" she asked suddenly.

I pulled my phone from my pocket. "Close to six."

"Dinner is at six-thirty, so we should think about heading back."

I frowned. "Skylar, I'm not entirely comfortable with this. It's nothing against your family, I just don't like situations where I don't know anyone."

"You know me. And Natalie will be there with her boyfriend, Dan. You can meet him, and our older sister Jillian, and my parents too. They are perfectly nice people with clean dishes. And we don't use sharp knives for fried chicken, so you don't have to worry about stabbing anyone. But if you do, stab Dan. Natalie thinks he might be cheating on her."

"That's not funny."

She lowered her chin and looked up at me. "Yes, it is. You're not going to stab anyone. You gotta lighten up a little, Sebastian. I'll help you." She leaned back on her hands and stretched her feet toward mine, batting one of my ankles with her toes. "Think how proud your therapist is going to be when you go in there next."

"He will be," I admitted. "He told me I should talk to you."

"Oh? Why's that?"

I exhaled slowly, nervous to share this with her but feeling like I owed her something good. "Because the day I saw you at the beach, a lot of…feelings surfaced that triggered a relapse."

"What kind of feelings?"

Fuck, this was embarrassing. "Old feelings. I used to…have a crush on you. In high school."

She beamed. "You did?"

"Yeah. Along with every other guy there," I said under my breath. "I had no chance."

"Stop." She kicked me gently. "You never said anything about it."

"How could I? You were surrounded all the time. And I was so fucking awkward and shy."

"You *were* shy. You're still shy. Sort of."

My face burned. "Yeah. I guess."

She didn't say anything for a minute or two, just stared out across the water. I was about to start rowing us back when she asked a question that surprised me.

"Why me?"

"Huh?"

"Why did you have a crush on me? Was it because you thought I was pretty?"

I had to think about it. Of course I thought she was pretty—everyone did. But that wasn't all of it. "It wasn't just your looks," I said. "I was an observer back then, not really a participator, so I saw a lot of what went on without actually being involved. I saw that you were nice to everyone, that you didn't bully or cut people down, that you went out of your way to smile and say nice things to people. I liked that you weren't shy about raising your hand in class to admit you didn't understand something. I liked that you sometimes asked me for help." I paused to take a breath.

"Wow. That's like the most I've ever heard you say at one time." Her smile lit up her face. "And I'm totally flattered."

That smile. It was like a drug—I wanted to say anything, do anything to keep it there. "So yes, Ken—that's my therapist—told me that if talking to you was a fear, then I had to conquer it."

She met my eyes. "And you did."

"I did."

"So now," she said, "you're going to conquer fried chicken, potato salad, and cherry pie with the Nixon family."

Taking the oars in my hands, I shook my head. "You're much bossier than you were back then."

"I'm not bossy," she said indignantly. "I'm just good at seeing what needs to be done." She grimaced. "Except when it comes to myself. Then I'm horrible."

I began rowing us back toward the dock. "I'll help you. Maybe we can help each other."

chapter sixteen

Skylar

I watched Sebastian row us back toward the cabin, the muscles in his chest and arms working hard. Even though our brief romantic interlude had been a little frustrating, what happened afterward had been good for us. Truthfully, I wasn't sure what had made me act the way I did, insisting he grab me by the throat—it could have backfired terribly. But I was so sure he wouldn't hurt me, I needed him to know it. And maybe it hadn't solved the problem entirely, but I felt like we at least gained some ground.

He was so different—for most guys, it would be the other way around. They'd be all over the sex part, and then when you asked about their thoughts, they'd go silent. Sebastian had those silent moments too, and moments where he snapped, but I felt like I understood him better. He was just so hard on himself.

Now if only I could get him hard on me.

Stifling a smile, I recalled how divine it had felt when he'd let himself relax for a few minutes with me on the bottom of the boat. I probably pushed it too quickly with the hand thing, but I couldn't help myself—and he'd felt so good beneath his shorts. Thick and long and solid. Lust zinged between my legs and I pressed my thighs together.

Damn. Sebastian needed time to work through whatever had his mind all jacked up when it came to touching me, and I wanted to be patient for him, but lord almighty I had some frustration to work off.

The thought made me wonder what he did to relieve that kind of tension, and right away I pictured him naked, lying in that bed in the loft getting himself off, the muscles in his arms working hard, his abs flexed.

Oh crap. I better look away from him right now.

Maybe I'd get the vibrator out tonight. The way I felt right now, it wouldn't take more than a minute.

• • •

While Sebastian cleaned up, I sat outside on the patio and tried very hard not to think about him in the shower.

OK, somewhat hard.

After about fifteen minutes, he came out to the patio dressed in khaki pants and a fitted navy blue button-down with the sleeves cuffed up. "This OK?"

"Of course. You look great."

"I didn't have time to shave." He rubbed his chin.

"Sorry."

"Stop it. I like the scruff. And we are very casual, I promise. I texted my mom that I was bringing a friend to dinner, and she was delighted. But we better hurry so I have time to change."

We pulled up between the big house and my guest house right at six thirty. Sebastian waited in the living room while I stealthily scooped a clean pair of panties from a drawer and flipped through casual dresses I had hanging on a rack beneath some corner shelves.

"That your closet? Very clever," he said.

"Gotta make use of every inch of space in a place this small. OK, I'll be right out." I grabbed a flowy little dress with cami straps and a deep V neckline and ducked into the bathroom. Tossing my shorts, panties, socks and t-shirt in the hamper, I threw my hair up in a clip and quickly showered, then slipped on the new panties and the dress. Crap, was it too sexy? The neckline was low and I didn't wear a bra with this dress, but the dress wasn't tight or short, and the pretty floral pattern gave it a touch of innocence. I put on some deodorant, fluffed out my hair, and added a dab of perfume behind each ear. A quick swipe of pink lip gloss was the only makeup I had time for.

"OK, dressed," I said, sliding open the repurposed barn door that now served as bathroom door. "Now shoes and we'll go."

Sebastian was standing by the window, hands in his pockets. He turned to me, his eyes traveling down my body. A muscle in his jaw twitched, and he cleared his throat. "You got the bin pulls attached. I like them."

"Me too." I hurried over to the corner shelves, beneath which I had shoeboxes stacked, and dug out my light brown wedge sandals. "Actually, I'm happy with the whole place. Wish my mother wasn't kicking me out of it next week. It's rented for the summer," I went on when I saw the question on his face. I shoved my feet into the sandals and tugged the straps over my heels.

He nodded in understanding. "So you need to find an apartment?"

"Yes." I grabbed my phone off the table and led the way out, pulling the door shut behind him. "But before that happens, I'll need to find that better paying job. Working for Natalie is fun, but it won't pay my rent."

Sebastian fell silent as we headed across the drive toward my parents' house, and he walked sort of slowly and stiffly, like a prisoner headed for the guillotine.

"Hey." I grabbed his hand. "No worries, OK?"

He looked down at our hands, his mouth set in a grim line.

"Are you nervous?"

"A little."

"You know what I used to do when I'd get nervous before auditions?"

"What?"

"I'd imagine the very worst thing that could happen. Like forgetting my lines or falling on my face. Wetting my pants. Those things still wouldn't kill me."

He stopped walking right before we got to the

front porch. "Except when I imagine the worst thing that could happen tonight, Skylar, I'm not wetting my pants. I'm stabbing someone."

I turned to him. "Who are you stabbing?"

"I don't know. Whoever's closest." His worried expression told me he was serious, and I was tempted to hug him, tell him he didn't have to come to dinner if he didn't want to, assure him I understood. But somehow I thought that wasn't what he needed.

"Well, remind me not to sit next to you, then." I headed up the steps. "Come on. Let's do this."

• • •

My family welcomed Sebastian warmly, Natalie giving me a smug smile behind his back as he shook our father's hand.

"I take it things are going well," she whispered on our way to sit down at the big antique table in the dining room, which was already laden with platters and serving bowls full of food.

I shrugged. "They're OK."

"I want details!"

"Tomorrow at work," I promised.

"Sebastian, why don't you sit here next to Skylar?" my mother suggested, pulling her usual chair for him. I sent her a grateful look.

Natalie sat on Sebastian's other side, and Dan next to her. I wondered if she'd confronted him about the text messages yet. We'd have to talk about that tomorrow, too.

"Sebastian, did you have an older brother?" asked Jillian, who was seated across from him. "I went to school with a Malcolm Pryce."

He nodded. "Yes, that's my brother. He's three years older than I am."

"Does he still live around here?"

"Traverse City. He's an attorney in my father's practice, also."

OK, so far so good. He wasn't exactly relaxing in his chair, but his tone of voice sounded normal.

Jillian picked up a salad bowl. "Oh, are you a lawyer?"

"Yes." He swallowed, maybe bracing himself for more questions about his past, and I put my hand on his leg to remind him he had a friend at the table. I wasn't going to let the conversation go anywhere that would embarrass him. I might not have a college degree but I was a master at manipulating a crowd. He patted my hand, and I smiled at him.

Suddenly I could feel my mother's eyes on me, and I could just imagine how pleased she was—not only had I brought a handsome new friend to dinner, but he was a lawyer too. Imagine that, Skylar did something right! Frowning, I picked up my wine glass and took a big sip.

The rest of the meal went smoothly, and even if Sebastian remained a little tense, he fielded questions politely and complimented my mother on her cooking. I winced once when Dan asked him why he'd moved back here from New York, but he simply said he missed the area and wanted to be closer to his family. My shoulders wilted with relief, and I put my hand back on his leg under the table. He covered it with his again, and this time, he left it there.

Our eyes met in the mirror above the sideboard

on the opposite wall, and something about the look we exchanged made my panties get a little wet. Maybe it was just the candlelight playing tricks on me, but I liked the fire I saw in his eyes, which looked darker in the dim room.

After coffee and dessert, my sisters and I helped my mother bus the table, and then they shooed me back into the living room, where Sebastian sat with Dan and my father discussing the lack of skill in the Tiger bullpen.

He stood when I entered. "I should get going."

"I'll walk you out," I said, hoping our evening wasn't over but unsure how to keep it going.

Sebastian thanked my parents for dinner and shook everyone's hands—I wondered if handshakes still bothered him—and we walked outside. The sun was setting, bathing the farm in beautiful amber light. Row after row of cherry trees in bloomed on the hills, and I inhaled the lush air, which was much cooler than it had been all day.

"So was it torture?" I asked as we strolled toward his truck, wrapping my arms around myself to fight the chill.

"Yes."

I elbowed him, and he elbowed me back.

"Your family is very nice."

"They are, thanks. Sorry for all the questions. They can be so overbearing sometimes."

He smiled slightly. "That's OK. Nothing I couldn't handle tonight."

"I'm glad."

We reached his truck and he took his keys from his pocket. Part of me wanted to invite him in to my guest house for a beer, but another part said that wouldn't be wise. Maybe it was enough today that we'd spent time alone, that we'd kissed, that he'd had dinner with my family.

"Well, goodnight. Thanks for coming." Rising up on tiptoe, I put my hands on his chest and kissed his cheek. He kissed mine too, and then pulled me in close for a hug. I held him tight, my arms around his neck, our chests pressed together. I could smell the clean, masculine scent of his skin, feel his breaths start to come faster, igniting the hum inside my body. My thoughts strayed to my vibrator.

"It's the craziest thing," he said in my ear, his voice low and raw.

"What is?"

"I don't want to leave you."

My heart nearly burst open with longing for him. "Oh God, I don't want you to, but this house is, like, right next to my parents, and—"

"Come home with me." He released me slightly, keeping his arms around my waist and looking down at me. I saw that fire in his eyes again like I had in the mirror, felt the heat radiating from his body. "Give me another chance to make up for this afternoon."

"Yes," I said without any hesitation. "Just give me a second."

"Skylar, wait." He grabbed my arm, and I worried that he'd changed his mind.

His face was grave. "I want you so bad I can hardly breathe, but I have to be honest. I'm not looking for—"

"Shhh." I put a finger over his lips. "I'm not

asking for anything, Sebastian. I just want to be with you."

Heart pounding, I ran into the house and pulled Natalie aside. "Can you grab my phone from the kitchen? If Mom asks, just tell her Sebastian and I went for a drive."

"Awwwww," she said, her voice rising like I'd been caught doing something naughty. "I'm gonna tell."

I slapped her arm. "Shhhh! Just grab it please."

Laughing, she ducked into the kitchen, where my mother was blasting Pavarotti and loading the dishwasher. Not that she'd have cared what I was doing—she'd probably have been happy, actually—but I didn't want any questions tonight.

A moment, later Natalie returned with my phone. "Here you go. Have fun. Details tomorrow," she said forcefully.

"Promise." I scooted for the door.

"And don't be late for work!"

I rushed back outside, where Sebastian was waiting for me at the open passenger door of the truck. "Everything OK?" he asked, helping me up.

I smiled at him. "Yes. Everything is perfect."

"Good. Now buckle your seatbelt. I'm planning to speed."

chapter seventeen

Sebastian

I drove back to the cabin with a heavy foot, one hand on the wheel and the other on Skylar's lap. She held it in both of hers, almost like a child clings to the string of a helium balloon. I knew why—she was scared I'd change my mind.

But I wanted Skylar in my bed more than I could remember wanting any woman there. Maybe it was the ten-year crush, maybe it was the way she kept touching me during dinner, maybe it was the smell of her hair when I'd hugged her or the feel of her breasts against my chest. Maybe it was her willingness to be patient but also to push me to do things I was reluctant to do.

I still couldn't get over the way she'd made me grab her throat this afternoon. What had possessed her to do that? Why did she trust me more than I trusted myself? What did she see in me?

Whatever it was, she'd silenced the voice within me. I knew better than to think it would last forever, but I hadn't had one disturbing thought at dinner, unless you counted thinking about fucking Skylar with my tongue while her parents were at the table. That was kind of disturbing. But it didn't scare me—in fact, when I was hugging her goodbye, the only fear I had was, What if I don't touch her tonight and tomorrow I'm a prisoner of my own mind again?

I couldn't waste this chance. I'd dreamed of her for too long, and I was tired of being so fucking alone. I wanted her. I needed her. Tonight. Now.

I took my hand and put it on her bare leg, just above her knee, tempting the voice to tell me to stop.

Nothing.

I slid it higher up her thigh, heard her breath catch.

But in my head, exquisite silence.

She widened her knees, inviting me, and I slipped my hand to her pale inner thigh, beneath her dress. The skin there was silky beneath my fingertips, and I traced a little spiral pattern, moving toward her pussy.

"I'm going to kiss you here," I told her, never taking my eyes off the road. "And here." I brushed my fingers over the crotch of her panties, and she spread her legs farther. "And especially here." Edging my fingers inside the silk, I teased her open. She moaned lightly as I circled my fingers over the hot little button. "I want to feel your clit get hard against my tongue."

"Oh God," she gasped, tilting her hips toward my hand.

It was so fucking sexy I nearly pulled over. But I didn't want to rush this. I'd been dreaming about her for ten fucking years. The first time had to be perfect, slow and sensual and romantic. Candles and wine and soft, clean sheets.

If I made it home.

"I love that you're wet already," I said, sliding one fingertip inside her, the other hand gripping the wheel tightly.

"I've been wet since you took your shirt off on the dock," she breathed. "God, that feels so good. I want more." She grabbed my wrist and pushed my finger deeper inside her, nearly causing me to run off the road.

Breathing hard, I fingered her as she moaned softly, imagining my dick sliding between those soft, snug velvet walls. It swelled inside my pants, bulging against the seam. "My cock is so hard right now," I told her, trying to keep my voice steady as my foot pushed harder on the accelerator. "I want to fuck you with it. I want it right here." I plunged two fingers inside her.

"Sebastian," she panted, gyrating against my hand. "I want you so badly. I want my hands on your cock, and I want it inside me. Hurry."

My mouth fell open. Jesus Christ. I'd never been with a woman who talked that way, ever. And the fact that it was Skylar had me jumping out of my skin.

OK, fuck the candles and wine.

I turned off the main highway on to my driveway, tires screeching, gravel spitting, and flew fifty feet through the woods toward the cabin before slamming on the brakes.

Before I even had the truck in park, she was slipping her shoes from her feet.

I undid my belt and jeans and shoved them down enough to free my cock. "Shit, I don't have a—"

"I don't care." Eyes on my erection, she slid her panties down her legs. "I'm on the pill."

"Then come here." I reached for her, flipping her onto my lap.

Reaching beneath her dress, I fisted my cock as she straddled me and positioned the tip between her legs. For just one second, I had a flash of doubt. Not an obsessive thought, but just a concern. *She's so small.*

"Don't you fucking dare." Lowering herself, she took me in deep, slowly sliding all the way down, her eyes steady on mine, her hands squeezing my shoulders. "I want this, Sebastian. I want this so badly. I fucking need it. Give it to me."

My name on her lips as she glided over the most sensitive part of my body set fire to my blood. With her tight, wet pussy sheathing my cock, any thought of turning back was abandoned. My body took over, yanking down the loose straps of her dress and taking her breasts in my hands. They were perfect— not too big, but round and plump and creamy white, with pert little light pink tips. "Yes," she breathed when I sucked on one taut peak, her hips beginning to move over mine. "Oh God, that feels so good."

Oh fuck.

This could potentially be over ridiculously, tragically fast. She was too beautiful, too warm, too wet, too fearless. And the way she was looking at me, like my cock was the best thing she'd ever felt inside her, like she couldn't get enough and yet it was too much, like she wanted this as much as I did. Was that even possible? I slid my hands beneath her dress, clutching her to me as I flicked her nipple with my tongue and thrust up inside her.

"Yes, yes," she murmured, rocking against me, her fingers digging into my arms. "I love your mouth on me, and your body is so hot, and your face is so beautiful, and your cock is so big—"

"Fuck," I seethed, sucking air between my teeth. "Goddammit, Skylar. I wanted to take my time, give you everything you want. You keep moving like that, talking like that, I won't be able to last."

"I'm getting everything I want." Grinding against me, she arched her back and swiveled her hips in some clever little female maneuver that had me groaning in agony. "Right now. Right here. Right there…fuck yes, right there."

"Yeah? You want it right there?" I tilted my lower body to give her a deeper angle, and she cried out, her eyes closing, her movements small but fast and frantic and fuck she was so beautiful when she came, her head thrown back, her mouth open wide, her pussy clenching my cock in tight, hard contractions.

Heat buzzed through my arms and legs, centering in my groin as I grabbed her hips and worked her up and down my cock, my eyes fastened on her perfect tits as they bounced in front of me. God, she was so wet and tight and her little noises were so hot and this was so much better than my fantasies because she was here and I was coming inside her *right. fucking. now.* I growled, my body seizing up as the climax hit, but she kept moving, sliding up and down my shaft, crying out every time her ass hit my thighs, taking every last drop I had to give.

When my body had gone still, she ran her hands through my hair, down my arms, up my chest, finally taking my head in her arms, pulling it to her chest. I lay my cheek against her breasts and listened to her heartbeat, closing my eyes and thanking whatever gods existed for letting me have this, even if it was only for tonight.

"Did I rush you?" she asked breathlessly, her lips against my forehead.

"No." I slid my hands up the back of her dress and locked my arms around her. "Believe me, I'm happy I held out as long as I did."

She laughed. "I like hearing you're happy."

Then stay with me, I thought. *Stay with me.*

chapter eighteen

Skylar

Holy shit, who is this guy?

He was so different. So relaxed and at ease in his skin, so unafraid. I wondered if it was stress relief—the sex itself—or if it was that he'd broken down a barrier—sex with me. But I didn't dare ask about it. Don't look a gift horse in the mouth, right?

We went into the cabin and cleaned up, Sebastian offering the bathroom to me first. "There are clean washcloths in the bottom left drawer, towels under the sink, soap in the shower. Use anything you want."

I felt pretty wet and sticky, so I decided to take a quick shower. I hung my dress and panties on the door and washed up with a bar of soap in his shower that smelled delicious and looked like it had honeycomb in it. After drying off with a fluffy navy blue towel, I hung it up and slipped back into my panties and dress.

When I emerged from the bathroom, Sebastian was just coming in from the patio, his feet bare. "I thought maybe we could lie in the hammock. It's cool out there, but the sky is clear. Good night to see stars."

"I saw stars twenty minutes ago in your truck," I told him with a smile. "Right through the roof."

He grinned back at me before pulling a thick charcoal gray fleece blanket from an old trunk serving as a coffee table. "We'll take this blanket out, but if you're too cold just tell me."

"OK." I picked up a framed photograph on a side table. "Who's this?" I asked, turning it so he could see the photograph of the two grinning little girls, one missing both front teeth.

"Emily and Hannah. My nieces. They gave that to me last Christmas." He switched off the living room lamp as I set the frame down.

"Ah. They live around here?"

He nodded and turned the kitchen light off. "Malcolm and his family live in Traverse."

"I bet they're happy you moved back."

He opened the sliding door and waited for me to go through it, then he tucked the blanket under his arm and followed me out before closing it behind us. "Yeah, they are. They worry about me living alone up here, though. Like I'm a kid. Drives me crazy."

I shivered walking across the stones toward the hammock, my skin prickling in the chilly night air. "*Do* you get lonely living by yourself?"

"Sometimes. Not tonight." He lowered himself into the hammock and stretched out on his back. "And that's all that matters to me right now. Come here."

Smiling, I took off my shoes and carefully climbed on beside him, tucking myself in against his warm, hard body. Together we spread the blanket over our feet and legs, and he pulled it up over my shoulder.

"Warm enough?" he asked.

"Yes, thank you." I snaked one arm across his stomach, beneath his shirt, taking the opportunity to feel up his abs again. "Hey, what's that honeycomb soap in your bathroom? I love it."

"My sister-in law Kelly makes it. Malcolm's wife."

"Really?"

"Yeah, she makes all kinds of stuff with honey. Her family keeps bees."

"How cool. I'll have to find out where to buy it. Maybe my mom will stock some products in the guest houses. I want her to have all local things."

He squeezed me. "That's a great idea."

I asked more about his extended family, and Sebastian recited for me the names and ages of all five of his nieces and nephews.

"I'm impressed," I said. "Do you know their birthdays too?"

"Yes, and my brothers' and their wives' and my dad's if I thought about it, maybe even yours."

I picked my head up and looked at him. "Shut up. Really?"

He narrowed his eyes. "You have a winter birthday, right? Is it in December? Maybe the twenty-first?"

I gasped. "Yes! How do you know that?"

"I have a good memory for facts, especially involving numbers." His mouth hooked up on one side. "Want me to recite two hundred decimal digits of pi for you? Would that turn you on?"

"It might," I said, and I was only half kidding. "God, you really do have thing about numbers, don't you? But how did you remember my birthday?"

He shrugged. "I probably saw it written somewhere, although it's an odd number and I don't like those. You should have an even birthday."

"What?"

He chuckled. "Nothing. Just a joke."

I loved hearing him laugh. Putting my head on his chest again, I snuggled in a little closer. "This is so nice. I'm so glad you invited me back here."

He kissed the top of my head and brought one hand to my hair, twining one long wavy strand around his fingers. "I wasn't sure you'd want to come."

I wanted to look at his face, but I loved his hand in my hair so much I stayed where I was. "Why not? I was here all day, just about."

"I know, but…I send a lot of confusing signals."

"You do," I agreed. "But seeing as I like your company and I have no better offers these days, you'll do."

He pulled my hair, making me squeal. "Very funny."

Melanie Harlow

I giggled, picking up my head to look at him. "I'm teasing. I want to be here. I needed this."

"Needed what?"

"Just…this." Even I wasn't sure exactly what I'd meant, but something about being there in his arms, feeling wanted and beautiful and free and sexy—it gave me hope. I'd felt so bad about myself for so long that I'd forgotten it was possible to feel this good, this excited about life and its twists and turns. Maybe it was just a physical thing between us, but it was enough, and if it fulfilled a need in him too, then all the better.

We kissed, slowly and lazily, his tongue parting my lips. After a moment, one of his hands stole up to my breast, squeezing it softly, and I moved a hand between his legs, stroking him like I had earlier in the boat, feeling him come to life beneath my palm. "I'm glad you're here too," he whispered against my lips. "Otherwise I'd be upstairs in my bed jerking off to you right now."

My core muscles tightened at the image, and I pressed my hand over his erection. "You just put a very naughty thought in my head."

"What's that?" His fingers teased my nipple through the thin material of my dress, making them both stiffen and tingle.

"I want to watch that."

He went still. "You do?"

I bit my lip. "Sorry, is that too dirty? I've never watched anyone do it before, I just think it would be hot to watch you. But it's probably too dirty."

"No. No. You just surprised me is all." He kissed me again, deeper this time, his tongue more

162

demanding, sliding between my lips with a skill that started a hum between my legs. "Want to come upstairs?" he asked, his voice low and playful.

"Yes."

He stood and took my arm, helping me up. I went to pick up my shoes, but he yanked me toward the cabin

"Leave them." He pulled me roughly across the patio and through the sliding door. A minute later I was breathlessly climbing the ladder to the loft. When I reached the top, I was surprised at how light it was up there—the moonlight shining in the huge window bathed the entire room in silver. Sebastian came up behind me and lifted my dress by the hem, and I raised my arms. He slipped the garment off my head and when I turned to face him, he was turning it right side out, as if he were going to hang it up or something.

"Really, Sebastian?" I grabbed the thing and threw on the floor.

"It's a nice dress."

"Oh, God. You're so cute. But fuck the dress. And fuck your shirt too." I started unbuttoning his shirt, my fingers trembling with the need to touch him. He helped me finish and I shoved it down his shoulders, dropping it next to my dress. Grabbing his white t-shirt at the neck, he tugged it off, adding to the pile of clothing on the floor. Immediately, I threw my arms around him, pressing my breasts against his warm, bare chest and crushing my mouth to his. He wrapped his arms around my back and lifted me off the floor, and I instinctively circled his trim waist with my legs. His muscular torso felt hot and hard against my inner thighs.

"Your body is incredible," I panted as he moved his hands beneath my ass. "I've been dying to get my hands on it all day."

"I've been hard for you for two days," he said, his fingers kneading my flesh. "And we both know that two is better than one, so I win."

Turning us toward the bed, he knelt on the mattress, laying me down gently on my back before pulling my drenched panties down my legs. I propped myself on my elbows, excited to watch him take his pants off and get started on the show. But after removing his shoes, he crawled up my body, lowering his mouth to my chest.

"Hey." I fidgeted impatiently. "You said I could watch."

"You can. You can watch me do this." He drew a circle around one hard nipple with his tongue before sucking it hard. "You can watch me do this." He dragged his tongue in a line straight south, making my clit tingle. "And you can watch me do this."

Pushing my legs apart, he buried his tongue in my pussy, stroking up through the center and lingering at the top before doing it again.

"Oh, God..." It felt so fucking good, and watching him do it made me so hot, I couldn't bring myself to protest. My mouth hung open as he slowly circled my clit with his tongue, dizzying, decadent arcs that made my toes curl and my hands claw at his crisp white bedsheets. Then he sucked it into his mouth, rubbing his tongue against it.

"You taste even better than I imagined, Skylar Nixon." He picked up his head for just a second. "And I imagined it a lot. So you have to let me have this." Dropping his mouth to me again, he pressed my thighs wider as he worked his tongue and lips and teeth over me until the room was spinning and I could hardly breathe.

"Fuck, Sebastian," I panted. "You're amazing. You're gonna make me come so hard."

"Good. Let me feel it."

I gasped as I felt one finger slide inside me. Then two. Somehow his fingers and tongue worked in some sort of tandem magic that had my back arching off the bed, my toes pointing.

"Oh God! What are you doing to me?" Dropping my head back, I fisted my hands in his sheets and writhed beneath his agile tongue and dexterous fingers.

Actually, writhed doesn't even begin to cover it.

I thrashed and moaned and cursed and grabbed his head and rocked my hips, grinding against his greedy mouth until I exploded in feverish bursts of white hot madness, crying out with every rhythmic pulse around his fingers and against his tongue.

When my body had stopped convulsing, he straightened up and unbuckled his belt. "Still want to watch?"

"Fuck yes, I do." Panting, I braced myself on my elbows, watching as he stepped off the bed and got completely naked. Moonlight dusted his shoulders and hair, outlining the powerful masculine lines of his body. The front of him was in shadow, but I could make out the serious expression, the flat hard stomach, the fully erect cock. It stood out from his body as he came toward me, and I nearly lunged for it, mouth open.

He knelt on the bed again, legs apart, and took himself in his fist. Slowly he began working his hand up and down its thick, hard length. I was breathing hard, my heart pounding in my chest. "God. I could watch you all day."

"I can still taste you." His voice was low and gravelly. "You're on my tongue, like honey."

"Oh, God." Desire ignited again inside me. I sat all the way up, knees wide, one hand moving between my legs. "I'm so wet. You've got me dripping."

"Yes," he hissed, his jaw clenched. His hand moved faster. "Drip all over your fingers. Let me watch."

Without tearing my eyes from his body, I rubbed my clit in hard, steady circles, widening my knees and arching my back. The second orgasm built even quicker than the first, gathering momentum inside a minute. "Christ," I whispered, working my fingers faster, watching the muscles in Sebastian's abs and forearm and shoulder flex. "You're going to make me come again. And you're not even touching me."

A few seconds later his body was sprawled over mine, his cock pushing easily inside my slick wet center. "I can't take it, you're too beautiful," he whispered, driving deep. "And I've thought of this so many times—I can't have you in my bed and not be inside you."

"I want you inside me." I clawed his back, his arms, his ass, digging my fingers into his flesh, pulling him closer. "You feel so good there." And he did—so good I was starting to panic this was the best sex I'd ever have and I'd never feel this way again. What if this was a one-time deal? What if tomorrow the voice in his head told him he'd smother me in my sleep if I stayed the night? He reached behind me, tilting my hips up so he could rub the hard base of his cock against my clit as he rocked into me. I was both amazed and terrified by his skill, by his size, by the way he knew exactly what I needed to feel. Deep inside me, something began to tighten.

Too deep.

That deep.

Oh Jesus. Oh no.

Please, please don't let Sebastian Pryce own the one cock that can reach The Spot.

But he did. The tip of Sebastian's cock was hitting The Spot, territory uncharted, unknown, unreachable by all prior cock owners who'd attempted to scale the surrounding heights.

This couldn't be.

No! No! No!

"Yes, yes, yes," I breathed against his neck, my entire lower body seizing up, my nails clawing at his skin. Fucking hell, Sebastian...you're so amazing and generous and hard and deep and fuck—"Oh God, you're perfect. Don't stop, don't stop, don't stop!"

"Never," he growled, thrusting faster and tighter to me. "Come again for me, let me feel you."

My second climax hit me hard, and I dropped my head to the side, mouth open, gasping as my core muscles tightened around him, again and again and again.

He came before my orgasm had even ended, throbbing long and deep inside me, his body going plank stiff above me. My hands felt the muscles in his ass flexing, causing a fresh wave of contractions in my lower body, and I rode them out on a long, blissful sigh.

Perfection.

chapter nineteen

Sebastian

Perfection.

Every moment.

From the front seat of my truck (who'd have guessed Skylar Nixon had a dirty mouth?) to the hammock (her hair pouring like liquid gold through my fingers) to my bedroom (better than any fantasy I'd ever had about her, and certainly better than any reality I'd ever experienced), every single second with Skylar had been perfect.

I'd been able to stay in the moment ever since she'd agreed to come home with me, so focused on her that there was no room in my mind for anything else. It was enough to make me utter those two little words to myself, the scariest two words I knew…*What if?* Only this time, the words didn't frighten me because I was anxious about causing harm—the question wasn't What if I hurt her? The question was What if I could make her happy?

And that was fucking terrifying.

How had she done it? I lay atop her now, our bodies still connected, our breathing still synced, our skin still slick, and wondered what spell had she cast to make me think after just two days that she could be mine and I could be hers and we could have this little place in the woods on the water where no one would bother us? Where we would love each other and explore each other and hurt each other and forgive each other and find grace in one another's bodies and souls? Surely there had to be something enchanted about tonight—some sort of witchcraft that was bound to fade and break once the sun came up.

Because I knew better than anyone that this feeling never lasts, not for people like me. It's an illusion that makes you feel good for a time, but it makes the fall that much worse when you realize it was only a tease. *See what it could be like? See what you can't have?*

Skylar shifted beneath me, and reluctantly I rolled off her, stretching out on my back, hands behind my head. I locked my fingers together, refusing to let myself touch her the way I wanted to. Expecting her to get out of bed, I was surprised when she turned toward me and laid her cheek on my arm. I wanted nothing more than to hold her, but I couldn't—I had to steel myself for the inevitable crash that was coming after such a high. I closed my eyes, inhaled and exhaled, desperately trying not to think about how hurt she was going to be when I pushed her away again.

She lay next to me for a minute before nudging my side. "Hey."

"What?"

"What are you thinking?"

That I wish tonight would last forever. That I knew how to love someone without disappointing her. That I believed in happily ever after. "Nothing. I'm tired." Her disappointed "oh" softened my heart, but I willed iron into it. "I should take you back."

Slowly, she sat straight up. Looked at me in disbelief. "That's it?"

"What's it?" Like I didn't know.

"That's it for tonight? I don't want to leave you, come home with me, I'm so glad you're here...and after everything we did tonight, all you can say is I should take you back?" She threw my words back at me.

"Yeah. I guess so." I shifted uncomfortably. "You were expecting something else?"

"Oh my God. Whatever. Fine." She got off the bed and scooped her panties off the floor, stepping into them before throwing her dress over her head. The silhouette of her curvy breasts and hips against the window made my jaw clench. "Your sheets are a mess," she said, fluffing that cloud-of-gossamer hair I loved. "Do you have a spare set to sleep on?"

"I have seven spare sets."

She stopped moving and looked at me. "You have eight sets of sheets?" Then she threw her hands up. "What am I thinking? Of course you do. Do you want help stripping the bed?"

"No." Did she think I didn't want to sleep with her honey-and-almond scent next to my skin? I knew

171

it was my soap she'd used but damn if it had ever smelled that good on me.

"OK then. I'll meet you in the car." She went for the ladder and started down.

Fuck. FUCK.

"Skylar, wait." I sat up, dragged a hand over my hair. "Don't go."

"Too late, asshole." She continued down the ladder and I heard her jump to the floor.

"Fuck!" I thumped a fist into the mattress, hard. Then I did it again, and again. I knew I shouldn't take my frustration with myself out on her, but if I didn't harden my heart against the what ifs, they'd drag me under. She'd drag me under. I'd be fooled again into thinking I was capable of being the person a woman like her deserved, of loving her the way she needed to be loved. And I knew—*I knew*—I wasn't.

So fuck the big, sad ending. I could stop this bleeding at the source, and I would.

Angry and sad, I threw my clothes on and jogged out to the truck, where she was already waiting in the passenger seat, legs tight together, arms crossed. I knew she was really mad because it was the first time she was totally silent for more than five minutes. We were almost to her parents' place when finally she broke down.

"I'm sorry," she said shortly, her tone cold.

I glanced at her, but her pose hadn't changed. "What are you sorry about?"

"For thinking I could do this. It's too frustrating. You're too frustrating. You're hot and cold too fast."

I pressed my lips together. Stared straight ahead.

"This is what I mean!" She glared at me but I

kept my eyes on the road. "If you'd just tell me what's going on in your head, maybe I could help!" she snapped.

God, she was so maddening—how could I explain that I had to keep her at a distance for both our sakes?

"You told me earlier today that you wanted to let me in. To give you time to let me in." Her voice had softened a little. "And I wanted to. I was willing to. It was you who asked for more tonight."

She was right. I felt some of my hardness crumbling, and I fought back. "Look, this is me. This is what I do. And if it's too frustrating for you, then it's better to end this now."

"End what? We never started." She looked away from me again.

A few minutes later, I pulled in her parents' driveway. She had her hand on the door handle before I even put the truck in park.

"If you just wanted the lay, Sebastian, you could have said so," she said bitterly. "You're a great fuck."

Then she jumped out, slammed the door and marched angrily over to her little house. When she disappeared inside without even pulling out a key, I realized she hadn't even locked it tonight. *Damn it, Skylar! You should lock your doors!* The ferocious need to protect her growled and bit at me beneath my skin, and I thumped the steering wheel hard twice, fighting the urge to go make sure it was secure now.

The urge won. Furious, I strode to her door and tried the handle. Locked.

"Fuck you!" I heard her cry from inside. "Go away!"

Back in the truck, I threw it in reverse and tore out of there, tires spinning.

• • •

When I got home, it was after midnight. I went straight up to the loft, where her scent still lingered. After undressing, I lay on my stomach atop the sheets where she'd offered herself up to me, no questions asked. I closed my eyes and she appeared…sultry and brazen as she straddled me in the truck, shivering and sweet as she lay with me in the hammock, hotter than fuck sprawled under me in my bed.

Hurt and angry on the ride home.

Groaning, I punched the pillow twice and flipped over onto my back, staring at the sloping ceiling as my thoughts turned resentful.

Did she really think I'd used her just for sex? How could she, when I'd confessed to her how I used to feel about her ten years ago? When I'd told her today I wanted to let her in but needed time? Did she think I hadn't meant the things I'd said?

It was just like a woman to say she understood about needing to give a guy time and then demand to know his feelings at every turn. What the fuck did she expect from me? I'd told her before things even got physical with us that I was bad at relationships and not interested in one. What else was there to tell her? If she didn't want to hang out anymore, fine. Good. I didn't need her. I didn't need anyone. Better to be alone than a constant disappointment to someone.

At least she thought I was a great fuck.

chapter twenty

Skylar

"Wow. You look kind of rough. Late night?" Natalie's brows lifted suggestively.

"Sort of." Listlessly, I stacked coffee cups behind the counter. I'd hardly slept, and I was so tired when my alarm went off I'd nearly called in sick.

"Did you have fun?" Natalie prompted, loading muffins into the display case.

"Yes." I sighed. "And then no. I need coffee."

"Help yourself." She nodded toward the pot. "Why no?"

As we went through the morning routine, I filled her in on what I'd learned about Sebastian over the last couple days—his OCD, his fear of harming people, his past, his cabin, his family, his aversion to relationships, his former crush on me...everything I knew. I even told her about snooping in his notebook.

She gasped. "What? That's awful! I can't believe you did that!"

I grimaced. "I know. I shouldn't have. But I was so curious about him, and he wouldn't talk to me! He still won't."

She looked confused. "What do you mean? You just told me a crap ton of info about him. Didn't he tell you all that?"

My chin slid forward. "Well, yeah, he tells me that kind of stuff. But he doesn't—" I stopped. He *did* talk to me, it wasn't that so much. "OK, it's not that he won't talk, it's that he will, and he says these sweet, crazy things, and then stuff happens, and he freaks out and turns into an asshole. He's too hot and cold."

"What kind of stuff happens?" she asked, her eyebrows lifting.

I sighed. Of course she focused on that part. "Sex stuff."

She gasped. "You had sex?"

"Yeah. And it was amazing," I said sadly. "Best I've ever had."

"Wow." The first customers were starting to arrive, so we had to get to work, but we agreed to go for a drink that night to talk, and I texted Jillian to join us too.

All morning and afternoon, I mulled over what had happened, and by the time we closed the shop I had to admit there'd been a lot more good moments than bad last night. Had I jumped down his throat too quickly? All he'd done was suggest driving me home.

But no. No.

I could tell that something was different with him after that last time in his room. I didn't really think he'd used me for sex—I'd only said that to hurt him. But something had happened to make him close off by the end of the night. The guy who'd driven me home was not the same guy I'd lain in the hammock with.

So who was it? And how could I get the other one back?

• • •

After we closed, I went home and took a long nap. When I woke up, I felt more rested but had no better understanding of Sebastian's motives for shutting me out. Maybe my sisters would have some insight.

We met at Trattoria Stella at seven and sat at the bar, Jillian flanking me on one side and Nat on the other.

"So what's new?" Jillian shrugged out of her jacket. She looked professional and mature in her dress trousers, pumps, and sleeveless silk blouse, and I immediately felt childish next to her in my ripped jeans and sandals.

Quit being stupid. It's not about clothing.

"Skylar had amazing sex last night," Natalie announced breathlessly, leaning forward with her elbows on the bar. "And she's gonna tell us about it."

"Amazing sex. What's that like?" Jillian asked wistfully, picking up the wine list.

"I wouldn't know either," Natalie replied.

"Why?" I looked at her. "The text messages?"

Natalie shrugged, her mouth in a grim line. "He says those are nothing. We're just in a dry spell, I guess."

"Everything seemed fine at dinner last night," Jillian offered, "and speaking of dinner." She elbowed me. "I take it the amazing sex was with Sebastian, the guy you brought to Mom and Dad's?"

I nodded glumly.

"You don't look too happy about it." Jillian tilted her head. "What's up?"

We ordered wine and some appetizers, and while we nibbled and sipped, I spilled to Jillian the story I'd told Natalie this afternoon.

"OCD is really rough. I've got a few patients with it." Jillian swirled the last ounce of chardonnay in her glass. "And you're never really cured of it."

"I know. He said the same." I took a bite of calamari and didn't even taste it. "But is it the OCD that's making him so moody? One second he's sweet and talkative and laughing, and the next he's a total dickhead."

Jilly shrugged. "It could be. Obsessive impulses can pop up at any time or they can be there all the time. If he's struggling with something in his head, he might not be able to just ignore it and keep up the chatter. Maybe going silent is one of his strategies for dealing with the thoughts instead of trying to bury or avoid them."

"Yeah." I set my fork down, feeling full although I'd barely eaten. "Makes sense, I guess."

"Did he say anything about the fiancée?" Natalie asked.

"Not much." I didn't feel like blabbing the details he'd told me about their breakup—in fact, I felt strangely protective of them.

"Maybe he's not over her?" Jillian suggested.

"No, I don't think it's that." Suddenly I just wanted to go home and get back in my bed.

"Maybe he'll call you to say sorry," Natalie said, her blue eyes wide and sympathetic.

"He doesn't even have my number. And he already said sorry." My throat felt tight, which made me angry. Why should I cry over him? "He just didn't say anything else."

"Well, what did you want him to say?" Jillian looked at me like I was a little crazy. "It was pretty much your first date, wasn't it? Maybe you're expecting too much."

"Just forget it," I snapped. "It obviously didn't mean anything." I felt bad that I was being so prickly when my sisters were only trying to help, but I was getting more depressed by the minute. Without the fun distraction of Sebastian on the horizon, I was right back where I started.

chapter twenty-one

Sebastian

The day after I slept with Skylar, I had an appointment with Ken, which I wasn't looking forward to. In fact, I nearly canceled it, but then I remembered how easy it was to backslide and justify when I got this way. I'd avoided therapy in the past because of something I didn't want to face, but that had only made it—and everything else in my life—worse.

So after a hike at Old Mission Point Park and a quick session at the gym, I showered, dressed, and went to his office.

"I slept with someone last night," I announced as I slumped onto the couch in his office.

Ken, who hadn't even sat down yet, looked a little taken aback at my choice of openers, but recovered quickly, lowering himself into his leather chair. "Oh?"

"Yes. That girl—woman—I mentioned a couple weeks ago. The one I used to have the crush on." I stared at my jeans, an older pair that had been washed so many times the denim had faded to that blue color I loved.

He flipped back a page on his notepad. "This is the one you were going to approach again because you'd had the setback the first time?"

"Yes. I approached her the next day." I could still see the happy surprise on her face when she ran to the door to let my dripping wet ass in.

"It went well, I take it." Ken's tone was amused.

"Yeah." I frowned. "Too well."

"How so?"

"I went out with her Tuesday night, then spent almost all day yesterday with her, then last night we—" I rubbed the stubble on my jaw, still feeling her satin thigh against my cheek. "You know."

He kept a straight face. "Go on."

"At first I was troubled by the thoughts of harming her, and I can't say that's entirely gone away. But over the course of the day, it was replaced with this...I don't know. Wanting."

"Wanting for what?"

"To be someone else." *To be the kind of guy who can touch her every day without fear. To be the kind of guy who can get on a plane and fly her somewhere romantic. To be the kind of guy whose mind doesn't convince him of things his heart knows aren't true.* "To be different."

He lifted his shoulders. "Sounds like she likes who you are. Does she know about—"

"Yes," I interrupted. "Right up front I told her about my anxieties and why they make it tough to be close to me." I sighed, closing my eyes for a second. "She said she was willing to try."

"Good." He sat back and pushed his glasses farther up on the narrow bridge of his nose. "So why do you want to be someone else?"

"I want to be someone that could make her happy," I said, crossing my arms in frustration, hands fisted. "And I can't because my mind won't let me."

"There's more to your mind than OCD," Ken reminded me. "A lot more than that."

I studied my legs, seeing her straddling them. Fuck. I closed my eyes again, but she was there too. "I'm not right for her. She deserves better, or at least normal, and she'd realize that fast. She could have anyone. Why would she want me?"

Ken crossed an ankle over a knee. "So let her make that decision. Fear of intimacy is not OCD, by the way. Neither is being afraid to commit. There's no reason why you can't give this a try, Sebastian."

"Yes there is," I said, annoyed with him. Ken was probably married with three kids and thought it was all so fucking easy when you met someone you wanted to be with. "My entire being is the reason. All the shit in my head. She says she likes me, but she also said I frustrate and confuse her. That shit doesn't go away."

"She's confused by your thoughts? Your compulsions?"

"No, I mean those would probably get to her eventually, but right now it's my moods. My silences. Whenever I sense myself letting my guard down, I retreat into myself and push her away. But I have to, because I know how this ends."

Ken's brow furrowed and he set his notepad aside in favor of crossing his arms just like I was. "I'm not sure I understand. You're scared of physically harming her? That's why you push her away? Or you're scared of getting emotionally attached to her? Those are two very different things. Let's figure out which we're dealing with."

I hesitated. Some part of me didn't want to admit to Ken that I was scared for my own sake—that I saw myself falling for Skylar, that I was half in love with her already, but that I'd be unable to make it work, and losing her would destroy me.

"What happens when I have a bad day?" I asked. "When I make us miss dinner reservations for the tenth time because I have to check the locks again and we're halfway there? What happens when she asks me to slice the turkey at Thanksgiving and I can't pick up the fucking knife because I think I'll stab someone? What happens when she needs to fly somewhere and it's an odd day and I get down on my knees in the airport and beg her not to get on that plane?"

"I don't know, Sebastian. Because that's just fearcasting. It's not real. And you've got ways to cope with those things."

"Well, I know what happens." I stared Ken dead in the eye. "I drive her mad. She leaves."

"But that's not what happened with your last relationship, is it?" he pressed. "You broke things off. You realized you didn't actually want to marry Diana. That means your doubts were not inconsistent with your true feelings. That's not OCD, Sebastian. That's stopping yourself from making a mistake." He held up his hands. "Now. Maybe you went about it all wrong, but that's another matter entirely."

I dropped my gaze to my legs again, spoke a little more quietly. "It won't work in the end. I don't know how to make it work. She leaves, Ken. I know she does."

"And then you're alone again," Ken said. "Probably forever."

"Exactly."

"Because you're a horrible person who doesn't deserve to be happy."

I nodded. This guy knew me way too well by now. It was aggravating as fuck.

"Bullshit, Sebastian."

"Huh?"

He shrugged. "Bullshit. If you truly believed you're a horrible person, you wouldn't be here talking about her. You'd have given up already and holed up somewhere to be alone and miserable for the rest of your life. And you do know how to make it work—you're just scared."

I swallowed, unsure if I should tell Ken to fuck off or keep talking.

"The truth is, you're letting guilt from the past and fear of the future poison the potential of this relationship already, even though you really like this woman and she likes you." He pushed up his glasses again and leaned forward, knees on his elbows. "But you have to be willing to try, Sebastian. You have to be willing to fail. And that takes guts."

My arms came uncrossed. Was he calling me a coward? "I have guts," I said defensively. "I'm just trying to think things though. I don't want to make the same mistakes I've made before, Ken. This girl is...special to me. She's different." I took a breath. "She's perfect."

Ken shook his head. "Nobody's perfect. Not her, not you, not me...I don't even think this is all stemming from OCD. Mostly, I think this is just a man scared to let himself be emotionally vulnerable to a woman he cares about." He smiled wryly. "Oldest story in the book."

• • •

Later that afternoon I took the boat out on the bay and thought about what Ken had said. Was he right? Was it plain old fear of rejection rather than my OCD getting in the way of my taking a risk? How could he know, anyway? He didn't hear that voice in my head that made me doubt everything. God, what I wouldn't give for some fucking *conviction* about something.

The truth was, I didn't want to be closed-off and miserable for the rest of my life. Maybe I'd thought I could be alone, but that was before I knew what it was like to be with Skylar, to feel that kind of connection to someone. And it wasn't all sexual— well, it was a lot sexual—but it was also emotional. She made me want to share things with her I'd never talked about outside therapy. She made me want to change the way I lived my life. She made me want to deserve her, or at least try.

But I'd fucked up already…Would she forgive me if I apologized again?

Probably. That was the kind of person she was. But she might not be willing to take another chance on me without some assurance that I wasn't going to keep doing this. And how the fuck could I offer her that kind of assurance when I had none of it myself?

All I could do was try harder, and as I rowed hard back toward the cabin, muscles aching, I vowed that I would.

• • •

The following day, I spent the morning at my father's office, getting caught up on some files he'd assigned me, and the afternoon covering the front desk for Lorena, his assistant, who had to go pick up her sick child at school. My dad had offered to call in a temp, but I assured him I could handle the job. Mostly I spent the time thinking of things I could do for Skylar, ways I could make it up to her for being such a dick. I still hadn't contacted her, but I had an idea in the back of my mind.

Around three, a couple came into the office that I'd never seen before. She was little but curvy, like Skylar, with a thick head of wavy light brown hair and a friendly smile. He was dark-haired and taller than his wife—they both wore rings, I noticed—but not really a tall guy. I wondered if she was pregnant, because as soon as they entered the lobby, she sank into a chair and put both hands over her stomach. "Oof," she said, closing her eyes.

"Are you OK?" the guy asked, putting a hand beneath her chin. "I can run you home, Mia. You don't have to be at this meeting."

"I'm fine, just woozy. We're already here so let's get this done."

He straightened up and approached me at the desk. "Hi. We have an appointment with Malcolm Pryce at three fifteen. Lucas Fournier."

I noticed he had a slight accent. "Of course. I'll let him know you're here." But after fumbling for a moment with the complicated phone on Lorena's desk, trying to use the intercom, I gave up. "OK, forget this thing. I'll just go back there and tell him."

"Thanks." He smiled, but quickly turned his attention back to his wife.

I went down the hall and knocked on Malcolm's open door. "Your clients are here. Fournier?"

"Oh, right. Fuck. " He pushed back from his desk, which was a mess. It drove me crazy how disorganized he was. How the hell could he find anything in this shit pile? "I need a few minutes. I'll meet with them in the conference room. Can you show them in?"

"Sure."

"Great, thanks." He stood up and straightened his tie before stacking some paperwork together.

Back up front, I found Lucas Fournier seated next to his wife, her hand in his. "Malcolm will be right up," I told them. "In the meantime, I'll take you into the conference room. I'm Sebastian, Malcolm's brother."

"Nice to meet you." Lucas got to his feet and shook my hand before helping his wife rise slowly from her chair. "This is my wife, Mia."

"Hi." She shook my hand as well. "Sorry I'm a little green in the face. This pregnancy is killing me."

"Oh." I wasn't sure what to say. "Congratulations?" I tried.

She smiled. "Exactly."

"This way, please." I showed them to the conference room and got them each a water bottle from the fridge in the kitchen across the hall.

"Thank you," Mia said gratefully, unscrewing the cap and chugging the water. "I'm so thirsty all the time."

"It's because you're working too much," scolded her husband. But he did it gently. "You need to hire someone to help you."

"Yes, I know. I'll get around to it. But I haven't found anyone I trust yet, and I like things done a certain way." She tipped back the water bottle again and probably didn't see him roll his eyes.

"Yes, I know. But you said you'd hire someone by the end of the month, and if you don't, I will."

"What do you do?" I asked, mostly to be polite.

"We own Abelard Vineyards," he answered, pulling out his wallet and handing me a business card.

"Oh, nice." I studied the card, my mind clicking. "I've heard of it. You took over from another winery a few years ago, right?"

"Yes, and bought some property adjacent to it, which is why we're here. There's a dispute over the property line with a neighboring farm, and we've already planted the area in question." Lucas glanced at his wife. "We're also expanding our tasting room and events schedule this summer, which is why we need to hire more help now."

She ignored him. "Can I use your bathroom please?"

"Sure." I gestured behind me. "It's just down the hall to the left."

"Thanks." She looked at Lucas. "Be right back."

He watched her leave, shaking his head. "She just went at the doctor's office. It's insane."

I had no fucking idea what to say to that. What possible appropriate comment was there to make about his wife's bladder? Luckily, he saved me.

"This is our third, so you'd think I'd remember all this."

"Wow. Three." I'd never pictured myself with kids, and Diana hadn't wanted any, so I couldn't imagine life with one, let alone three.

"Yeah, that's why she needs an assistant. But she's so damn stubborn." He shook his head.

"What sort of help does your wife need? I know someone who was the assistant tasting room manager at Rivard, but she's looking to do a little more."

"Really?" Lucas looked interested. "What's she doing now?"

"She's working at Coffee Darling currently. That's her sister's shop. But I know she'd like something else."

He nodded. "I know that place. They have good croissants." Pulling out his wallet again, he gave me another card. "This is Mia's card. Pass this along to her, and have her give Mia a call to set up an interview." He smiled wryly. "Although my wife's so picky and so moody these days, I almost don't want to send your friend into lion's den."

"She can handle moody," I assured him. "And I think your wife would like Skylar—she's beautiful and smart, and she works really hard."

Lucas grinned. "Is her last name Pryce?"

"Ah. No." The tips of my ears burned. "It's Nixon."

"Well, what are you waiting for, Pryce? Marry that girl." His grin widened before he tipped up his water bottle again.

I rubbed the back of my neck, which suddenly felt hot too. "Yeah, it's probably too soon for that. We've only been on one date."

Mia came back in the room, and his eyes lit up at the sight of her. "Sometimes that's all it takes," he said.

chapter twenty-two

Skylar

The Saturday before Memorial day, which was also the day of the reunion, I got off work a little early and moved my things into my parents' house.

Back in my old room, I plugged in my laptop and phone, shoved a few boxes under the bed, hung dresses, skirts, blouses, and coats in my closet, and stacked shoe boxes beneath them. Into the drawers of my old dresser went underwear, socks, pajamas, bottoms and tops, workout clothes and a couple bathing suits. I tried not to feel too depressed about having to live with my parents, but it was hard. Every noise I heard, from the slam of the dresser drawers to the squeak of my old bed springs, reminded me that I was right back where I'd started ten years ago. Even the smell of the house hadn't changed—furniture polish and pie. There was *always* a pie in the oven because my mother sold them at the little farm stand on the road.

Once everything was moved and unpacked, I went back to the guest house and helped my mother give it a thorough cleaning. She praised everything I'd done with it, from paint colors to linens to small finishing touches like the bin pulls, and thanked me for my hard work. I could tell she suspected something was up with me, because she kept eyeing me strangely. It was the look she used to give us before checking to see if we had a fever as kids.

"Everything OK?" she asked after I sighed for the millionth time, glancing over at me from the window she was washing.

"Fine." I continued wiping down the counters.

She was quiet a minute, her cloth squeaking on the glass. "Sebastian is nice. He going with you to the reunion tonight?"

"No."

"Why not? I thought you graduated the same year."

"We did. He doesn't want to go." I finished with the counters and moved on to the oven, which I hadn't even used that much because I really didn't cook. Yet another adult skill I lacked.

"Oh. What about Dani and Kristen?"

"They couldn't make it in. Dani's due in like two weeks, and Kristen's in-laws were visiting or something."

"Are you going alone, then?"

"I guess."

She stopped what she was doing and came over to the kitchen. "You don't sound very excited about it."

"I'm not."

"So why go at all?"

I shrugged. "Maybe I won't."

"Skylar."

I finally turned and looked at her.

"What's with you?" Her brow furrowed. "You're not acting like yourself."

Exhaling, I leaned back against the oven. "I'm just trying to figure out some stuff and it's stressing me out. I'm not much looking forward to the reunion because I'm embarrassed about being on Save a Horse and the whole dethroning thing, but I haven't done anything else worth talking about."

"You've done a lot of things!" She threw up one hand. "You've traveled, lived in New York City, been on television...how many people can say that?"

"I don't know. Doesn't seem like much compared to what I *said* I was going to do." I threw the rag onto the counter. "Or compared to what Nat and Jilly have done. I just feel like an asshole, OK? That's what's with me."

"Skylar Elizabeth Nixon, you listen to me," she said so forcefully I had to meet her eye. "I did not raise any assholes, and more importantly, I did not raise my girl to talk that way about herself. So you went to New York to chase a dream and it didn't happen, so what. You know what I always say about failure."

"It builds character," I mumbled.

"That's right. Failure builds character, and character is what you need right now. Character and confidence. This is no big thing! You think you're the first small-town girl with stars in her eyes that got disillusioned with the reality of trying to make it in that world?"

"No," I said through clenched teeth.

"Of course you don't, because you're not stupid. Now, your entire life everyone's been telling you what a special snowflake you are—but the truth is, you're just like the rest of us, honey. That means sometimes you're gonna get what you want, sometimes you're not. Sometimes you're gonna get it only to find out it's not what you thought it was gonna be. It's all part of the journey. Do you understand?"

"Yes," I said, even though part of me was like, *What do you mean I'm not a special snowflake?* Was your mother supposed to say this stuff to you?

"Good. You can walk into that reunion tonight and be proud of who you are, Skylar. You're a beautiful girl with a great big heart and a lot of potential. Good Lord, if we all had the answers by age twenty-seven, life would be pretty boring, don't you think?"

I curled my upper lip. "I hate boring."

She laughed, coming around the counter to give me a hug. I let her, wrapping my arms around her plushy middle and taking comfort in her pie-crust-and-Windex scent. "You always have. Go have fun tonight. You can think about life's opportunities tomorrow."

• • •

The reunion was being held at The Corner Loft downtown. I got ready in my old bedroom, feeling a little like I was leaving for the Prom, only without a date. In the spirit of being more responsible, I'd decided to take back the outfit I'd purchased to wear to the reunion and wear something I already owned—a fitted LBD with cap sleeves that hit me about mid-thigh. It was a little more conservative than I usually dressed for parties, but I wasn't feeling all that festive. For me it was all about the shoes anyway, and I wore black strappy Louboutin heels with a satin bow at the back.

I took an Uber downtown, arriving early as promised to help with decorations. The reunion committee was there already, placing centerpieces on tables, setting up a photo booth, and giving a photo montage a test run on a large screen against one wall.

Jennifer Krege, the committee head, greeted me warmly. We hadn't been close friends, but I remembered her as an outgoing high-achiever. "You look beautiful," she said. "You haven't changed a bit."

"Thanks. You look beautiful too." She was very pregnant, but looked adorable in her dress and flats, and I was jealous of the way she could wear an Audrey Hepburn updo. My ears made me look like a muppet when I tried it. "What can I do to help?"

She put me to work setting out votive candles, and when that was done, she asked me to help her move some tables to make room for dancing. Other committee members said hello, and while no one squealed with joy when they saw me, no one spit in my eye either. I began to think maybe the evening would be OK.

I relaxed even further after a couple glasses of wine, and even managed to have some fun reminiscing with former classmates about school plays, favorite teachers, choir trips, Homecoming parades and bonfires. Maybe I was a little bit careful whenever I talked to someone to keep the conversation focused on the past, but other people seemed more interested in reliving the old days rather than talking about their current, everyday lives too. Only a few asked about Save a Horse, and when I confessed that pretty much everything they saw was staged, they said (much to my relief) that's what they figured since I'd never been anything like that in school, and we went on to talk about other things. (Only one creeper asked about the mechanical bull, but I quickly excused myself to the ladies room after that.)

As the evening wore on, I found I actually enjoyed hearing about the different paths my classmates had taken, and I didn't resent their happy marriages or adorable kids or professional lives. In fact, I was genuinely happy for them. There were even a couple divorces and failed start-ups and one juicy affair rumor, so I didn't feel completely terrible about my mistakes or lack of direction. When people asked what I was doing now, I simply said I'd moved to New York for a while but missed home and family, so I was working for Natalie and the family farm while I figured out what to do next.

Far from being judgmental, some of my married-with-kids classmates expressed envy at my having so much time to myself, at all the possible avenues still open to me. I smiled and agreed, but inside I thought it would be nice to owe a little time to someone. It made me think of Sebastian, and I wondered what he was doing tonight. I hadn't heard from him since I got out of his truck three days before.

"I mean, seriously, you could like take off tomorrow and go to Rio or something and no one would even bother you," Katelyn Witzke was saying to me, although her eyes were scanning the room behind me. "Ooh! There's Sam Schatko. He looks bad. Did you hear about his wife? I heard she's screwing his boss. Can you imagine?"

"No. Hadn't heard that," I murmured. Katelyn and I had run with the same popular crowd, but even back then I remember her always gossiping about someone. I hadn't liked it much then and found it even less tolerable now.

"Anyway, I can't even go to the bathroom at home without the boys following me in there. A shower by myself feels like heaven. And speaking of heaven, what god is that?"

"Huh?"

"That guy right there, behind you. He's gorgeous. Did he go to our school?"

Confused, I glanced over my shoulder and saw Sebastian walking through the crowd, looking right at me. My breath caught in my throat—he *did* look like a god. Gorgeous and serious and totally focused on me. Wearing a dark blue suit and white dress shirt without a tie, he turned every female head in the place as he crossed the room. My stomach flip-flopped madly.

Wait, I was angry with him. I narrowed my eyes.

But as he came closer and I saw the uncomfortable, almost pained expression on his face, I knew I wouldn't have the heart to brush him off when he got to my side.

Still, it had been three days. I could make him sweat five more minutes. I turned back to Katelyn.

"Do you know who that is?" she whispered, staring over my shoulder, her dark eyes like saucers.

"Mmhm." I lifted my wine glass to my lips nonchalantly, trying not to betray the hammering in my chest. A moment later, I felt the warmth of his body at my back.

"Hey." His voice was low in my ear.

A shiver moved up my spine. I looked at him over one shoulder.

Then I waited.

For an apology. A how are you. A nice to see you. Anything that would indicate he knew he'd hurt my feelings and felt bad about it. Seconds ticked by and he remained silent, so I looked at Katelyn again, who was standing there with her mouth agape. "I'm sorry. You were saying?"

Then I felt it—his forehead dropping gently onto the back of my head, and resting there. Something squeezed my heart, but I refused to give in. Then I felt the hand on my hip, heard him whisper my name, and I knew I was lost.

Katelyn was positively riveted. "Is—is this your husband, Skylar?"

"No. This is Sebastian Pryce. Sebastian, do you remember Katelyn Witzke, used to be Katelyn Ellis?" He didn't move. "Say hello to the nice lady, Sebastian," I said firmly.

Sighing, he came out from behind me and held out his hand. "Hello."

"Hi," Katelyn said uncertainly, taking his hand. I could tell she was struggling to place him, just like I had, and I could also tell the moment it clicked, because she blinked, her mouth falling open again. "Wait a minute—you're not the Sebastian Pryce from our graduating class, are you?"

He nodded, looking more uncomfortable by the minute. Unable to stay mad at him when he seemed so miserable, I took his hand. "Sebastian moved back about a year ago, and we ran into each other at Coffee Darling. He's an attorney now."

"Oh," she said, recovering somewhat. "For what firm?"

"My father's."

She waited for him to elaborate, but he didn't, and I scrambled to cover the awkward silence. "Hey, would you mind getting me another glass of white wine, Sebastian?" I asked him. "I'm empty."

"Sure." He took my glass. "And then maybe we can talk?"

"OK."

He looked at Katelyn. "Can I get you anything?"

"No thanks." She held up her half-full glass. "I'm good." As soon as he was out of earshot, she pounced on me. "Oh my God! Is that really Sebastian Pryce? The crazy one? Are you guys dating? He's so hot! Is he, like, normal now?"

Irked by the word crazy, I was already frowning by the time she got to normal. "Don't say that about him. He wasn't crazy, he was just…shy. And a little anxious."

She shrank away from me, screwing up her face. "Are we thinking of the same person? He was totally nuts. Remember all the weird things he used to do? The washing his hands thing and the way he'd arrange all his pens and pencils on his desk so they were the exact same distance apart and the way he wouldn't sit in an odd row in any classroom? I remember this huge fight he got into with Mr. Parlatto because he wouldn't sit in the first row." She lifted her wine to her lips, her eyes lighting up at the promise of fresh gossip. "He was a total freak."

I was furious now, my hands fisting at my sides. "I remember how he used to get teased for being a little different," I snapped. "And I realize now how tough it must have been for him to go through school without any friends. I wish I'd have shown more compassion, something I think we all could use a little more of. Excuse me."

I found Sebastian in line at the bar, fending off the advances of a drunk Cassie Callahan, our prom queen and head cheerleader. A girl who probably wouldn't have given him the time of day ten years ago. Fierce, territorial desire for him ignited inside me. "Ready to go? I need a ride home."

"Yeah," he said. "You don't want your wine?"

"No. I'm done." Without a word to anyone else, I took Sebastian's hand and pulled him through the crowd, well aware of the stares we got. At the coat check, Sebastian held my coat for me and I slipped into it, then he tipped the woman two dollars before taking my hand again. My heart was pounding as we descended the stairs, and I had the desperate urge to kiss him, to wrap my arms and legs around him, to cover his body with mine and protect him—which was ridiculous. I was half a foot shorter than he was, even in my heels. And he was a grown, gorgeous, strong man, not the misunderstood child he'd been...but still. Something inside me just wanted to get him alone and hold him, whisper to him, take him inside me and make him feel good. He'd come here for me, even though he hadn't wanted to. Even though he'd known how people would gossip and wonder.

We didn't speak until we got outside on the empty sidewalk. "Fucking hell," he said, rubbing the back of his neck as we turned the corner. His truck was parked on the street a few cars down. "How did you stand it in there that long?"

I didn't answer. Instead I moved in front of him and threw my arms around his neck, kissing him hard, my feet coming right off the ground. His arms looped around my back

"What are you doing here, anyway?" I whispered against his lips.

"I came for you."

Gratitude made my body tingle, but I wanted more. "Why?"

"Because I'm sorry." He set me on my feet and looked me in the eye. "Because it wasn't just about sex, and I treated you like it was. I was wrong." Lowering his lips to mine, he kissed me before whispering in my ear, "Give me another chance. Please."

"Oh, God, Sebastian." Taking his face in my hands, I rose up on tip toe and looked up at him. "I don't even feel like I have a choice. I want you too much."

He exhaled, his breath warm on my mouth. "Come home with me. Stay the night."

I kissed his lips. "Yes." The side of his jaw. "Yes." The base of his throat. "Yes."

chapter twenty-three

Sebastian

Somehow I managed to drive home, although I don't know how, since the moment I turned the key in the ignition, Skylar unbuckled my belt, undid my pants, and stuck her hand inside my boxers.

"Move your seat back," she said, pulling my cock out and slipping it through her fingers.

I did as she requested, looking around to make sure no cops were in sight.

"Now drive," she demanded. "Or I'll stop."

Groaning, I put the truck in drive and tried to concentrate on the lines and lights and signs and traffic rather than on her hand working up and down my shaft, or her thumb circling the head, or the way she watched what she was doing, a little moan escaping her mouth. And speaking of her mouth.

When I turned onto the dark, quiet highway on the peninsula, she unbuckled her seatbelt and leaned toward me. "Careful now," she whispered. Before I could stop her, she fluffed her hair back behind her shoulders, fisted my dick, and put her head in my lap. The next thing I felt was her tongue swirling around the tip of my cock like it was an ice cream cone and she didn't want to waste a single drop. Oh fuck, oh fuck, now I was picturing her with my cum dripping off those round pink lips like melting vanilla ice cream.

I garbled something unintelligent, but what I meant to say was, *I can't drive, I can't drive.* It got even worse—better?—when she took just the head in her mouth and sucked, first gently and then hard, her fingers closing tight around the base.

My leg muscles tightened up. "Jesus, Skylar. Easy." I tried to relax my lower body muscles, which wanted to flex and thrust and push deeper into her mouth.

She took her lips from me with a little pop and giggled. "No, it's hard. And I think it's getting harder."

"Oh, fuck. Fuuuuuuuck," I moaned as she slid her lips down to her fingers, enveloping my cock in hot, wet heaven. She kept it there, half in her mouth, half in her hand and worked it from both ends, jerking and sucking until I was positive I was going to lose control of my truck, my orgasm, and my senses.

"Mmmmm." She lifted her head again. "I can taste you," she whispered. "I love it."

My jaw ticked. "You are a very bad girl."

"I know." She rubbed the tip in circles against the flat of her tongue, and I cursed again, making her laugh.

God, that laugh. I'd never grow tired of it. And then I made the mistake of glancing down at that blonde hair. I'd seen her first from behind tonight, the moment I stepped into the room. I'd hated every step of the walk to get to her, feeling the eyes of everyone there on me, but I'd kept my focus on that hair and those curves in her tight black dress and those alabaster legs that had been wrapped around my body just a few nights ago. When I'd gotten close enough to see her shoes, blood rushed to my groin at the sight of the bows tied above the high heels.

That was bad, right? That I'd gone there to apologize, to show her I wanted to be there for her, to make an effort at being the kind of person she deserved—and then all I could think about was fucking her with her shoes on?

And that was if I could hold out.

"Wait," I begged her as I felt myself nearing the point of no return. We were getting close to the cabin, although I could hardly feel my foot on the pedal. "I don't want to come yet. Just wait."

"Not. Waiting," said the little vixen, taking me all the way in. My cock hit the back of her throat and my legs seized up.

Fuck, I have to pull over. Veering to the shoulder, I braked hard and came to an abrupt stop, my breath coming fast, my heart pounding inside my chest. *Please don't let a cop come by here tonight*—at least not for the next thirty seconds, which was all I'd have before—

"Jesus. Skylar." Turning off the ignition and the lights, I grabbed her hair, gathering it in my fists.

"Yes," she whispered, yanking me hard and tight and fast with her hand. I could feel her breath on my cock, teasing me, and it made me want to tease *her* a little.

I tightened my fingers in her hair, not pulling too hard, but not letting her get her mouth back on me either.

She gasped. "Oh, you're so mean. Let me. Please. I just want to taste you." She looked up at me with those big, soft eyes and I swear to fucking Christ I almost lost it right there in her face.

"You're a very bad girl, Skylar Nixon."

Her lips widened into a wicked smile. "Let's play a game."

Oh, Jesus. "What kind of game?"

"Just a little something I've been thinking about." She licked me, and I let her. "Let's pretend we're back in school and we're skipping class."

I closed my eyes, willing myself not to come too fast, but the fact that she wanted to indulge in a little fantasy was liable to put me right over.

"And I've never given anyone a blowjob before. You're the first, Sebastian." Her voice had changed. It was higher-pitched, more girlish.

"Yeah?" I managed, relaxing my grip in her hair a little.

"Yes." She brought her legs up beneath her so she was kneeling on the passenger seat. "Tell me what to do to make you come."

"Uh, hearing you say that would've made me come already."

She gave me a dirty look, then pouted. "Come on. Play with me." A dirty little grin stretched her lips. "I just want to please you."

When she lowered her mouth to me again, her ass in the air, I put one hand on it as she took me in deep again, slowly gliding her lips and tongue and teeth down my cock and back up, again and again and again.

"Fucking hell, Skylar Nixon. If this is your first blowjob, you are a goddamn prodigy."

She giggled, pulling me from her mouth. "You like it?"

I licked my lips and palmed her perfect ass. "Yeah."

"Have you seen me around school?" She arched her back, batted her lashes at me. "I've seen you."

"Every day," I growled. "And every day I want you just like this. On your knees for me."

"Really?" She smiled shyly. "Tell me what to do."

I inhaled. "Put my dick in your mouth," I told her. (Somewhere inside my head was a skinny, awkward teenager screaming *Oh my God, you just told Skylar Nixon to put your dick in her mouth!*) "Yes, just like that." She took me between her lips and resumed the slow bobs of her head, the tight squeezes with her hand. "It feels so good when you take my cock in deep like that. I love your tongue on it." She paused with the tip hitting the back of her throat and I groaned, lifting my hips off the seat.

"Yes, yes…" I whispered. "Fuck yes, like that. You're so beautiful, and I've thought about this so many times…" I loosened my grip of her hair further and she moved her hand and head faster, making my lower body tingle and clench and burn. Oh fuck, I was close—did she really want it this way?

"You're gonna make me come in your mouth...are you sure?" In answer, she went even harder at me, moaning and sucking and jerking me with tight, hard pulls, keeping me deep inside her mouth. *Oh God oh God oh God—fuck yes!* I spanked her ass hard, left my hand there as my climax ripped through me and I came in her mouth, my cock throbbing hard, my breath escaping me in loud, strangled growls.

When it was over, she swallowed and straightened up to her knees, wiping her mouth with the back of her hand. "Was it good?" she asked, all wide-eyed innocence and full, puffy lips.

"Uhng." Yes, that's what I said. Uhng.

She smiled slyly. "I hope so. I liked it. Maybe you'll let me do it again sometime."

"Maybe." Grabbing her jaw with one hand, I pulled her face to mine. "You. Are. Very. Naughty."

Her eyes gleamed with blue fire. "I was naughty, wasn't I?"

I kissed her lips. "Yes."

"It was your fault. Wearing that suit and coming to surprise me that way." She buckled herself in while I did up my pants, and as we drove the short distance to the cabin, I kept looking at her legs...and her shoes.

It gave me an idea, something I'd always wanted to try but never had the nerve to attempt because of who I was. But Skylar was different.

She understood me.

chapter twenty-four

Skylar

"Are you hungry?" he asked once we got inside.

"Sort of." I slipped out of my coat, setting it and my purse on the couch. I had no idea if I was hungry—my stomach had been doing all kinds of crazy acrobatics since he'd walked into that reunion.

He went into the kitchen, flipped on the light and started rummaging around in the fridge. "Will you eat if I make something?"

"Sure. You cook?" Surprised, I went over to the little breakfast bar and sat on a stool.

"Yes." After washing his hands, he pulled out a carton of eggs and a green bell pepper. "Are you impressed?"

I nodded. "Definitely."

"Good." He pulled two small tomatoes, a bag of shredded mozzarella cheese, and a package of bacon from the fridge. "Do you cook?"

I pursed my lips. "I'm more of a sous-chef."

He grinned and grabbed milk, butter, and a bag of basil from the fridge before closing the door. "You can help."

"OK." Excited, I joined him in the kitchen, washing my hands at the sink. "What should I do?"

"Can you chop the basil and slice the tomatoes?"

"Sure. Knife?" I looked around for a knife block but didn't see one.

"They're in the cupboard above the fridge. I'll get you one."

"Why the hell are they up there?"

"No reason." He opened the cupboard, and I saw the block tucked inside it.

Liar.

"Hey," I said. "Bring the entire block down."

He froze.

"I mean it. Get the whole thing."

He pinched the bridge of his nose a second, but then he reached in and lifted the block down, setting it on the counter.

We both stared at it.

I pulled out the biggest butcher knife he had. "Take it."

Grimacing, he took it from me and held it in his hand.

"Are you going to stab me?"

"No."

"Good. Are you going to stab anyone, ever?"

"No." He stared at the blade. "No, I'm not."

"Then why do you have to keep your knives way the fuck up there?"

He shrugged. "Old habit."

"Well, break it. If I ever come over to cook again, I need to be able to reach things. I'm high-cupboard challenged."

He handed me the knife, taking a breath. "You're right. I'll move them down."

"Thank you." I located a cutting board and got to work, while he melted some butter in a pan on the stove.

"Did anyone ever tell you," he said, "you'd make a good therapist?"

I laughed. "No. But I'm glad you think so."

"Hey, do you like champagne?" He opened the fridge and pulled out a long-necked green bottle. "My brother and sister-in-law got me this when the cabin was finished and I never opened it."

"I love it," I assured him. "Pop the cork."

• • •

Sebastian had no dining table, so we ate Caprese omelets and drank champagne sitting next to each other at the breakfast bar, a lemon beeswax candle burning between us.

"That smells so good. I've got to get your sister-in-law's information," I said between bites. "Don't let me forget."

"I saw her yesterday. She gave me some samples and a card for you. Oh," he said, as if he'd just remembered something. "I have something else for you too." He set his fork down, stood up, and reached for his wallet, which was on the kitchen

211

counter. "Here," he said, handing me a business card.

"What's this?" I took it from him and studied it. "Abelard Vineyards, Mia Fournier."

"I met her and her husband yesterday at the office. My brother Malcolm is helping them settle a property line dispute." He sat down again and resumed eating. "They're new owners in the last couple years or so, and they've expanded. She's pregnant, and she's looking for an assistant. Someone to help with the tasting room and special events." He glanced sideways at me. "I thought of you."

I couldn't keep the smile off my face. "Thank you. That's so sweet."

"He said she's picky, but I know she'd like you."

My heart sank a little. "Picky? I bet she wants a college degree. Or more experience." I set the card down and picked up my champagne.

"Her husband didn't say anything like that. He just said she's choosy about who works there. You should call her."

I bit my lip, bubbles lingering on my tongue. "You think so?"

Sebastian set his fork down again, grabbed the back of my neck and pulled me toward him, kissing my lips hard. "I know so. Who wouldn't adore you?"

A blush crept up my chest. "It does sound perfect. I'll think about it."

• • •

When we'd finished eating, we poured the rest of the champagne into our glasses and went out on the patio. This time we shared one of the Adirondack chairs Sebastian had put together, me sitting on his lap.

"Are you cold?" he asked me, and I loved the way his forehead wrinkled with concern. "I'm sorry. I'm in a suit, but you have bare arms and legs."

"I'm OK. I'll let you know if I get cold." I kissed his forehead, my right arm around his shoulders, my left holding my wine glass.

We were quiet for a moment, and it was a comfortable silence. I wasn't even the one to break it.

"I'm glad you're here," he said. "I thought maybe I'd fucked things up too much the other night."

"I was a bit thrown," I admitted. I took a sip of champagne. "Can you tell me what happened?"

He didn't speak right away, and I didn't force it. "I panicked."

I looked at him. "Why?"

"Because you...do something to me I didn't expect. Something I don't even really understand." He dropped his eyes from the water to my legs. "Sorry, I know I owe you a better explanation," he started, but I hushed him with a kiss.

"You know what? Not right now you don't." I kissed him again. "You really don't. I know what you mean." In all honesty, I didn't even really understand what was happening between us, and I sure as hell hadn't expected it either. Maybe tomorrow we'd talk. Tonight, I just wanted to be with him.

We kissed again, sweet and slow and searching, and eventually Sebastian set down his glass to brush my hair back from my face. "Do you know," he whispered, "how many nights I dreamed about you?"

I shook my head, my pulse quickening.

"Countless. And in countless dreams, you weren't as beautiful as you are in real life, and I don't mean just your face."

I smiled. "You liked the blow job."

He groaned. "Fuck yes, I did. But I like even more than that about you. You make me want to take chances I never thought I'd take again."

"What kind of chances?"

"Being close to someone. It's never easy for me, but you make it feel that way. And every time I'm with you, it gets easier."

After a deep breath, I asked, "So in the car tonight…no bad thoughts?"

He shook his head. "None. You managed to shut down my brain entirely—at least, *that* part of it."

"You thought with something else?" I asked playfully.

"That's the fucking amazing thing. I didn't think at all. I just felt." Then he kissed me again, and again, and again, his tongue parting my lips, his hand traveling up my leg to my waist. "You have no idea what that's like for me—to just feel. It's heaven." He put his hand on my face and kissed his way across the opposite cheek to whisper in my ear. "You're an angel."

I smiled at the sweet words, at the tingle between my legs, at the way I could feel his cock stirring beneath me. "An angel, huh?" My eyes closed as his mouth traveled down one side of my throat, his hand pressing the other side. His warm, wet tongue on my skin sent darts of lust straight to my core.

"Yes," he said, his voice low and rough. "But this little angel has to answer for her earlier disobedience."

My heart stopped for a second, then raced. "She does?"

"She does." He slipped an arm beneath my knees and stood, cradling me as we walked toward the door. "And she better not talk back this time."

I laughed, although a funny tickle that felt a little like fear was fluttering in my belly. "Where are you taking me?"

"Shhh. My turn to play." He went up the steps, opened the sliding door, and set me on my feet inside the cabin. "No questions. Go up to the loft and wait for me. Don't get undressed and *don't* take off your shoes." His light eyes appeared black and shining in the dark.

"OK," I whispered, wondering what he was planning to do with me up there. "Should I be nervous?" It was a joke…sort of.

"Should have thought of that before you tried to run us off the road tonight." He leaned in, one hand on either side of the doorway. "And before mentioning you like it a little rough."

My mouth fell open as he shut the sliding door and walked away. Oh my God, where the hell was he going? And what on earth was he planning? This was a guy who had some pretty violent images in his head from time to time…did they ever merge with his fantasies? I bit one knuckle, hesitating for just a second before hurrying over to the ladder.

My heart thumped hard as I carefully climbed the ladder in my heels, wondering if it was wrong to be so turned on by the fact that I wasn't one hundred percent sure being the object of someone's fantasies was entirely safe. I trusted Sebastian...but still.

What was he going to do to me?

chapter twenty-five

Sebastian

I hurried through the dark to my tool shed, where I knew I had some thick cotton rope left over from stringing the hammock. My heart was beating fast, both from nerves and excitement. I wanted to follow through with this, but I also hoped my brain wouldn't trip itself up. Indulge Bondage Fantasy with Skylar Nixon wasn't on the SUDS list, but it was definitely something I'd imagined and never thought I'd have the nerve to try.

It was a risk, but I was getting better about taking those.

After picking up the wine glasses off the patio, I went around to the front door, solely for the purpose of making Skylar wait and wonder a little longer. She was so fucking adorable, and the look on her face when I'd told her to go up and wait for me was priceless.

I fucking loved that she liked to talk dirty, to fantasize out loud, to play a little. I'd never been with anyone like her before, and I'd never felt comfortable enough with anyone else to show that side of myself. Given my struggle with guilt and shame, I was always so worried that they'd think I was sexually aberrant or perverse.

Although I felt a little perverted right now, sneaking in my own front door with coiled rope in my hand, setting the glasses on the table and switching off all the lights. Why did I even have this fantasy, this desire to render her helpless for the purpose of pleasure?

Don't fucking overthink this, Pryce. Just do it.

I climbed the ladder slowly, drawing out the suspense. When I reached the top, I found her sitting primly on the edge of the bed with her hands in her lap, legs together and feet flat on the floor. She hadn't turned on the light, and since the night was slightly overcast, the moon didn't offer much in the way of illumination either. Still, her eyes went right to the rope in my hand, and I heard her breath catch.

But she didn't ask.

God, she was so fucking perfect. My heart was hammering, and the crotch of my pants was hot and tight. I set the rope on the nightstand and slipped off my jacket, tossing it next to her on the bed.

"Did I tell you how much I like your shoes tonight?" I said, removing my cuff links. After slipping them into my pocket, I cuffed my sleeves, fighting the urge to rip off that black dress, throw her legs in the air, and fuck her into oblivion with my hands wrapped around her ankles.

She shook her head.

"I love them." Moving closer to her, I switched on the bedside lamp.

"Thank you." She looked up at me, her eyes wide and trusting, but just a little bit worried.

"Are you nervous, angel?"

She glanced at the rope on the table. "Maybe a little."

Was she playing or serious? She was an actress, after all. Maybe she knew how hot it was to play the innocent. Either way, her answer made my cock even harder. I tipped her chin up. "Stand up."

She stood and gazed up at me through her lashes.

"Turn around."

She presented me with her back, and I moved her hair aside and slowly unzipped her dress. Black lace appeared as the two sides separated, and my breath stopped.

"What's this?"

"It's a corset."

"With straps?"

"Yes. It keeps everything smooth and in place under a fitted dress like this...plus I like nice underwear." She shimmied the dress down her arms and legs and stepped out of it, laying it on the bed.

My legs felt like they might give out—below the corset, which laced up the back, she wore a matching black thong. I let my eyes wander from her long blonde hair to the cinching of the corset to the perfect ivory curves of her ass down her slender legs to those fuck-me-I'm-adorable heels. *Jesus. I don't care what anyone says, NO MAN is good enough to deserve this.*

But since I was here.

I moved up behind her and kissed her back, rubbing my lips softly against her skin. Her perfume was slightly floral, slightly sweet, like orange blossoms, and I inhaled, taking her scent into my head and chest. "You smell good enough to eat," I said, running my hands down her arms from shoulder to fingers. "But first…" Pausing to grab the coil of rope from the nightstand, I brought her hands behind her back and crossed her wrists. As I wound the rope around them, I spoke to her in a low, soft voice. "You're so beautiful, angel. The most beautiful woman I've ever known. That kind of beauty has a strange power over men—it makes us feel strong and yet weak. Protective of it and yet defenseless against it." Her breath was coming faster, her chest rising and falling. I completed the knot and turned her to face me. "Does that make sense?"

She swallowed. "I don't know."

I slipped my fingers into her hair and lowered my mouth to hers, tasting her lips with my tongue. It made me hungry. I dropped to my knees in front of her, as all men should. "Open your legs."

She widened her stance and I kissed my way up each inner thigh, dragging my rough jaw along her smooth skin. "You have to remain standing. That's my rule." Then I put my lips on that black lace, fastening my mouth on her pussy, my hands running up the backs of her legs.

She whimpered, her legs trembling. "Oh God, oh God. Your mouth…"

I worked the little scrap of lace aside with my tongue, keeping my hands on her ass. She tasted like honey and oranges and I couldn't get enough. Burying my face between her legs, I plunged my tongue inside her and then stroked it up her center, finally moving the lace aside with my hand so I could get at her clit.

The second I licked it, her knees buckled a little. I circled her thighs with my arms to hold her up as she moaned and cursed me.

"Enough, please," she begged. "I can't stand anymore."

"Come for me, and I'll let you lie down," I whispered.

"I don't know if I can, standing like this. My legs…" Her tone was pleading, desperate.

"You want to come. I know you do. Come on, angel." I circled her clit with my tongue, sucked it into my mouth. I did all the things I'd done the other night that had made her gasp and sigh and moan, slipping two fingers in side her and twisting them the way she liked. The knowledge of her body, of her mind, intoxicated me. *I know what makes her come.*

And I did make her come, her pussy clenching around my fingers, her voice crying out in waves that matched the rhythmic spasms. When her legs finally gave way, I flipped her onto her stomach so her upper body lay across the bed, bound wrists at the small of her back. Her slender arms were pale against the black satin corset. *God, her ass is all mine. And fuck, those legs. Those shoes.* "Don't move," I told her, yanking her wet underwear off. Then I stood and unbuckled my belt, undid my pants.

"Yes," she panted. "I want it."

"Yes, what? What exactly do you want, angel?" Oh Jesus, I would probably go to hell for tying up Skylar Nixon and making her beg me to fuck her.

But right now, my soul's eternal damnation seemed a pretty fair price.

"I want you, Sebastian," she said breathlessly. "I want you to fuck me. Hard."

"Hard?" I took my dick in my hand, stroking it as I took in the image of her bent over my bed, hands tied, legs straight, feet apart. I teased her pussy with the tip, smearing wetness from front to back, sliding it in the crack of her ass.

"Yes." Her eyes were closed, her mouth open.

"Apologize."

"Huh?" Her eyes popped open.

"Apologize," I growled, pushing inside her. "For being so beautiful. For making me want you so badly. For breaking me down. For making me so fucking hard for you all the time." Words slipped from my mouth as I grabbed her hips and thrust slowly in and out. "From the moment I saw you again, I knew you could undo me. I knew I should stay away from you, but I couldn't. I can't. The only thing I can do is make you mine."

"I'm not sorry," she rasped, her bound hands clenching into fists just like her pussy was tightening around my cock. "I'll never apologize. Never."

"So you want this?" I pulled her back onto me, slowly but not gently. I watched myself disappear inside her body, mesmerized.

"Yes," she said. "Yes, I want this. I *want* to break you. I want to be yours. I want you inside me." Her voice hushed to a whisper. "I want everything."

"Fuck. *Fuck*." It was too much—all of it. The rope around her hands and her pale skin and curvy body, her words and the memory of her, the possibility of us. I held her hips and fucked her fast and hard and deep, and nothing—nothing—in my entire life had ever felt as good. Strength and power and indestructible certainty that I could do *anything* flooded my veins, and as I reached the breaking point, my entire body seizing up and then exploding deep within her, all I could think was taking *her* inside *me*, caging her within my bones, enclosing her within my ragged, imperfect puzzle of a heart.

Mine.

• • •

Later, after I'd unwrapped her wrists and kissed the tender red marks on her alabaster skin, we undressed each other and slid between the cool white sheets in my bed, arms wrapped around each other tight. She fell asleep first, and I lay there stroking her hair, ignoring the ghosts that tried to fill my head with punishing dread, filling it instead with the scent of her skin, the softness of her breath, the weight of her head on my chest. Then I closed my eyes and held her as I drifted off to sleep.

In the morning, I woke first, facing away from her, one of her arms slung over my torso. I picked up her hand and kissed it before sliding out of bed and pulling on a pair of jeans and a t-shirt from my dresser. Soft, golden morning sun was just starting to come in through the skylight, and I smiled at the way it fell across her features. I could get used to seeing the first light of day on her face.

It reminded me of a poem I liked by Robert Frost about the ephemeral beauty of the beginnings of things.

Was this our beginning? Would we always remember the first night we spend together? The first morning here at the cabin?

Don't be fucking melodramatic, snapped the voice. *You have no idea what she's feeling. You think the things she said to you when you had her tied up and defenseless were real? It was a fucking game.*

Fuck. It had been kind of a game, but I hadn't sensed any guile or pretense in her. It felt like she was speaking the truth. I *wanted* it to be the truth.

Could this work between us? I wasn't ever positive about anything, but something tempted me to think maybe, just maybe Skylar Nixon could be the one woman who was strong enough, sweet enough, forgiving enough to be with me. The thought was both terrifying and beautiful.

Quietly I climbed down the ladder, used the bathroom, put the coffee on, and took my notebook out onto the porch. I felt rested, but throughout the night I'd woken up repeatedly with words scattered in my head, and I wanted to see if I could make some sense of them on paper. Sometimes letting the voice have his way in writing demystified it—lessened its foreignness inside my mind. These were *my* thoughts, *my* words, *my* feelings, and I owned them. I wasn't their victim. Pulling the pencil from the spiral where I'd tucked it, I looked out into the woods for a few minutes, letting the raw words weave themselves together.

Some Sort of Happy

Skylar

You fall softly
like snow
mine

I am beneath you (I fall hard, like stone)
so I will catch you
on my tongue
You melt there like sadness
mine

I tied your hands (*mine*)
a vain, exquisite endeavor
to break you
mine

Shards of bone and soul
mine
littered the bedroom floor this morning
I stepped carefully around them
for fear of injury
mine
but you are brave, I think

You will gather them close
and try to smooth their jagged edges
mine
with the fearless, infinite grace
of your foolish heart

mine

chapter twenty-six

Skylar

Guess he wasn't kidding about the sunrise.

I had the day off, so arising at dawn hadn't exactly been my plan, but when I woke up and found myself alone in Sebastian's bed, I missed him right away. Holy hell, last night had been amazing. From the blowjob in the car—I don't even know what came over me, I'd *never* done that before—to the sex in his bedroom to the things he'd said…my mind was spinning. Jesus, had he really tied me up? Sebastian Pryce, who was so nervous about hurting people he kept his sharp knives hidden above the fridge, had actually tied my hands behind my back with rope?

Spying the rope on the floor, I brought the sheet up to my mouth and giggled silently. God. He was such a study in contradictions. But I loved that he felt comfortable enough with me to do it. I loved the things he said while he did it. I could still hear his low, intense voice in my mind.

Apologize… For breaking me down… The only thing I can do is make you mine.

Every second of it had been perfect. I'd meant what I said—I'd never apologize for wanting him—but I didn't see it as breaking him. And as for being his… my stomach tightened at the thought. What did he mean by that? Like *his* his? The forever kind of his? Or was it just great sex? Maybe he was the kind of guy who said things in the dark he wouldn't repeat in the light. I wanted to talk about it, but it would probably be like pulling teeth. Tugging the sheet from what were assuredly perfect hospital corners, I wrapped it around myself and managed to get down the ladder without slipping.

The smell of freshly made coffee filled my head as soon as I started to descend. I didn't see him in the kitchen or living room, but I noticed the front door was open. Through the screen door I heard the morning song of the birds, and I remembered he liked to watch the sun rise from the front porch. I set the sheet aside and scooted into the bathroom, where I found a new toothbrush and washcloth laid out for me. *God. He's the sweetest hot-and-cold asshole ever. This could be really good between us…will he try?* After using the bathroom, brushing my teeth and scrubbing off what was left of last night's makeup, I poured two cups of coffee from the full pot, and waddled to the door, holding the sheet tight under my armpits.

"Hey," I said through the screen. He'd been sitting there writing, and jumped at the sound of my voice. "Sorry, didn't mean to disturb you."

"No, it's all right." He quickly closed the notebook, stuck the pencil inside the spiral, and set it on the porch floor before standing. "I didn't expect you up so early. Here, I'll get the door."

"Thanks," I said. "Wow, it's so beautiful out there."

He opened the door and took the cups from me. "I like your outfit."

"You're not mad I pulled the sheet off the bed?" I stepped past him onto the porch and took one cup from his hand.

"Uh, no." He let the screen door slap shut and brought his coffee to his lips. "I'm particular, but I'm not totally insane." He paused. "Usually."

Smiling, I swished over to the other rocker, sat down, and looked around. "So this is sunrise."

Sebastian laughed. "This is sunrise. Ever seen one before?"

"Yes. But not after a night's sleep. The bars close late in New York, as you know, so if I worked till close, sometimes the sun was coming up by the time I got off. But it didn't look like this. Or sound like this or feel like this." I inhaled, the scent of dark roast coffee mixing with the fresh, woodsy air. "Or smell like this."

Nodding, he sat in the other chair, and I tried—I really tried—not to bombard him with personal questions right away. But there was just so much I wanted to know about him! Everything from *What do you like to eat for breakfast* to *What do you write about in that notebook* to *What did you mean last night that you wanted to make me yours* to *Are you ready for another round?*

But I didn't want to spook him too soon, and anyway, it was nice just sitting here. I could get used to this.

Whoa. Whoa there.

Somewhere inside me, rational sense suddenly spoke up. *You just spent your first night together, so don't go getting all attached to him or this or anything else. He already told you he moved here to get away and doesn't want a serious relationship, so don't go thinking one night of great sex was going to change his mind about that. You are not a special snowflake.* I lifted my cup to my lips.

"Hey. No frowning at sunrise."

I sipped and smiled at him. "Sorry. Didn't mean to. I was just thinking too hard."

"Bout what?"

Inhale. Exhale. "About last night."

A dark look crossed his face, and he looked out into the trees. "It was too much for you."

"No! No, not at all. I liked it."

"Did you?"

It was cool on the porch, but my body warmed. "I loved it, actually." I dropped my eyes to my coffee. "I've never done that before."

"Me either."

I looked at him, surprised. "No? My God, you knew exactly what you were doing! You seemed so sure of yourself."

"I know how to tie a good knot. And I'd certainly thought about doing it plenty of times." He looked away from me for a second. "I've just never met anyone I felt comfortable enough to do it with."

"Not even your fiancée?" I couldn't resist.

"Especially not her."

Oh my God, what did that mean? I was trying to work it out in my brain when he reached over and tugged on the sheet. "Hey. Stop analyzing. Last night was fun. Let's leave it at that."

What? Was he fucking kidding? I couldn't leave it at fun! What about all the things we'd said? Didn't they mean anything? "But—"

"No buts. Come here."

A little frustrated, I got up, coffee and sheet and all, and went over to his chair, where he opened his arms and motioned for me to sit onto his lap. His chest was warm, and I leaned back against it, trying not to feel disappointed that he wasn't going to tell me anything else.

And then the notebook at our feet caught my eye.

"Are you a writer too?" I ventured.

"No. Not really."

"I noticed you have that notebook with you a lot."

He hesitated. "It's part of my therapy."

"Oh." I paused for a sip of coffee, wishing I could see his face. Could I keep asking or was I pushing it? "Like a journal?"

"Sort of."

And that was it. We talked a little about the reunion and the job at the winery he wanted me to apply for, but nothing more personal. When our cups were empty, Sebastian offered to refill them, and I stood. He kissed my cheek. "You're even prettier with no makeup on. Do you know that?"

I blushed. "Thank you. I appreciate the things you left out for me in the bathroom. You do that for all your dates?"

"Stop it. I've never had a woman here, Skylar. You're the first."

As I watched him go inside, the thought of another woman here with him struck me with a jealousy so fierce it knocked the wind out of my chest. Shit. I really liked him. I wanted this to *be* something. Why wouldn't he talk to me? I looked down at the notebook again, the powerful urge to peek inside it overwhelming me.

No. Don't do it.

But when I heard the bathroom door open and shut, I acted without hesitation. I wanted to know— was he feeling anything like I was? Was he just too scared to tell me? Crouching down, I flipped quickly to the last page and looked to see what he'd written. My heart was already beating madly when I saw my name.

Skylar

You fall softly
like snow
mine

I read through the words on the page quickly, gooseflesh covering my skin, and when I didn't hear the door open again, I read through it once more, savoring the words this time. Tears welled in my eyes—I did want to gather the broken pieces of him close to me. But what did he mean by my "foolish" heart? Was he saying I was dumb to think this could work?

I flipped back a couple pages and the word *kissing* caught my eye. As I began to read, my stomach turned over.

I'm kissing her. We're on the couch, and she's sitting beside me. My hands are in her hair, and it occurs to me that I could have the urge to put my hands on her neck and squeeze her throat, cutting off her air. I am weak and will give in to this urge. I pull back from the kiss and she smiles at me. I wrap my hands around her throat and watch the confusion come over her face, her blue eyes widening in concern. She is vulnerable and helpless and trusting. Helpless to control the impulse, I squeeze hard, so that she cannot breathe. Her pale complexion purples as she struggles to breathe, and her eyes are terrified. In a moment, it's done. I've crushed the life out of this beautiful creature, and I deserve to die for it.

The screen door opened. "What the fuck?"

I jumped up, my face burning hot, my skin prickling with shame. "Oh God, Sebastian. I'm sorry, I—"

"Godammit, Skylar. This is personal." He set the cups on the wood floor so hard coffee sloshed over the edges and picked up the notebook, which was still open to the page I'd read. As he glanced at it, his complexion darkened. "Fuck. Fuck!"

"I'm sorry," I said, tears spilling over. "I just wanted to know how you felt and you wouldn't tell me. But…what is that stuff about choking someone?" Those words…what the hell was that about? Was it some kind of fantasy? Or was it therapy?

He slammed the notebook shut and stared at me. I'd never seen such rage in his eyes. "Did you need to see if I was the monster I say I am? Got your fucking answer, didn't you."

"Please. I don't think you're a monster." I yanked the sheet up higher and wiped at the tears coursing down my cheeks.

"Yes, you do. I can see it on your face."

"No. It was so wrong of me to look in there, Sebastian, and I'll never do it again. Please say you'll forgive me."

He closed his eyes, inhaled and exhaled loudly.

"Talk to me!"

He opened his eyes and stared hard at me. "I'm going to ask you something, and I want the truth. Did you look in it the first time? The time I left it at the shop?"

Oh fuck. This really sucked. I wasn't even wearing clothes—I had no armor at all. Taking a deep breath, I nodded. "Yeah. I did."

"What did you see?"

I swallowed hard. "I saw the list of things with the numbers, and I saw that Talk to Skylar Nixon was written."

"Anything else?" The cold fury in his voice made me tear up all over again.

"Yes. I saw a poem you must have written about me the day we saw each other again at the beach. It was so beautiful, Sebastian. I was so drawn to you after reading it."

He laughed bitterly. "Really."

"Yes! At least I'm being honest!"

"You got caught. You have to be honest *now*."

I bit my lip, torn between wanting answers and knowing I should shut up. "What was that about choking a woman? Was it therapy? Was it about me?"

"Fuck off. Not everything in my life is about you." He turned and stormed into the cabin, leaving me to sob uncontrollably on the porch.

God, why couldn't I have minded my own business? Why hadn't I just asked him directly what I wanted to know? Why couldn't he and I make this work, and was it even worth trying? If our start was this rocky, should we just forget it?

I collapsed onto the porch steps and cried hard into my arms.

chapter twenty-seven

Sebastian

Up in the loft, I threw the fucking notebook on the floor and sat down hard on the edge of the bed. I was mad as fuck, and I was horrified. Skylar had seen really fucked-up things that I'd written—things that I wasn't comfortable sharing with her yet, so I'd lashed out. The SUDS list was one thing, I might have talked with her about that eventually anyway, but the stuff about her…God. She'd seen the exercise Ken had recommended where I imagine the worst— I'd written that the night I'd seen her at the beach in the attempt to lessen the impact of the thought, to wrest control away from it. I'd written in graphic detail about strangling her—my God, what she must think? She was probably down there calling the police!

It was a matter of time, anyway.

I squeezed my eyes shut. Maybe that was true.

Still, I'd treated her cruelly. As if I didn't know what it was like to mess up and be sorry for it. And yet she'd apologized and asked my forgiveness.

I *was* a monster.

You warned her. She can't say you didn't.

"So now what, asshole?" I muttered, rubbing my face with my hands.

From downstairs I heard the screen door shut, and a moment later I saw her messy blonde head coming up the ladder. She got to the top, struggled with the sheet, then stood up tall. Her face was tearstained and her eyes were red, but the set of her chin was defiant.

"Here's the thing," she announced. "I'm not letting us ruin this."

"Ruin what?"

"Our beginning. I don't care what you wrote in that book, you are not a monster and I'll never think that. So if that's what has you all in knots right now, let's just get that out of the way."

I was too stunned to say anything.

"And I was completely wrong to look in your notebook the way I did. I'm sorry." She lifted her shoulders. "I wanted to know how you felt."

I'm falling in love with you.

"Sebastian." She walked toward me, and I focused on the sheet wrapped around her body. "How do you feel?"

"I don't know," I said lamely. I stared at her bare feet, toe to toe with mine.

"Yes, you do. You're scared. I am too." She put her hand under my chin and forced me to meet her eyes. "I was there last night, remember? I heard the things you said. I said things back to you, and I meant them."

Finally, I looked up and met her eyes. "I meant the things I said too."

"OK." She rubbed my arm. "Then we have something worth fighting for, something young and a little unsteady on its legs, but it can get stronger."

"What if this is just too much work?" I blurted, hating myself for sounding like a coward.

"For who?"

"Both of us. What if I keep fucking up and you get tired of having to forgive me?"

"Hey." She knelt at my feet. "I don't want you to be anyone other than who you are. I don't know how else to tell you that. And look, it was me today that fucked up and needed forgiveness, right?"

"I guess so."

"And I'll never do that again. Your journal is your business. Your therapy is your business. I was totally wrong to look in it." She hesitated. "Even if your words about me did give me goose bumps."

I laughed a little, embarrassed but pleased. "Did they?"

"Yes." She looked up at me with wide, searching eyes, and I felt my dick begin to stiffen. "But why did you say I had a foolish heart? Do you think I'm a fool? Sometimes I think I'm not smart enough for you."

My chest caved. "Skylar. I didn't mean it like that." Leaning down, I took her head in my hands and kissed her softly, then reached for the sheet wrapped around her. She stood and let it fall, and I grabbed her beneath the arms, tipping her back on the bed. I stretched out over her, covering her naked body with my clothed one, brushing her hair back from her face.

"I don't think I'm good enough for you, you know that. And I'm going to frustrate and confuse you, just like you said. Maybe it's the OCD, maybe I'm just difficult—I have no fucking clue. But I won't deserve all the chances you'll have to give me."

She wrapped her legs around me and took my face in her hands. "I'm going to give them, though. And if that makes me a fool, well..." She smiled. "At least I'll be your fool."

I buried my face in her neck, not at all sure I wouldn't tear up. "Mine," I said hoarsely, kissing my way down her chest.

"Yours," she whispered, arching her back when I took the tip of one breast in my mouth. "Yours," she whimpered a few minutes later when I licked two fingers and circled them over her clit, slid them inside her pussy. "Yours," she cried a few minutes later as I brought her to orgasm with my hand, my teeth biting down on one hardened nipple.

I hated taking my lips from her skin even briefly, but somehow she managed to pull off my shirt, and undo my jeans. After shoving them off, I settled between her thighs again, sliding my cock along her clit.

She dug her heels into my legs and clawed at my back. "Inside me. Please. I miss you there already."

Another time I might have teased her, made her wait a little longer, but this morning I just wanted to do as she asked. Our mouths were open and hot and panting against one another's as I slid inside her and began to move, slowly at first, reveling in every inch of slick, tight friction. She writhed and bucked beneath me, grabbing my ass with both hands, pulling me in deep and gasping in pain when I stabbed too deep.

"Too hard? I don't want to hurt you," I whispered, but my hips rocked harder and faster, taking orders from her hands.

"You won't, you won't," she said, her eyes shiny and wild. "I love it deep like that. You have no idea how good it feels."

I almost laughed. "I do, I promise."

"Oh, God." She picked up her head, burying it in the crook of my neck, licking my throat, lifting her hips to meet mine thrust for thrust, driving me to the breaking point. "You make me come so easily, it's like fucking magic."

"Yes. Come with me," I growled low in her ear, feeling that invincibility surge inside me. "Come hard on my cock, let me feel it."

"Yes!" Her climax hit and she dug her nails in deep and held on tight, her lower body going stiff as I drove inside her, again and again. Then I buried myself as deep as I could, coming long and hard, and still felt like I wanted more of her, wanted to give her more of me. *I miss you there already*, she'd said, and I hadn't even been inside her yet. But I knew exactly what she meant.

Even as I held her trembling body close to mine, I mourned the inevitable loss of her.

Nothing gold can stay.

chapter twenty-eight

Skylar

"Hello?"

"Hello, I'm calling for Mia Fournier." I tried to sound less nervous than I felt. Sebastian and even Natalie had encouraged me to make this call on Monday, but it had taken me three more days to work up the nerve. I wanted to be prepared in case she asked about experience, a college degree, why I'd been fired from Rivard, or even Save a Horse, on the off chance she'd watched.

"This is Mia."

I took a breath. "This is Skylar Nixon. I got your card from my friend Sebastian Pryce, and—"

"Oh, at the law firm! Yes! Lucas mentioned you might be calling."

I smiled, relieved that she knew who I was. "Yes. I understand you're interviewing for an assistant?"

"I am. Are you interested in the position?"

"Yes," I said, biting my tongue before I added, *but I'm not sure I'm qualified.*

"Great. Can you interview next week?"

I told her I could, and we set up an interview at Abelard for nine AM Tuesday. I'd have to make sure I got that day off from Coffee Darling, but since Natalie was so supportive, I didn't think she'd mind.

I went to bed that night happy but fretful, making a list on my phone of all the things I needed to do—print out a resume, plan my outfit, research Abelard Vineyards. Frowning at the screen, I tried to think of what I was missing.

"Stop worrying. She's going to love you." Sebastian turned back the sheet and climbed into his bed, where I was sitting up cross-legged, my phone in my lap.

I didn't look up. "Maybe. We'll see."

"Stop." He grabbed my phone and hid it behind his back.

"Hey!" I got to my knees and tried to get it back.

"Enough," he said, holding it out of reach. "You have to get up too early to be doing this right now."

"Come on, give it back. I need it." I made several unsuccessful attempts to get it, and he laughed.

"You don't. You need to relax, I can see it on your face. Don't make me tie you up."

Sighing, I sat back on my heels. "Very funny."

"You're fucking adorable when you pretend to be angry with me." He set my phone on his nightstand and tackled me, throwing me onto my back. Now that we spent so much time together, I knew why his body was so hot—he went to the gym every fucking day! I was a slug compared to him. And he worked at the law firm a lot too. He'd worked a full day every day this week, and then worked out after that. We didn't see each other until dinner time or later, which was why I ended up spending the night so much.

It wasn't that I missed him so badly the two nights we spent apart I could hardly sleep. Nope. No way.

I squealed as I landed, grappling with him but laughing as he pinned my wrists to the bed near my shoulders. "Not a fair fight at all."

"Nope." He kissed me, his lips and tongue a soft contrast to the hard strength of his hands cuffing my wrists. "My sister-in-law wants to meet you."

"Oh?" A little thrill moved through my body.

"Yes. She came into the office this afternoon." He kissed me again, on the lips first, then the neck and chest over the t-shirt of his I'd taken to sleeping in. "She asked if I'd like to bring you to their house for dinner."

"And what did you say?"

He barely took his mouth of me. "I said fuck no, you have terrible table manners."

I rolled my eyes and kicked my legs at him. "You're so mean. Get off me."

"OK." He flipped to his back, dragging me on top of him, holding my wrists above his head. "Better?"

"Mmmmm." Was I mad at him? I forgot. I drew my legs astride his hips, and slanted my mouth over his. As the kiss deepened, I rocked my hips against his thickening cock, feeling desire spark at my center. God, I was beginning to think I was a fiend, the way we'd been going at it almost every night this week. Last night I'd slept alone in my old bed, and I'd been so lonesome for him I had to get myself off with my fingers like a lust-crazed teenager, and I still felt totally unsatisfied.

I'd been really good about taking my pill, but even so, in the back of my mind I wondered if any hormonal treatment would be strong enough to fend off his crazy smart, super ripped sperm. And holy shit, what would I do then? "I'll be right back," I whispered.

He didn't stop me from going for the ladder, which told me he probably knew what I needed to do. My pills were in my purse, which was downstairs, so it was a couple minutes before I climbed up again. The lamp was still burning, and the sight of shirtless Sebastian waiting for me in bed, on his back, the sheet pulled up to his hips, outline of his cock clearly visible, nearly made me trip over my own feet.

Grinning, I jumped on him, straddling his hips again, my hands on his warm, hard chest. He grabbed the hem of the shirt I wore. "Not that I don't love seeing you in my clothes, but I love it even more when you're naked."

I happily whipped off the shirt and tossed it aside, leaving only my panties between us. Sebastian, I discovered, always slept naked.

No complaints here.

His hands moved to my ass as I leaned down to kiss him, my breasts brushing over his chest. He moaned, his tongue stroking between my lips, his hips lifting to push up against me. I moved my body over his, sliding my clit along his thick, hard cock, feeling my underwear grow damp.

"Take them off." His voice was low and firm.

I smiled down at him. "Fiend."

"For you I am."

I bit my lip. "Did you miss me last night?"

"So much I could hardly stand it."

Shaking my head, I said, "Me too. What's with us? Is it because the sex is so good?" Then I panicked. "I mean, it's good for me...I hope it's good for you."

He spanked me lightly. "Stop. It's amazing for me, and you know it. I can't get enough."

That put the grin back on my face and I swung one leg over so I could work my panties down my legs. I was so anxious to feel his cock hit The Spot I left them hanging around one ankle as I straddled him again. But he had another idea.

Shimmying down the bed until his head was between my knees, he looked up at me. "I used to lie awake at night and think about doing this to you." He kissed one inner thigh and then the other, rubbing his scruffy cheek against the sensitive skin there before wiggling down even further and dragging his tongue up my center.

I shivered, falling forward to grip the simple wooden headboard. "Oh God, Sebastian. Your tongue is just..." But I couldn't even find a word for it. Light and colors danced behind my closed eyelids as I dropped my head back, undulating my hips over his mouth. His arms looped over my legs, pulling me tighter to his face, and when I looked down I almost lost it at the sight of those gorgeous green eyes in the V between my legs.

"Fuck," I breathed as he worked my clit with the tip of his tongue. "I didn't even know enough to imagine this. I had no idea it was even possible to feel this good." It was true—I'd been with some really good-looking guys, but somehow being incredibly handsome didn't always correlate to being that skilled in bed. Natalie and I had a theory that slightly less attractive guys were probably better lovers because they had to work harder for it. Like she once confessed that Dan had kind of a small dick but was pretty good with his hands.

Sebastian, however, had everything.

Everything.

Including his tongue buried in my pussy.

And when the tension at my core whirled into a vortex too powerful for my body to contain, he moaned along with me as I rode out my orgasm above him, grinding unabashedly against his face.

When the spasms had stopped I moved down his body, prepared to take him in my mouth, but he deftly flipped me onto my back and pinned my wrists by my head. In the lamplight I could see his shiny lips and chin, and my insides clenched with aftershocks. He kissed me hard and deep, his mouth open wide over mine. I tasted myself and him and us and sex and it was warm and sweet and I opened my legs for him, desperate to feel him enter my body and drive us both into another mad frenzy.

He glided in easily, and I tilted my hips to take him deep. When he was buried inside, he paused and looked down at me, and I thought he was going to say something but he didn't. He just kept his eyes on mine as he started to move, his hips rolling like ocean waves over mine. I strained up against him, pressing closer with my chest, lifting my hips.

"I missed you so much last night," I whispered, every nerve ending in my body on fire. "I touched myself and thought of you."

"I did the same," he said, the muscles in his arms flexing as he braced himself above me. "Twice."

I smiled, deliriously happy. "You win."

• • •

I spent the weekend working for Natalie and preparing for my interview. On Saturday after work, I went over to Jillian's condo and she helped me put together my resume and print it on good paper. I wasn't even sure Mia Fournier would ask for it, and it wasn't terribly impressive anyway, but at least it had some references on it and accounted for my education and the last five years of my life.

Kind of sad I only needed half a page for that stuff.

"Are you sure I should list Miranda Rivard?" I scrunched up my face when I saw her name on the test copy we'd printed.

"She said it was fine, right?" Jillian set down a cup of tea for me.

"Yeah. I guess so." I'd called her the day before to ask her permission, and she'd said it was fine and she'd be honest about my good performance and the reason I was asked to leave. I didn't love that second bit, but I had to list *someone* from Chateau Rivard if I wanted to put my time there on my resume, short-lived as it was. "What do you think?"

Jillian looked over my shoulder, sipping her tea. "Let's go a little bigger with your name and move your contact information here." She pointed to a different place on the page.

"OK." It was small stuff, trivial even, but everything about the way I presented myself would be important, I knew that. After making the suggested changes, I printed it again. "Now how does it look?"

She picked it up off the printer and studied it while I got up to fetch the honey from her cupboard. I spooned some into my tea and stirred it up, then I sucked on the spoon. *Oh Jesus. My tongue is sore.* I laughed quietly to myself, turning my back to Jillian as I recalled the spectacular feats of fellatio I'd performed last night in the rowboat, which we'd taken out for a late night cruise.

When I turned around, Jillian was looking at me funny. "What?"

"What are you laughing about over there?"

"Nothing." I dropped my eyes to my tea and quickly sat down again.

"That is not a nothing face. That is an I-did-something-naughty face. Trust me, I'm the big sister. I know that face of yours."

I grinned, lifting my tea to my lips. "Guilty."

"So?"

"I have a very sore tongue muscle today."

Jillian's dark, high-arched brows shot up. "You *do*? And how's his tongue?"

"I'd be surprised if he can talk normally. I can barely *walk* normally."

"Oh my *god*," she groaned, fanning herself. "You're so lucky. Damn."

"I know." I picked up the resume. "So this looks good, you think?" It wasn't that I didn't want to spill to her, I just felt protective of what Sebastian and I had together. It was so new, and felt so fragile.

"Yes. It's fine. I want to hear more about the guy." She propped her chin on her hand and looked at me dreamily. "I need to live vicariously."

"Jill. Come on. You're beautiful. You're a doctor. Where are all the beautiful male doctors I see on soap operas?"

She rolled her eyes. "Married. Or fucking nurses. Or fucking anyone else they want to because they're too busy to have a relationship." Sighing, she sat up straight again. "And I guess I am, too. It just gets a little lonely sometimes."

"So fuck a hot doctor for fun."

"A year or two ago, I would have. I did. But now I think I'll hold out for something better. What about you? Is this going somewhere, you think?"

I shrugged, but couldn't keep the smile off my face. "I don't know. Feels like maybe."

"Like maybe? Is there long term potential there?" She brought her cup to her lips.

I rolled my eyes. "Jillian, it's only been like ten days. I don't even know what he's thinking long term for himself. And he... once said something about not believing in the one."

Her brow wrinkled. "The one?"

"Yeah, you know. *The one.* The idea that there's one perfect person for you and you have to find her or him."

"Ah, a soul mate," she said. "Very romantic idea. But I'm not sure it's real, either."

Glancing around at her clean, modern condo, I wondered if she ever pictured living here with someone else, or if she was content to live alone. "I don't know what I believe. But I do know he sends mixed signals...when he first talked about his cabin I got the feeling he really enjoyed the solitude, but he always wants me to sleep there now, even if I have to get up crazy early for work the next morning and he has to drive me."

"Sound like he really likes you too, then."

"I think so. I hope so."

"It also sounds like you need your own car."

I groaned, dropping my head back. "Yes. A car. An apartment. A job. Grown up things."

"Well, here you go." She set the resume in front of me. "Step one. Go get it."

I took a deep breath. "You think I can?"

"I know you can." She lifted her tea with two hands. "What's with the insecurity? Since when have you ever lacked confidence about something?"

I squeezed my eyes shut. "Since Mom told me I wasn't a special snowflake."

Jillian choked on her tea. "What?"

"Don't laugh! I know it sounds ridiculous, but Mom gave me this *pep talk*"—I made little air quotes—"last weekend, the day I moved out of the guest house, basically telling me that I need to quit whining, go out, and get a life for myself, because

I've spent years getting everything handed to me and being told how pretty I am."

Jillian shrugged. "Kinda true."

"Thanks," I said flatly. "Jeez, no wonder I like being around Sebastian. He's always telling me how amazing and beautiful I am."

"And you are." Jillian patted my hand. "But you're gonna have to work for what you want, too. Nothing comes free."

chapter twenty-nine

Skylar

Later that night and all day Sunday, I spent a good amount of time researching Abelard Vineyards, and consequently, the Fourniers. On the About the Owners page of their website, I discovered that they'd met while she was vacationing in Paris and married in Provence. There was even a wedding picture, and I gasped when I saw it.

"What a beautiful couple!" I angled my laptop toward the kitchen Sebastian so he could see. He was putting dinner together for us while I took notes on the winery. "This is her? The woman you met?"

"That's her," he confirmed, going back to slicing potatoes.

"Look, they got married at his family's villa. Isn't that romantic? A villa," I said dreamily.

"Maybe you should start with an apartment," he teased, throwing the potatoes onto a baking sheet.

"Hahaha. I don't even mean to live in—just to visit a place like that would be amazing." I clicked on the picture to make it bigger. "I've always wanted to go to France. Have you ever been?"

"Nope. That would require getting on an airplane."

I looked up at him, surprised. "You don't fly?"

He shook his head. "Never."

"How'd you get back and forth from New York?"

"I wasn't back and forth all that much, but when I was, I drove." He stuck the tray in the oven and set a timer.

"Oh." I stared at the picture for a minute, not really seeing it. I was kind of bummed about this. "Are you scared of flying? Or you just don't like it?"

"I don't like it. In general, all forms of transportation make me edgy. Too many possibilities for tragedy to strike. But driving a car, at least I have some control. There's enough anxiety in my life without adding airplanes to the mix." His movements had gotten stiff and his voice sounded a little testy, so I decided to drop it.

"Got it. OK, it says here that she got her business and master's degrees at Michigan State and ran an event planning business in Detroit for years. And he was a professor in New York. A master's," I mused. "And married to a professor. I bet she wants someone better educated than me."

"Stop it. Or you get no meat tonight." He looked at me threateningly over one shoulder as he turned the steaks in their marinade.

I held up my hands. "That is a serious threat. Stopping."

"Tell me what else it says." He tossed the chunks of potatoes in some olive oil.

"OK, let's see. Here's some press clips about the winery." I read the sound bites out loud, followed links to full articles, and took plenty of notes. Apparently, Lucas Fournier purchased the land from a grower who was trying to expand the red wine scene in Northern Michigan, which hadn't taken off the way the white did. He was particularly interested in making Gamay and pinot noir, so the next thing I did was research those grapes. I also read that Lucas Fournier had opened a successful absinthe bar in Detroit, and I read an interview in which he talked about being modern without sacrificing authenticity. About being willing to take risks. About trusting your gut even when common sense tells you otherwise.

Before I knew it, an hour had passed and Sebastian was asking if I was ready to eat.

"Yes, I'm sorry," I said, sliding off my chair at the breakfast bar. "What can I take out?" We were going to eat on the patio, at a little outdoor dining set he'd bought at an antiques store this weekend.

"It's all ready." He opened the door for me and I stepped out, gasping with delight when I saw the little dining nook under a tree in one corner of the patio. He'd put a light blue tablecloth on the round table, set it with candles, and strung lights in the branches above. "It's not a villa in France, but I hope you like it."

"Oh my goodness! This is perfect!" I clapped my hands and grinned at him. "Thank you so much for making dinner. Sorry I wasn't better company tonight."

"I'm just glad you're here. I know your mind is elsewhere." He pulled out a chair for me, and I sat down.

"I'm learning a ton. Did you know that the Duke of Burgundy banished the Gamay grape from his kingdom in 1395 because it competed too well with pinot noir, which was his favorite? He called it an evil, disloyal plant." I laughed, spreading my napkin in my lap. "Kind of funny that those are the two grapes Lucas Fournier has."

"I did not know that," said Sebastian, sitting across from me. "Tell me more, since we are drinking the Duke's favorite tonight, an Abelard Pinot Noir, in fact."

My heart fluttered as he poured. I loved the way candlelight played with the light green of his eyes. I loved that he'd just made steak and potatoes and salads for us and set up this beautiful, romantic little spot. I loved that he'd encouraged me to go after this job, which I was even more excited about now that I knew more about the forward-thinking young owners. I loved the way he touched me, like he still couldn't believe I was there and might disappear at any moment. I even loved that he looked at me with sadness in his eyes sometimes, because I knew it meant that he was struggling with things in his mind but letting his heart win. He hadn't had any episodes the entire week.

At least not that he'd admitted.

But I'd given up trying to guess at every expression on his face, every silence he retreated into, every tense one-word response to a question I was hoping he'd answer in elaborate detail. I accepted him for who he was, and how hard he was trying. The chance he was taking with me. I knew how difficult it was for him, and I loved him for it.

Holy shit, what?

You heard me. I love him for it. Just a little. Shut up and let me.

I picked up my fork, dropping my eyes to my plate. That was OK, right? To admit to yourself you'd fallen for someone? I mean, it didn't have to be a big deal. It was just a feeling. A nice feeling, in fact. A nice, deep feeling. Who wouldn't fall hard and fast for someone like Sebastian?

And God knows I like things deep, hard, and fast.

I stifled a laugh as I stuffed my face with potatoes, and Sebastian looked at me a little funny but didn't say anything, which only made my feelings stronger.

But I wouldn't say anything to him. Jesus Christ, I could only imagine what he'd do if I told him I loved him. I didn't really have any hang-ups about it—I came from the theater world where everyone loved everyone, loudly and proudly (of course you could *hate* someone in that world and still love them loudly and proudly too, but that was a different matter)—but I felt that Sebastian wasn't the type to use or hear a word like love lightly.

"So what do you think I should wear to my interview?" I asked with mock seriousness. "The navy and white striped skirt or the black dress? This is life or death, so think hard. I really want this job."

"Hmm." He sliced off a piece of New York strip and chewed while pondering. "I'm a little partial to the black dress for obvious reasons, but I also like the striped skirt. You were wearing it the day I saw you at the beach."

My jaw dropped. "You remember that?"

"Of course I do. With a white blouse and bare feet."

"Well, I actually had shoes, just not when I ate sand in front of you. God, that was so embarrassing. I wish I could go back and undo it."

"Don't you dare." He picked up his wine glass. "If you hadn't fallen on the sand, I never would have talked to you."

"Never?" I asked incredulously. "Come on. Yes, you would have. You came in to the shop later that day."

He shook his head. "I came into the shop because I'd just come from my therapist's office. And the reason I'd called an emergency meeting with my therapist was because of my run-in with you."

I set my fork down. "So you're saying if I hadn't fallen on the beach, you wouldn't have talked to me, you wouldn't have needed that appointment, and you wouldn't have been in the shop that afternoon?"

"Exactly."

I sipped the wine and let the flavors mingle on my tongue. "Do you think we'd have found each other eventually?"

He shrugged. "Hard to say. I probably would have done my best to keep avoiding you."

"Why?" I set my glass down. "I thought you always liked me."

"Fear. It's powerful."

"Yeah. I guess." But I hated the idea that we'd been such a near miss. In my mind we were destined to meet. Fate was powerful too, right? "So maybe…it's a good thing I got fired? I mean, that's what led me to the beach."

"Maybe."

My mind was already working backward. If Sebastian and I were the real deal, not only was it a good thing I'd gotten fired, but it was a good thing I'd done Save a Horse, a good thing I'd hated New York, and a good thing my career as an actress hadn't taken off. Not only that, but it was a good thing he hadn't married that tart in Manhattan. My God—Sebastian could be married right now! Eating dinner in some New York apartment with some other woman across from him! Someone who didn't understand him at all.

For the first time, I felt grateful for the crappy decisions I'd made in the last year, because they'd all led me to this table, this man, this moment. It gave me a little boost—maybe, somewhere deep inside me, there was a woman who knew what she wanted, and what's more, she knew what to do to get it.

• • •

Tuesday morning dawned bright and sunny. A good omen, I thought. Per Sebastian's advice, and because I thought it would bring me good luck, I dressed in the navy striped skirt, pairing it with a bright pink blouse this time. Based on the web site and the wardrobe I'd seen in pictures, Mia Fournier looked like a woman who appreciated color.

I'd spent Monday night at home since I'd wanted to get a good night's sleep and look refreshed, and Sebastian and I tended to stay up too late when we were together. My mother made me eat breakfast (a cherry turnover, which I ate standing up and leaning over my plate so I didn't drip on my blouse) and wished me luck before heading out.

While I was brushing my teeth, my cell buzzed with a text from Natalie. **Break a leg this morning! Love you!**

When I was almost out the door I texted back thanks, and noticed I'd missed a message from Sebastian too. **You don't need luck today, but I bet it's with you. Let me know how it goes. I'm thinking of you.**

I smiled, pulling the door shut behind me. I did feel lucky, but I also felt confident for the first time in weeks.

Abelard Vineyards—named, I'd learned from an interview with the Fourniers, for a medieval French scholar who had a tragic but passionate love affair with a young student of his—was only about a ten-minute drive from my parents' farm, about midway between it and Sebastian's cabin. As I drove up the tree-lined drive, my heart started to pound. The place was absolutely breathtaking.

The architectural style was French, but rather than the dark, formal faux-chateau style of the Rivard family, the Fourniers had built a Provencal-style villa of light weathered stone with a faded red tiled roof and shutters painted a soft blue. It was luxurious without being imposing, authentic but not stodgy.

The gravel drive circled in front of the main building, and I followed signs to visitor parking. When I got out of the car and looked around, I saw that the vineyards stretched out behind the buildings, a big red barn sat off to my left, and a sign pointing to the tasting room was straight ahead. Since I was meeting Mia Fournier in the tasting room, I followed the sign down a narrow gravel path around the side of the villa, admiring the flowers and herbs planted along the way.

Around the back was a large patio with tables and chairs, where guests could sit and watch the sun set over the rolling fields. Jutting off the stone building was a covered, tiled area lined with built-in upholstered benches and long picnic tables on either side of double doors. Six chairs lined the other sides of the tables, and adorably chic little topiary trees in clay flower pots rested on the tables. It was absolutely stunning, and already I wanted this job so badly I could taste it.

The glass doors to the tasting room off the patio were propped open already, allowing for plenty of natural light and a soft breeze. When I walked in, I noticed right away how the two-story ceilings and ample windows let in plenty of natural light, and the colors in the light stone walls were echoed in the neutral couches and chairs, which were grouped in one large sitting area in front of a huge fireplace at one end of the room. The plank floors were a medium-toned wood, as were the large square coffee table and several end tables. The one bright spot of color was a massive floral centerpiece on the coffee table—probably three dozen roses in various shades of pink.

Guess I wore the right thing, I thought with a smile.

"Hello! You must be Skylar."

I turned and saw a petite, curvy woman with long, wavy brown hair walking toward me from the other end of the room, where a curved wooden bar lined with stools took up one entire wall.

I smiled, moving toward her. "Yes. Good morning."

"Good morning." We met in the center of the room and she held out her hand. "I'm Mia. Welcome to Abelard."

I took her hand and met her eyes, noticing we were probably about the same height, although I wore heels and she wore flats. "So nice to meet you. The place is stunning. I'm in love."

"Thanks. It's been a long road to get here, but we're happy with it. Can I offer you something? Coffee or tea? A glass of wine?" She laughed, putting a hand on her slightly round belly. "I can't join you, but it's never too early for wine."

"Congratulations. Sebastian mentioned you were expecting. That's wonderful."

"Yes, our third. I thought we were done after two, but my husband had other ideas." She rolled her eyes. "When we first met, he didn't even want kids. Now he wants an entire litter!"

I laughed, wondering how old she was. She was radiantly beautiful with lovely skin, little tiny smile lines around her eyes the only sign of aging on her face. I wondered what it was like to be as happy as she looked.

"So anyway." She fluttered a hand. "Can I get you anything?"

"No, thank you. I do love the Abelard pinot, but I should probably complete my interview before I indulge in it."

She smiled and started walking toward the couches. "Let's sit over here. I was going to do this back in my office, but it's such a beautiful morning." She sat at one end of a large couch and I chose a high-backed chair adjacent to it.

"It is. And I love the way you designed this so your guests have this gorgeous view, even when they're inside. And that air!" I inhaled, taking in the scent of the fields outside. "It's like you've made the sight and smell of the land the grapes are planted on part of the tasting experience. You're hitting all the senses."

"Oh God, my husband's going to love you." She smiled, settling back on the couch. "So tell me about yourself."

Taking a breath, I started with my roots on Old Mission and growing up here. I talked briefly about performing on cruise ships and my time in New York, but emphasized that I'd really missed home and my family and had decided to return this spring. "I didn't really love living in a big city," I confessed. "Maybe the shopping, but other than that, I prefer life here."

"I agree." She nodded. "Lucas, my husband, lived in New York when we were first dating, but when we decided to move in together, I was really glad we agreed on Detroit. It's a fun city, but it's less crowded and manic than New York."

"Yes, I read that he opened an absinthe bar there? The Green Hour?"

Her eyebrows lifted. "Done your homework, I see."

I lifted my shoulders, felt a blush warm my cheeks. "I figured I'd better. You run a pretty impressive operation here. If I want to be your assistant, I need to know my stuff."

She laughed. "Thanks. So what else did you learn?"

"Well, I know that you ran a successful event planning business for years in Detroit, so I figured you might want to expand the event schedule here…maybe start promoting Abelard as a wedding venue? Possibly host small corporate events?"

She looked amused. "Go on."

"I researched pinot noir and Gamay, the two red wines your husband makes here, and learned quite a bit about why those wines should do well even in a cool climate like ours, and how our position along the forty-fifth parallel mimics the growing conditions in other parts of the world where those grapes do well. Part of that I knew because of growing up on a cherry farm," I admitted. "Cherries do well here too for many of the same reasons—the soil, the hilly land, the water surrounding us."

"My goodness. You really have done your homework." She tilted her head and crossed her arms. "And you worked at Rivard?"

I shifted uncomfortably. I'd known it was coming and had rehearsed how to handle it, but it was still embarrassing. "Yes, for about a month. I really enjoyed the job, and I learned a lot there, but Mrs. Rivard had a problem with my performance on a reality television show, which painted me as a bit of a villain." *Please, please don't have watched the show.*

"Seriously?" She blinked. "What show?"

I screwed up my face and cringed. "Save a Horse (Ride a Cowboy)."

Mia burst out laughing and clapped her hands together once. "Oh my God, that's funny. Wow." Giggling, she tucked one leg beneath her and winked at me. "So did you? Ride a cowboy?"

"No." I shook my head. "The only thing I rode was a mechanical bull, and I only lasted seven seconds."

She gave me a sympathetic look. "Ouch."

"Yeah. The entire experience was pretty embarrassing, and I'd like to forget all about it. I asked Mrs. Rivard if I could list her as a reference, and she said I could. I don't believe she had any issues with my work there—it was simply a matter of my persona on the show not gelling with her vision of a good employee." I took my resume from my bag and handed it to her. "Her contact information is here, if you'd like it."

"Thank you." She studied the resume a moment. "Ah, you were a Cherry Queen."

I sighed, feeling like I should come clean. "Yes, I was, but they asked me not to advertise it. I put it on the resume because it's something I'm proud of, but after the show aired, they effectively dethroned me for bad behavior."

"Really?" Her eyes went wide. "What the heck did you do on that show?"

"I just wasn't myself," I said. "I acted a certain way because the producers wanted ratings, and they figured I'd get more attention if I played devious and mean."

"Did it work?"

I shrugged. "For a little while. But it sure backfired on my life. I shouldn't have done it, but…live and learn. On to better things."

She nodded. "I agree. We all make mistakes."

"There you are." The deep voice came from the far end of the room, and I looked over to see a ridiculously attractive man walking toward us. I think my jaw hung open a moment before I remembered to close it.

Mia looked over her shoulder at him. "Yes, I decided to sit in here. I didn't feel like climbing those stairs again and it's so pretty this morning."

He reached the back of the couch and placed a hand on her shoulder. "You OK?"

"Yes." She patted his hand and gestured to me. "This is Skylar Nixon, the friend of Sebastian Pryce. Skylar, this is my husband, Lucas."

I stood and he reached over Mia's head to shake my hand. He had dark eyes and hair, worn a little long and shaggy, and a fantastic smile. Christ, what did their children look like? "Very nice to meet you," I said. "You have a beautiful place here."

"Our little Provence." He glanced at Mia. "My family has a vineyard there and we tried to create some of that magic here."

"Oh, I bet she knows all about that." Mia's eyes twinkled. "She's done her research."

"Oh?" Lucas looked at me.

"Yes." I smiled. "I know the location, I know you grew mostly grenache, and I know you got married there."

"See?" Mia glanced up at her husband and pointed at me. "This is what I need. Someone who looks like this and has the brains to come prepared to an interview."

"Thank you." I rocked forward onto my toes, I was so happy.

"Sounds like this is going well, then. I'll leave you to it. Skylar, very nice to meet you, and you"— he leaned down to kiss her, the back of his hand in her hair—"take it easy."

"I will." She reached up and touched his scruffy cheek, and something inside me twisted a little. They had such an easy way about them, you could just tell how close they were, how much they loved each other. I wondered about how they met, and decided if I got the job and we became friendly enough, I'd ask. Lucas waved at me once more before heading out the glass doors.

"Well," Mia said, getting to her feet. "I suppose I should call your references, but unless I discover you robbed Rivard blind, I'd love to give this a try. The job involves assisting me in various capacities—from running tours to planning events to manning the tasting room to helping with marketing and PR. I'm very hands-on and I'll train you for that stuff myself, but you'll have to get some wine training from Lucas and the winemakers here."

"Sounds great."

"It pays hourly to start, eighteen an hour, but after three months we can revisit that number and even consider salary. I'll call your references this week and confirm with you after I've spoken to them." She made a face. "Not that I'm looking forward to speaking with that old bat Miranda Rivard, but I'll do it."

I laughed. "Thank you."

She walked me outside, waving hello to someone watering the flower beds. "How soon could you start?"

"I'm working for my sister right now, but she said she could find someone to replace me within a week."

"So Monday?" Mia asked hopefully. "Sorry to rush, I just want you to be as comfortable as possible before I have this baby, which is in the fall."

"No problem," I assured her. "Monday would be fine."

"Great." She held out her hand, and I took it. "So nice to meet you, Skylar. I'm glad Sebastian sent you my way. I have a feeling this is going to work out great."

I smiled. "Me too."

• • •

Later that night, Mia Fournier called and told me the job was mine if I wanted it. She said Miranda Rivard had praised my work ethic, performance, and attitude, and even admitted to feeling some regret at having let me go. When Mia heard that, she decided to snap me up right away, and asked if I could come in on Friday to fill out paperwork.

I was at Natalie's when I got the call, and she and I both squealed and jumped up and down once I hung up. The next day, a sign went in the window at Coffee Darling looking for help, and by Friday evening, she'd already hired a college student who was home for the summer.

Sebastian was thrilled for me, and took me out for dinner at Mission Table the next night to celebrate. When he showed up at my parents' front door, he presented me with a congratulatory bouquet of honey sticks tied together with a bright pink ribbon. I threw my arms around him and he lifted me right off my feet, laughing in my hair. If he'd have let go, I swear I'd have floated right into the sky.

At dinner that night, I laid out my summer plans, and he listened attentively. "I'm going to bust my butt to prove my worth there, and hopefully negotiate a raise after three months. At that point, I think I'll have enough saved, and a good enough income, to afford a nice apartment and maybe buy or lease a car. The other thing I was thinking of is offering to rent a guest house from my mother come fall when the tourist season is over. Then I could continue to save and maybe buy something next year."

"Sounds good."

Suddenly I realized I was doing *all* the talking. I eyed him carefully. "You're awfully quiet tonight."

"Am I?"

"Yes. What's up?"

He offered me a slight smile. "Nothing. I had a rough day, I guess. But it's making me feel better to see how happy you are. I'm glad you got the job."

"Yes. Thank you so much. It's because of you, you know."

He dismissed that idea with a wave of his hand. "Nah."

"It is! I'm so grateful. And I'm planning to *show* you how grateful later on." I swirled my tongue around the scallop on the end of my fork suggestively.

"In that case, I'll take the credit."

I smiled, smug and happy. "Good."

chapter thirty

Sebastian

Every day that summer, she was the first thing I thought about in the morning, and the last thing I thought of before I fell asleep, whether she was beside me or not. And as the weeks went by, I wanted her beside me more and more. I missed her when she wasn't there—her smile, her laugh, her smell, her voice, her kiss, her touch.

I began working full time for my father's firm in June, and I was doing well. The workload was manageable, challenging enough to be interesting but not overwhelming; I went to the gym most mornings before work and felt physically as good or better than I had in years; and I kept my weekly appointments with Ken, sometimes going in for a last-minute lunch appointment if I felt like the voice was causing my confidence in myself, my work, or my relationship to falter.

Emotionally, I felt more stable than I'd ever felt. The obsessive thoughts weren't getting in the way of being close to Skylar, and she had this way of getting me to open up without being pushy. She was so honest about herself, so accepting of me, that I found myself talking to her about things I'd never shared with anyone—my favorite childhood memories of my mother, my love for poetry, especially about nature, and how I sometimes envied my brothers their happy marriages and families, even though I'd never been sure about having one of my own. One hot August night I told her how it was more an envy of their faith in themselves—the way they were able to make a decision like getting married or having kids without all the constant second guessing.

"I know what you mean," she'd said, sucking on a honey stick. I kept a supply of them at my house now. We were lying at opposite ends of the hammock, our bodies tucked alongside each other's. "Those forever things are scary to me too."

I chuckled. "Forever things?"

"Yeah. Marriage, family. I mean, I like the *idea* of a family but I'm not sure I'd be a very good mother. Natalie's positive she wants kids, and I think Jillian does too—but whenever I think about it, it seems like something so far off in the future. Forever things are what *real* grownups do." She laughed softly. "I'm not one of those yet. Maybe after I get a car I'll feel more grown up."

We were quiet for a minute, and I put my hands behind my head, hoping to sound casual. "What *about* marriage? Do you ever think about that?" To my surprise, I'd been thinking about it a little bit lately, imagining what it would be like to be married to her, contrasting the peaceful life we'd have here with the frantic, noisy one I'd almost committed to in New York. How had I ever thought that would be right for me?

"All girls think about that at some point." She shrugged. "I suppose I'm no exception. What about you?"

"Nah," I lied. She hadn't exactly jumped at the idea, so I figured I'd better not sound too enthusiastic. Maybe she was thinking of us as a just-for-now thing until the real thing came along? The notion crushed me, not that I blamed her. She could do so much better. "I'd be a terrible husband."

She took the honey stick from her mouth and pointed it at me. "I was totally gonna tell you that. I mean, you can't cook, your house is filthy, and your dick is just meh."

I lunged for her and she screeched, jumping off the hammock and making me chase her onto the dock, where I threw her over my shoulder and carried her back into the cabin. She laughed and squealed, beating against my back in a futile effort to escape my arms. "I take it back, I take it back. I meant to say your dick is mehgnificent."

"Too late, angel. You ran from me. You know what that means." In the living room, I tossed her onto the couch, where she grinned up at me, breathless.

"But you don't have rope."

"No," I said, unbuckling my belt and sliding it off. "But this will do."

Her jaw dropped. "It will?"

"Uh huh. Stand up."

Poor little angel. I think her legs might have actually trembled as she stood naked at the end of the couch while I bound her ankles and bent her forward over the arm.

Mine did. They trembled with lust as I slid my fingers inside her pussy and then inside her mouth, listening to her suck them. They trembled with awe when I fisted one hand in her hair and teased her tight little ass with the tip of my cock, astonished at the way she let me desecrate her. They trembled with euphoria when I fucked her up against the wall, one hand rubbing her clit as she came and cried out my name over and over again.

My god, I love her, I thought as I flooded her body, my vision clouding at the edges. *I'm so in love with her I can't see. She's fucking perfect.*

Actually my entire life was pretty fucking close to perfect. I'd never been happier.

And I'd never been less sure that I could hold onto it.

chapter thirty-one

Skylar

"Come on," I said, pouting. "Look at the sheet. Did I get it right?"

It was late August, and we were sitting on a blanket on the dock with a bottle of Abelard Pinot Gris, and Sebastian was supposed to be quizzing me on the tasting specs. Recently, Mia and Lucas had asked if I'd be interested in repping their wines in the Midwest, meeting up with distributors, shop merchants, and sommeliers since Mia would be too busy with three kids to travel. I loved the idea, but knew I had a lot to learn about the wines at Abelard and the industry in general before I took on that role.

"Yes, you got it right." Sebastian set his glass and the binder aside. "But school is over for the day."

"I have to learn this by the weekend," I whined. "You said you'd help."

"I know." He took my glass out of my hand and set it next to the candle lanterns we had burning. "And I am. I'm going to help you relax."

"Oh?" I leaned back on my hands, legs stretched out toward him. The mischievous glint in his eyes made my insides flip.

The summer was flying by in a happy whirlwind of work, wine, and great sex...definitely the best summer of my life so far. I loved the job at Abelard, I loved working for the Fourniers, and I grew more confident each day that I was doing a good job. Mia was an exacting boss, but fair and helpful and so organized I was in total awe. If I made a mistake or a miscommunication, she was understanding, and she was quick to praise when I did things right or took the initiative on something. She definitely had her own ideas about the way things should be done, but after we got to know each other a little better, she wanted to hear my ideas too, and encouraged me to be brave about voicing my opinions.

I functioned as both her personal assistant and assistant tasting room manager, and many of the ideas I'd had for Rivard were welcomed at Abelard. Lucas had loved the idea about creating a YouTube channel for informal videos about their wines, and he'd thought I'd be a natural in front of the camera. Together with his chief winemaker, a French import named Gabriel Allard, Lucas and I outlined the video series to coordinate with events Mia had planned throughout the summer. I stayed late many evenings learning about the wines, and I took home a ton of additional reading about the grapes and the soil and the winemaking process. Many nights I fell asleep with books resting on my chest or my laptop still open beside me.

Often I was in Sebastian's bed.

We saw each other three or four nights a week, and on my days off, which were always during the week, Sebastian would try to come home early and we'd go hiking in the park or swimming off his dock or take the boat out on the water. When I'd worry aloud that I was encroaching on the solitude he'd claimed to crave when we first met, he'd hush me with a kiss or put his hand over my mouth, and once he just picked me up off the boat bottom and tossed me into the water.

He'd slowly opened up to me about his past, both his difficult childhood and the last ten years. I tried hard not to pry, but ate up every word he said, every memory he shared. Gradually his moods made more sense to me, and I'd learned when I could ask another question about something, when I could make a joke, and when I should just shut up and kiss him or hug him or better yet, do nothing but listen in silence. I became accustomed to his quiet moods, the occasional flare of his temper, and his infernal reticence about his feelings, and in turn, he endured my occasional insecurities about work, my eight million beauty products in his bathroom, and my ceaseless chatter about varietals, vintages, acidity, fruit, minerality and terroir—although he did tell me if I mentioned "floral notes" to him once more, he was going to ban me from drinking wine in his presence.

"Yes. Relaxing is very important for wine tasting." He circled my ankles with his fingers and spread them apart before lying on his stomach between my legs. Then he moved up so his head was beneath my skirt. "Lift up your hips."

Grinning, I did as he asked and let him slide my panties off, then I gasped when he pushed my thighs further apart and swept his tongue up my slit.

"Mmmmm." He did it again, lingering at the top. "Absofuckinglutely delightful on the palate."

I burst out laughing, dropping back to my elbows and bending my knees. "Is that right?"

"Yes." He flicked and swirled and savored. "My God, this vintage is magnificent. Light and refreshing with a fabulous fruit profile and balanced acidity."

"Oh Jesus." I clapped my hands over my mouth, laying all the way back, laughing and moaning with delight at the same time.

He sucked my clit into his mouth and nibbled on it, making my legs tingle all the way to my toes, which curled into the blanket. "Mmm, yes. An incomparable flavor and exquisite aroma. Full-bodied and delicious." Two fingers slid easily inside me.

"I thought you said it was light," I breathed, widening my legs even more, my hands seeking his head.

"It's everything I like. Do I even need to mention its elegant floral notes? And the lingering finish, well…it's indescribable," he teased as he fingered me deep and slow and my body arched off the dock. When he put his mouth back on me, I came so hard I yelled *way* too loud, my voice echoing off the water. I covered my mouth again, but Sebastian just laughed, licking up the lingering finish until there wasn't a drop left.

"Oh Jesus, I'm so loud," I whispered, embarrassed. "What if someone heard?"

"I really don't give a fuck." Sebastian got to his knees and undid his pants. "So come here and sit on my cock. I'll hold my hand over your mouth if you want."

I sat up, giving myself a moment to enjoy the sight of him there on his knees, his dick hard and waiting for me, his eyes dark and glowing in the candlelight. I loved the way his forearms looked when he cuffed his button down shirts. Crawling up on his lap, I put my hands on his shoulders and slowly lowered myself onto him, enjoying every slick, warm inch gliding deeper and deeper. When my ass rested on his thighs, his cock penetrating so deep I felt that wicked good twinge of pain, I wrapped my arms around his neck.

We stayed there a moment, eyes locked on each other, mouths open, breath mingling between us. The light, playful mood of a moment ago was gone, something heavier in its place. I threaded my hands into his hair, staring with wondrous disbelief at this man who was so beautiful, so smart, so strong, and yet still retained that sadness in his eyes, that lingering fear that he wasn't good enough for me. My heart was pounding so hard, it echoed in my head. I felt so full, so deliciously full with him that I knew I was going to burst right then—not an orgasm, but an emotional release.

"I'm so in love with you," I whispered, starting to roll my hips over his. "I'm *so* in love with you,

Sebastian." My eyes teared up, although it made me happy to tell him. I didn't care if he said it back or not—I felt it and I wanted him to know it.

"Skylar." He squeezed me tight, burying his face in my neck. "You're all I want. All I dream about. I think I've always loved you."

Tears dripped, although I smiled too. "Really? Always?"

"Yes." He used his arms to move my body against his, a slow, undulating rhythm that had my core muscles coiling again. "Because I can't remember what it feels like not to love you. Not to ache for you. Not to yearn for you."

The words he used to describe his feelings broke my heart. "You don't have to ache or yearn, love. I'm here." I covered his forehead in kisses, pulling his head back to force him to look at me. "I'm here, and I'm not leaving."

"You will," he said, that inexplicable sadness in his eyes. "You should. I should suffer for you."

"Shhh." I kissed him before he could say anything more, plunging my tongue into his open mouth, wrapping my legs around him.

He straightened up so the base of his cock hit my clit and grabbed my ass hard with his hands, grinding me against his body. "Oh god," I breathed against his mouth. "It's so good, so fucking good."

He groaned and thrust up hard and deep inside me one final time, using his arms to move me over him as we came together, our bodies pulsing in wondrous relief at the same time.

Afterward, he hid his face in my chest, and when a small sob made his shoulders twitch, my throat squeezed tight. Why was he so convinced I'd leave him? Why did he think he needed to suffer for me? Was it because no one had been understanding enough in the past? Had no one tried hard enough to break down his walls? Would he shut me out, retreat into isolation to protect himself?

"Sweet boy," I soothed as his tears dampened my blouse. I ran my hands over his shoulders, down his back, pressing kisses to the top of his head. "You'll never suffer for me. I won't let you."

"Don't make that promise. You'll regret it."

"No, I won't. What is this? What's wrong?"

"Fuck. Sorry." He quickly wiped at his eyes.

"Sebastian. Talk to me."

"It's nothing. I guess I just didn't realize I was holding in a lot of tension." He focused on pulling out of me, and the moment he did, I sat back and brought my legs together, covering myself with my skirt.

"Oh." Well, this was a letdown. Was he really shutting down on me right now? After what we'd just said to each other?

"I'm sorry about your skirt. I'll pay for the dry cleaning."

I stared at him, blinking twice. "My *skirt*?"

"Yeah. I got…stuff on it." He stood and did up his pants.

"Jesus Christ, Sebastian." I scrambled to my feet, feeling warmth trickle down my leg. "I don't care about the damn skirt. I care that you're closing yourself off from me, right after I told you I love you."

"I'm not." This without even glancing at me.

"You are. Why?"

He was silent for a second, staring out at the water, and I recognized the stubborn set of his jaw. He wasn't going to talk.

"Fine. Be stubborn." Instead of engaging in the argument, I leaned down to pick up my shoes and my binder and stomped off the dock and up to the cabin.

Inside the bathroom I cleaned up with a wet washcloth, fighting tears as I looked at myself in the mirror over the sink. *This is him. This is what you'll have to deal with every time your relationship hits a milestone that freaks him out.*

But what milestones would there be? He'd just said the other night that he doesn't want the forever things—getting married, having kids. I'd played that off, and then we'd gotten distracted with sex— amazing, hair-pulling, wall-thumping, name-screaming sex—but later, as we lay next to each other in his bed, I felt sad that there was a possibility he didn't want those *forever* things with me. Maybe he was just scared of that kind of commitment—a lot of guys were. Or maybe he worried about passing his OCD on to his children if he had any. *Maybe he's scared he'd stab me with the cake knife at our wedding. But who the fuck knows, because he won't talk to me!*

A gentle knock sounded on the door.

"Just a second," I said. "Actually, just come in. I don't care."

The door opened and a downtrodden Sebastian appeared behind me in the mirror. I met his contrite eyes before rinsing out the washcloth in the sink.

He entered and stood beside me, taking the washcloth in his hand. Without a word, he wrung it out and dropped to his knees, and turned me to face him. Then he gently ran the cool, wet cloth up the inside of one leg.

I sighed. "I already did that," I said, although it was so sweet that he wanted to do it, I didn't protest when he stood, rinsed and wrung again, and knelt down to wipe the other leg, and then tenderly washed in between them.

He looked up at me. "I do love you. More than I've ever loved anyone."

I cupped his jaw with one hand. "Then let me in, and let me stay."

"I want to." The fear in his eyes broke my heart. "I'll keep trying."

chapter thirty-two

Sebastian

I started slipping the night Skylar told me she loved me. I knew I would.

It was all kinds of fucked up, I knew that too. Because I'd spoken the truth—I did love her more than I'd ever loved anyone before. My heart knew the truth, but it was as if my head refused to cooperate. Refused to believe in a future with her. Refused to let me feel secure in the knowledge she was happy with me.

She hadn't brought work clothes for the next day, so I had to take her home that night. Halfway down the driveway, I had to go back and check the locks on the cabin doors. The second time, we reached the road, and I had to reverse to check them again. A quarter of the way to the farm, I felt the need to go back and check them again, and I nearly turned around. I was so agitated, my hands shook.

"Hey." Skylar put three fingers on my wrist. "Stop. You locked the doors. I saw you."

I swallowed. "OK."

"What's going on with you? Talk to me."

"It's nothing."

"Is it…what I said? Maybe that was too much." The worry in her voice was like a punch in the stomach.

"No, Skylar." I glanced at her, saw her chewing her bottom lip. I took her hand and kissed it. "I'm so glad you said those words to me, and I meant what I said to you."

Which was why I counted lines in the center of the highway, there and back.

And why I made sure I kissed her goodnight eight times and told her I loved her twice, praying she wouldn't catch on to what I was doing.

It was why I counted as I brushed my teeth, made sure I stopped reading my book on an even page, and switched the lamp in my bedroom off eight times.

In the dark, I lay my head on the pillow and worried with an intensity like pain.

I loved her, and she loved me.

Now it was my responsibility to keep her safe.

keep her safe.

keep her safe.

keep her safe.

keep her safe.

keep her safe.

keep her safe.

keep her safe.

• • •

Three days later I saw Ken, and he knew right away something was off with me. "How are things?" he asked, eyeing me warily from his chair.

"Fine." I kept all my answers short and offered nothing. When he asked about Skylar, I told him things were comfortable, and even as I spoke the words I tapped the side of my leg eight times, then dropped my head and blinked eight times. I'm sure Ken recognized I was not myself, at least not the self that I'd been in the past few months, but he didn't push. When I left the building I made sure I took an even number of steps to get out to my car. I hated what I was doing, felt sick and shameful and loathsome, but I couldn't stop.

Skylar was tougher on me than Ken.

"What's with you?" she whispered two weeks later when she caught me rearranging the place setting at my brother's house. I was trying to make sure the two forks were exactly the same distance from each other and the one nearest the plate was that same distance from it. Same with the spoon and butter knife on the other side.

"Nothing." I gave her a smile when she reached over and took one of my hands under the dining table.

"Are you nervous about something?" By contrast, she seemed cool and calm, although she was meeting my entire family for the first time today.

"No." Leaning toward her, I kissed her cheek to reassure her. The last thing I wanted was for her to think I had an issue bringing her around my family. I didn't—in fact, this had been my idea. Well, mine and my sister-in-law's. She and Skylar had met already because Skylar had arranged a meeting between Kelly and Mrs. Nixon about supplying her guest houses with products. Skylar had also arranged a meeting with Mia Fournier, and Abelard now stocked and sold Kelly's honey-based products as well. Kelly adored Skylar, and had encouraged me to bring her to dinner to meet the rest of the family. My father was here with his longtime girlfriend, my brother David was here with his wife, Jen, and my nieces and nephews sat at a kids table in the kitchen.

Skylar was her usual self, beautiful, relaxed, and outgoing, and it was wonderful to see how she fit in with my family. Diana had come to Michigan twice in our two-year relationship, and neither time had I felt as comfortable or proud as I did tonight. In fact, I quite enjoyed the impressed looks on my brothers' faces when they first saw her. My father, who'd met her once at the office, kept looking back and forth between us with a curious look on his face, and I wondered if he was thinking *How the hell did a guy like you get a girl like that?* Which is basically what I thought every time I looked at her.

"Your family is wonderful," Skylar said later as I drove her home.

"They loved you." I tried to sound relaxed, but I was horribly tense behind the wheel. Lately I'd been obsessing over her getting into a car accident. She'd purchased her own car last week, a little Mini Cooper, and I was terrified that it wouldn't protect her. It was so *small*. Even in the truck, I was nervous about a crash. Then I felt awful for even having those thoughts because my brain convinced me I might *cause* the accident just by thinking about it.

"I love *you*." She reached over and rubbed my leg. "Are you sure you're OK? You seem distracted lately."

"I'm fine. Just tired." Inside my head were multiple voices screaming at me. One warned me that by shutting her out, I was avoiding the issue of relapse and contributing to the relationship's demise, if not my own. Another cackled with I-told-you-so glee, finding delight in watching me fuck this up just as predicted. Another begged me to keep doing what I was doing because it was the only way to reassure myself that no harm would come to her.

"Seems like you're more than tired." Her tone was wary. "I—I've noticed a couple things in the last couple weeks, and I'm concerned."

"Oh? Like what?"

She took a breath. "Like the checking the locks thing."

I bristled a little. "I've always done that."

"And the outlets?"

"I live in a cabin. I worry about fire."

"And putting the knives back above the fridge?"

I'd been hoping she wouldn't notice that. "I just did it to clear the clutter off the counter. I hate clutter."

She didn't say anything until we pulled up at her parents' place. Right after Labor Day, she'd moved back into the guest house she'd lived in last May, and I'd spent a couple nights there, although I felt much more comfortable at the cabin. Being in my bed with her was the one place I felt completely at ease in my body—and in hers.

"Want to come in? I have to work early tomorrow, but I'd love for you to stay the night." She took one of my hands in both of hers. "If you're tired, we can go right to sleep, I promise."

I smiled, with effort. "That rarely happens with us."

"I know." She gave me a wicked grin. "But I like it."

"Why don't you grab your stuff and come to the cabin with me?"

She considered. "I'll need my car in the morning, though."

"I'll drive you to work and pick you up," I said quickly. "Tomorrow's Saturday. I'm not working."

"No, that's silly. I'll get my work clothes and meet you back at the cabin." She leaned over and kissed me quickly, and before she could get out of the car I grabbed her and kissed her again.

She caught on and grinned. "I know, I know. Two is better than one."

"Busted." I laughed a little, but inside I was dead serious.

Nothing could be done in odd numbers. Nothing.

chapter thirty-three

Sebastian

As autumn progressed, I fell more in love with Skylar every day, and knew if I could fucking let myself be sure of something, it would be that she and I belonged together. But the sense of impending doom, and the irrational fear that I would be the cause of it, tormented me.

I did my best to hide my anxiety from Skylar, but not all of my compulsive behaviors were easy to conceal. She knew something was up with me, but when she'd ask if I was OK, I'd lie and say I was stressed about work, or tired, or hadn't been eating right. She either believed me or pretended to, probably in order to give me space to work this out on my own, which made me feel even guiltier. I was lying to the woman I loved and she deserved better. *Don't believe me*, I wanted to tell her. *Don't let me shut you out. Don't take my silences for answers. Don't let me ruin this with fear.*

On my bad days, it felt like every step I took could trip the wire, every drastic thought I had would come to fruition, and every minute was sixty seconds closer to losing her. *Of course you'll lose her*, the voice taunted. *When have you ever been able to hold on to something good?*

But there were good days too.

When Mia Fournier had her baby in mid-October, Skylar was given a promotion, a raise, and a box of Abelard Vineyards business cards that said Skylar Nixon, Brand Representative on them. I sent her two dozen pink roses at work the next day and told her how proud I was of her that night. She asked if she could have a reward, and I said of course.

The wicked little thing asked if we could take a shower together, during which she begged me to jerk off in front of her and come on her chest.

Which I did.

Later on I blindfolded her and tortured her endlessly with my tongue for being such a naughty girl, her hands tied, her body stretched out on the bedroom floor.

On those kinds of days, I felt like a god. I could do anything as long as I had her. One chilly fall evening we dragged my sleeping bag out on the dock and spent the entire night out there, whispering and kissing and making love until the sun came up, when we finally went into the cabin and slept for hours in my bed. I came so close that night to asking her to move in with me, but I was too scared—if she was there constantly, it would be much harder to hide my rituals from her.

But God, how I loved her. Madly. Passionately. I wanted her with me all the time. I craved her with every fiber of my being. That night on the dock, I knew without a doubt I wanted to spend the rest of my life with her.

Finally, some fucking conviction.

In November, I started fantasizing about proposing. *This* was how you were supposed to feel when you asked someone to be your wife—wildly in love, every vein in your body running hot with blood when you're together, every beat of your heart an explosion. But the more I thought about it, the closer I came to asking her if she wanted to stay with me forever, the more fragile she seemed in my eyes, the more obsessive thoughts pummeled my brain, and the less I felt I was good for her. She wouldn't be happy with me, would she? She couldn't be. I was a liar. I was a coward. I was despicable, tying her up and fucking her just to make her feel defenseless and vulnerable the way I did.

But I couldn't stop.

Fear, guilt, and shame tortured me, and the more I fought it, the worse I felt in my skin. My life became a charade. I hid my relapse from Ken by canceling sessions for four weeks straight. I was able to hide it at work because my father let me keep my own hours—it never mattered if I was late. I stopped writing in my journal in the effort to hide it from myself, and I tried desperately to hide it from Skylar—but eventually it became impossible.

"What is *with* you?" she asked one cold, rainy November night after I'd driven back to the cabin for the second time to check the outlets and appliances. We were on our way to meet the Fourniers for dinner and were late already, but I'd made soup on the stove that afternoon, and it was an odd day, and even though I remembered turning the burner off, I didn't trust myself. What if that memory was from a different day and the gas was still on? I'd made up some story about forgetting my wallet and then needing one of my meds, but those were flimsy excuses and she knew it. "And if you say 'nothing,' I'm getting out of this car. I've put up with this behavior for too long."

I pressed my lips together, remaining silent. When I pulled up in front of the cabin, I told her to wait in the truck. Running through the driving rain, I went inside and began checking the appliances, and when I turned around she was standing there, arms crossed.

"Sebastian. Stop it."

"I fucking *can't*," I blurted, gripping the edge of the counter. *You didn't check the toaster.*

"Then tell me what's wrong. You've been acting strange for weeks now, and you won't talk to me. I don't know what to do when you shut me out like this. I feel helpless!" She was wearing a fitted black coat and a new pair of leopard print high heels. Even furious with me, she was beyond beautiful. *Too beautiful for you.*

Turning, my head, I stared out the window. I couldn't look at her. *You fucking coward.*

"God, it's like you're two people," she said, starting to cry. "The one that takes me to bed every night and says such sweet things and makes me feel so hopeful and good and safe, and this one that's just—"

"Crazy?" I finished, braving a sideways glance at her. "Told you."

"Confused," she said, shaking her head. "I have no idea what's going on with you, but unless you decide to let me in on it, I can't help you!"

Help me. Stay with me. Don't go. But I said nothing.

"God, you're so maddening!" She shook her hands in the air. "Why won't you talk to me? It's like you *want* me to leave you!"

I swallowed, part of me desperate to fall on my knees and beg her to stay and the other part anxious to get this over with. *You always knew she'd go, didn't you? At least let it be on your terms.*

"Christ, that's it, isn't it? You're doing all this to drive me away so you can hate yourself for it afterward." She shook her head. "Why do you think you don't deserve to be happy?"

"Because I don't!" I finally exploded. "I'm not right in the head, Skylar. I'm fucked up." The truth gnawed painfully at my gut, and I felt no relief in voicing it.

Tears dripped from her eyes. "My God. You're so intent on punishing yourself for something you have no control over, you can't see straight," she said. "Have you been going to therapy?"

I looked away again.

"Look at me. Have you?"

Reluctantly, shamefully, my eyes met hers. "No."

Drawing herself up, she wiped her tears and put both hands over her heart. "You don't know what this is doing to me. I love you, Sebastian, so much it kills me to see you hurting. I want to make everything better for you, and it breaks my heart that I can't. And I want a life with you, but I can't be the only one trying to make it happen."

"This *is* a life with me, don't you get it?" I snapped, hiding behind anger. "This is who I am."

"Bullshit. This isn't who you are, and you know it." She pointed a finger at me. "You're not an asshole, and you're not a freak, and you're not a monster." She took a step closer and the fresh tears in her eyes had my chest in a vise. "You're a beautiful, brilliant, complicated man, Sebastian Pryce. And I adore you. But if you want to suffer here alone with your tortured soul because you think for some fucked up reason you deserve it, fine. Choose suffering over me. But I can't watch. It will destroy me."

She turned and walked out the door, and I watched through the front window as she grabbed her purse from the truck and got into her car, not even trying to shield herself from the downpour. Instead of driving off in a huff, she sat sobbing in the driver's seat for a few minutes, which was even worse, and my hands gripped the cement countertop so hard I thought I might crack it.

Eventually she left, and I was so mad at myself I nearly put a fist through the kitchen window.

Voices warred inside me.

Go get her back, you asshole.

Let her go. She's better off without you.

You love her. You'll be miserable without her.

So what? It's better than making her miserable.

Women like her don't have to give second chances, you know. Get yourself the fuck together and go after her.

I wanted to tear my hair out. Claw my eyes out. Shred the skin from my bones. I wanted to punish my body, castigate my brain for what it was making me think and feel. Even though I'd already been to the gym this morning, I went back and put myself through another grueling workout. Then I came back to the cabin, where everything reminded me of Skylar. The porch. The couch. The shower. The kitchen. The bedroom.

I made a sandwich but couldn't even eat it because I saw the honey sticks next to the peanut butter in the pantry. The thought of her giving her honey-kisses to some other guy split my chest in two. I stood staring out the sliding glass door onto the rain-soaked patio, recalling the night last spring when I'd bought the chairs and the next day when she'd watched me put them together. The hammock was down now, but I could still see her lying there, still feel the way her body felt on mine when we'd lain in it together last summer. I looked at the dock, where she'd first told me she loved me. Fuck, why couldn't I just be normal? Any other guy would have just bought the ring and proposed by now. A woman like her was one in a million.

My cell phone buzzed, and I pulled it from my pocket. It was Skylar's number.

Thank God. I didn't even hesitate before pressing Accept. Even if she just wanted to yell at me, at least I'd hear her voice.

"Fuck. I'm such an asshole," I croaked.

"What? Sebastian?"

My heart stopped. The voice was familiar, but it wasn't Skylar's. "Yes. Who is this?"

"It's Natalie."

Gray fog clouded my vision, and I steadied myself with one hand on the counter. Why was Natalie using Skylar's phone to call me? Was she so mad she didn't even want to hear my voice? Or had something happened to her? "What's going on? Is Skylar OK?"

"She's OK. But she had an accident."

"Oh my God." The room spun, and for a second I thought I might get sick. *I caused it. I caused it. This time it's real.* "A car accident?"

"No. She slipped and fell on some wet cement stairs outside a restaurant. She broke her wrist and hit her head pretty good, but she's fine now."

"Jesus." I grabbed a handful of my hair and tugged on it. *So it wasn't a car accident, but it was still your fault. She went to the restaurant alone and you should have been with her.* "Where is she?"

"She's at Munson. But she doesn't want to see you."

"What? Why?" *You know why, you stupid fuck.*

"I don't know. She didn't elaborate, and she's exhausted and loopy from the pain meds, but when I asked if I should call you, she said no, she didn't want to see you and that if I called you she was never speaking to me again."

"Fuck that. I'm coming." I looked around for my keys. I hated hospitals more than odd numbers, but nothing could keep me from her.

"No! Please don't." Her tone was desperate. "Look, I called you because I knew you'd want to know, and I'm guessing she'll eventually speak to me again after I tell her I did, but really—she's got a bad enough headache right now. Whatever's going on with you guys will have to get sorted out another time."

My throat was squeezed so tight I didn't know if I could even talk anymore. "OK. Thanks."

We hung up, and I considered my next move for less than two seconds.

Skylar was hurt. I needed to be near her.

Despite the rain, I drove fast, praying hard that Natalie had been truthful with me and that Skylar's injuries weren't worse than she claimed.

At Munson, I parked and raced into the lobby without even hesitating outside the doors. Looking around wildly, I spotted the info desk and charged up to it. Once I got Skylar's room information, I headed for the elevators, my stomach churning a bit at the hospital smell in the halls. *Forget that. It doesn't matter. The only thing that matters is her.* I forced myself to inhale deeply. Again, and again, and again. After a minute, one elevator door opened and Natalie stepped out.

"Sebastian." Her eyes went wide. "What are you doing here?"

I squared my shoulders. "You have to let me see her."

"She's finally sleeping. Please don't go up there now."

My posture deflated a little. "Are you sure she's OK?"

"Yes." She looked at me, chewing on her bottom lip. "You look awful. What's going on with you guys?"

"I fucked things up." I closed my eyes and breathed deeply, not sure why I'd just blurted that out to Skylar's sister but oddly relieved that I had. "I fucked things up and now she's hurt and it's my fault."

"What? She slipped and fell, Sebastian. She was wearing ridiculously high heels and it was raining. How can that be your fault?"

Tears formed and I pressed a thumb and two fingertips over my eyes, embarrassed. "It just is. I know it."

"Good grief. Come on." She took me by the elbow and turned me around. "Let's go get a cup of coffee. It won't be as good as mine, but maybe it's drinkable." I let her steer me down the hall and around two corners, then over to a table in the near empty cafeteria. Dejected, I sank into a chair. "Don't move," she said.

I sat with my head in my hands, and a few minutes later she came back with two steaming white styrofoam cups and set them on the table. God, could I drink out of a hospital styrofoam cup? My skin crawled. "Thanks."

"You're welcome." She sat across from me. "Now spill. What happened?"

I shrugged and stared at my coffee. Where did I even begin?

She was quiet a minute, and I could feel her eyes on me. "I hope you don't think she betrayed a confidence, but Skylar has mentioned your OCD to me."

"I figured. I know you're close."

She picked up her coffee and blew across its surface. "Does this have anything to do with that?"

I sighed, feeling completely defeated. "Yes."

More silence. "Do you have a therapist?"

"Yes. But I haven't been honest with him about my relationship with Skylar. And I've been avoiding him for a month."

"Why?"

I exhaled heavily. "Because when she told me she loved me, I relapsed, and I was too scared to admit it."

She tilted her head. "Scared of what? Don't you love her?"

I met her eyes. "Of course I love her. Look, I can't even begin to explain the fucked up circuitry in my brain, but suffice it to say, I thought I was protecting her by saying nothing. By doing the things I did." *Solid thinking there, asshole.*

Nodding slowly, she sipped her coffee. "What about now? Can you talk to him now?"

"I don't know. I don't know if he can help me." I swallowed hard against the bitter bile rising in my throat, so sick and tired of that voice in my head I wanted to scream. Why wouldn't it just leave me the fuck alone? "I don't know if anyone can help me."

"I'm sorry." She leaned forward, elbows on the table. "Because Skylar is crazy in love with you, you know. Every other word out of her mouth is your name. And I don't think she's going to let you go."

"I love her too. But she already left me, and she was right to do it."

"Says who?"

The voice in my head. "Me."

"You're right. That is fucked up." She sounded so much like Skylar, I looked up sharply. "Sorry if that's harsh, but I agree with you. I'm the first person to say I think Sky's a great catch, but she's a handful too. Ever tried to share a bathroom with her? Good grief, she's a slob. Makeup and hair shit everywhere. And her shoe collection—good grief! Those boxes! Good luck to any man who needs any closet space at all in her house."

My lips tipped up a little. "Yeah. She does have a lot of shoes."

"She's a cover hog too. Ever notice that?"

I had, but it didn't bother me. I'd subject myself to subzero temperatures before letting her be cold at night.

"And she's pretty and all but have you ever seen her funny little ears? They stick way out from her head like a monkey's."

I found myself smiling at a memory—Skylar surfacing after jumping into the lake the first time we went swimming together, hands over her ears. I thought they were adorable, of course, but she hated them. "Yeah. But I actually like them."

"What about the way she's so obsessed with wine now? I never thought I'd get bored with wine, but Jesus, if I have to listen to her talk about *vines* and *terroir* and *fruit on the palate* any more, I'm going to strangle her."

I straightened up, feeling the need to defend her. "She's dedicated to her new job. I love that about her."

"Well then, I'd suggest you try harder to get over feeling like you don't deserve her, because believe me, all she wants is you, and any man that can put up with her bathroom mess and her closet hogging and cover stealing and fruit-on-the-palating *and* the Nixon ears…" She shrugged. "Seems like you guys should make this work."

Miserable, I slumped back in my chair again and regarded Natalie. "Her faults are so small compared to mine. Mine drive us both crazy and they probably would for the rest of our lives."

She tilted her head from side to side. "Maybe. Guess you won't know until you try it. But nobody's perfect, Sebastian. Give yourself a break."

I sat there for a minute, my hands on the table, wondering what to do next. "She won't even talk to me."

She pressed her lips together. "She's being stubborn. Of course she wants to see you, she just won't say that. Her exact words were, 'Not until he gets his shit together. And I can't be the one to get it together for him.'"

I frowned. She was right about that—I had to fix this on my own, if I could. But I was so worried about her. "What about her injuries? They're not serious?"

"No. Like I said, a broken wrist and a bump on the noggin, that's all. Since she lost consciousness briefly, they're keeping her for observation, but she seems fine."

The thought of her slender wrist broken and a bump on her head infuriated and saddened me. I wished there was some way I could bear it all for her. "Is she in pain? Will her new insurance cover this? She just got benefits last month," I worried.

Natalie scrunched up her face as she set down her cup. "Yeah, we're waiting to hear. Our parents might have to help her out."

My hand shot out and I grabbed her arm. "Please let me pay for it. I want to. I want to take care of her." *Forever.*

Forever.

Forever.

Forever.

Forever.

Forever.

Forever.

I didn't even feel that bad about counting it out. I'd have kept going, to infinity, but Natalie shook her head. "She'll never let you."

I set my elbows on the table and buried my head in my hands. I had so much work to do. So much ground to regain.

Natalie touched my wrist. "Go see your therapist, Sebastian. And try again. She's worth it."

"She is worth it." I looked up at Natalie, totally sure of what I was saying. "She's the one."

chapter thirty-four

Skylar

I woke up to the sight of Natalie reading a magazine in the chair near my bed. "Hey," I croaked.

"Hey. You're up." She set her magazine aside. "How do you feel?"

I made a face, tried to shift positions. "Haven't been this sore since I fell off the mechanical bull. Achey. Wrist hurts." I lifted my left arm gingerly. "God, I'm such a klutz. This really sucks."

Natalie nodded sympathetically. "How's your head?"

"Hurts. But still attached." I tried to move my neck, which was stiff as hell. "How come you're not at work?"

"I had Michael open for me."

"Did you talk to Mia?"

"Yes. She and Lucas are both very worried about you and said not to concern yourself with anything at Abelard. I wouldn't be surprised if Mia came by here today, or by your house tomorrow, if they let you go. She wants to see you."

I nodded, but that hurt, so I just lay still and moaned. "Uuuuuuugh, why did I have to wear those damn expensive shoes?"

Natalie laughed ruefully. "It was probably a damn expensive fall. Think your insurance will cover it?"

I groaned. "I hope so."

"If it doesn't, Mom and Dad will help you. Mom will be here shortly." She was quiet for a second, fiddling with the hem of her hoodie. "Sebastian was here last night."

At the sound of his name, my breath caught. "He was? He hates hospitals!" For a moment, I was sad I'd been so adamant with Natalie about not seeing him. *He must have struggled to walk through those doors, but he did it. Maybe there's hope.*

"He offered to pay your hospital bill."

"No. I don't want his charity." The offer was sweet, and so like him, but I'd never take him up on it. We were broken up right now, as far as I was concerned. The thought made my throat hurt. My chest. My heart. Everything.

"He was very upset. He wanted to see you."

Carefully, I turned my head to look at my sister. I could tell from her voice there was more. "What else did he say?"

She shrugged. "Not much. Just that he'd messed up. He seemed to agree with you about getting his shit together."

"Really? He talked to you about it?" Closing my eyes, I exhaled, scared to let myself be too optimistic but wondering if maybe the things I said last night had gotten through to him. The truth was, I didn't want to be without him in my life, and I'd do what it took to help him—but he had to *let* me.

"I think he was going to talk to his therapist. He said he would."

"He did? Thank God." Relief eased some of my pain, at least the emotional grief. Going to therapy was the best first step. My eyes filled. "He's so hard on himself. And I was really hard on him. But I love him—and he doesn't understand how frustrating it is for me to see him struggling and not know what's in his head."

"I don't know what's in his head, Skylar. But I know what's in his heart—you are."

My throat closed up completely, and my head began to throb with the need to cry. I closed my eyes and the tears slipped down my cheeks. "Was I wrong to walk out? Oh God, I'm awful. I should have stayed with him. Then I wouldn't have fallen. It's a sign I'm a horrible person after all."

Natalie stood, grabbed a tissue from the bedside table and dabbed at my cheeks. "Stop. I don't think you were wrong to leave. In my opinion, he needed that wake up call. And loving someone doesn't mean you have to love everything they do. But it does mean you forgive them a little more often, a little more easily."

I sniffed. "I once told him I'd give him all the chances he needed, and he called me a fool."

"We're all fools for love, aren't we?" Her voice was wistful.

I looked up at her. "Things aren't any better with Dan?" Last I'd heard, he'd admitted to a flirtation at the office, but nothing more.

"I don't know. I guess they are. He claims the fling or whatever it was is over and begged for another chance, and we do have a lot of history. I don't want to just throw that away." She sat on the edge of the bed and chewed her lip a moment. "But I also don't want history to be the *only* reason to give him another chance. When I see you talk about Sebastian, when I listened to him talk about you, when I saw the expression on his face when he said you were the one, I—"

"Wait, what? What did he say?" I didn't mean to interrupt Natalie's thought, and I did care deeply about her feelings, but I couldn't just let her gloss over that thing about *the one*. Had I even heard her right? My head was so foggy.

"He said you were the one." Her face contorted with worry. She put her hands on her head. "Oh no, I hope I didn't just blow what was supposed to be a really nice moment between the two of you by telling you that. He's never said that to you before?"

"No," I said slowly, my heart beating fast. Wasn't *the one* kind of a forever thing? "He doesn't believe in the one. Plus it's an odd number. He hates those."

"What?" She dropped her hands, her expression confused.

"Never mind. Just one of the quirks that makes Sebastian who he is." But right then, I actually found his number quirks kind of endearing. "So he really said that?"

She nodded. "Yes. He definitely said, 'She's the one.' But you can't tell him I told you first!" Her eyes were wide and panicked.

"It's OK. I won't." I pursed my lips. "But he better fucking say it to me eventually. Or I'll be the one that got away." Inside, my heart was tripping over itself—the one! the one! the one!

Natalie laughed. "Somehow, I doubt that. Give him a little time, sis. He wants to make things right."

A nurse popped in to take my vitals, so Natalie got off the bed. "Don't go, Nat. I want to hear the rest of what you were saying about Dan."

"Nothing more to tell, really. I suppose I'm just envious of the way you and Sebastian feel about each other. But all relationships take work, I know that. Maybe we just need to work a little harder." She dismissed the topic of her relationship with a shrug and a smile that didn't quite reach her eyes, and sat on the chair again. If I hadn't been so exhausted, I'd have pressed her to say more, but between the pain and the drugs, I was beat.

I lay back and let the nurse poke and prod me, and at first I had my eyes closed but I swear I could feel her staring at my face. When I opened one eye, stare was confirmed.

"Are you..." she began hesitantly, "by any chance... from that reality show?"

Oh, God. Really? After all this time, a Save a Horse fan? I squeezed my eyes shut again for a second. "Yes."

"I thought so!" Her reaction was so joyful I thought for sure she had me confused with another contestant.

"I'm Skylar Nixon," I said, as if she couldn't read the medical chart on the door.

"I know!" She rocked back on her heels gleefully. "My friend and I loved you on that show! You were the only fun thing about it! That time you threw the drink on Whiney Whitney? Priceless!"

I blinked at her. Was this for real? Or was this my brain on drugs? "Seriously?"

"Yes." Smiling, she finished up with my blood pressure. "We were so bummed when you left."

"But I was so horrible."

She shrugged. "It was fun to watch, though. Who wants to watch a bunch of people being nice to each other?"

"That's what I told her," put in Natalie.

Sighing, I shook my head. "Whatever. I'm just glad it's behind me. But thanks." I gave the young nurse a smile. "I appreciate it."

Some time during the afternoon, I was cleared for release and sent home with lots of pain meds and instructions to take it easy. My mother took me back to her house and insisted I stay there, even though I was a little desperate for some alone time. But it was nice to be fussed over and catered to, I'll admit. She made spaghetti and meatballs for me, which I ate on a tray table while snuggled in a cozy spot on the couch. Jillian came over with honey sticks, chocolate chip cookies, and my favorite shampoo and conditioner, and after dinner she helped me wash and dry my hair, then gave me a foot massage on the couch while I ate sweets and watched a Tiger game on TV with my dad.

I checked my phone only once and saw messages from Mia and Kelly Pryce, who must have heard about my fall from Sebastian, but there was nothing from him. Disappointed, I put my phone away and tried to enjoy the time with my family, despite my aching head and sore arm.

But before I fell into a drug-induced deep sleep that night in my old bed, I fretted that he'd changed his mind about me and gone back to thinking that a relationship was just too much work, even if I was the one.

chapter thirty-five

Sebastian

"I've been lying to you."

Ken took my characteristic bluntness in stride, regarding me silently, waiting for me to go on. If he was alarmed, he didn't show it, nor did his expression betray any surprise at what I'd announced. He had to know something was up—I'd never asked him to come in on a Saturday before.

"And I canceled all of last month's appointments to avoid facing the truth." Perched at the edge of the couch, I slid my hands up and down the tops of my legs, anxious about making this confession but knowing it had to be done.

"I was worried about that." He looked at me intently. "Did you have a relapse?"

"Yes. For months now, I've been backsliding."

He reached for his notepad and clicked his ballpoint pen. "Intrusive thoughts?"

"Yes. And the rituals. And anxiety, the worst anxiety I've ever felt."

He made a note and flipped back a few pages. "Months, you said? About when did this start?"

"August twenty-fifth."

Ken looked up. "What triggered it?"

"Skylar told me she loved me." For a second, I blamed Skylar for telling me she loved me for the first time on an odd day. Didn't she know nothing good happened to me on odd days?

"And what about that was traumatic for you?"

I stared at my hands on my legs. "The weight of it. The responsibility."

He made another note. "Tell me about the responsibility of loving someone."

God, didn't he understand me at all? "It's not the responsibility of loving someone. Loving her is easy. It's effortless." I took a breath and tried to put into words how I felt. "It's the responsibility that comes with letting someone love *you*. It means you're beholden to that love. You have to sustain that love."

"You have to deserve that love."

Aha. He did understand me.

"Yes," I said quietly. "And no matter how much my heart feels for her, my head just keeps convincing me I'm doomed to disappoint her, or worse."

"You will disappoint her, Sebastian. That's human nature. In any close relationship, there will be hurt and disappointment." He set his notepad aside. "But there is also forgiveness. Redemption. No one expects you to be perfect."

"Except for myself."

"You're going to have to let that go, Sebastian.

We all know what it feels like to want to be a better person for someone, but aiming for perfection is a mistake." He shifted in his chair, sat up taller. "Think back to when I first started seeing you. You set goals. You made progress. Things have changed now that you've fallen in love, but there's no reason why we can't adjust those goals, adjust your therapy to help you. You respond well to therapy, Sebastian. You're disciplined and tough on yourself and determined. Let's use those qualities to help you get back on track."

I nodded, glad to hear his faith in me.

"Now tell me what happened in the last month."

Sitting back on the couch, I described my last few months to him in detail, explaining how falling more in love with Skylar had triggered the faulty wiring in my brain to convince me the rituals would protect her. "Instead they drove her away," I said. "She accused me of doing it on purpose, and I wonder if she was right. Maybe I wasn't doing it to protect her—maybe I was doing it to make her leave so that it would be less painful. I'd have control over it, you know?"

Ken nodded. "You'd be alone by choice then, rather than be abandoned."

"Right." I exhaled, closing my eyes for a moment. "You know, I spent all last night wondering if those shrinks were right about my issues stemming from my mother's death. Deep down, am I just scared of being left alone? Did I isolate myself in school because I was afraid to make friends? Did I choose Diana because I knew subconsciously there was never any danger of losing my whole heart to her?

And did my feelings for Skylar trigger this relapse because I swam out past that danger?"

"Those are good, introspective questions, Sebastian."

I sighed, rubbing the back of my neck. "But then I wonder if that's all bullshit and it's just neurological, not psychological."

Ken nodded. "Also a valid question."

I pinned him with a stare. "I need answers, Ken. I need help. I don't want to lose her. Tell me what to do."

• • •

Together, Ken and I discussed strategies for getting back on track, some that had been successful for me in the past, and some that were new to me. He told me to schedule an appointment with my doctor to see about changing up some of my meds and specifically asked me to mention being treated for depression as well as anxiety. I promised I would, and I meant it. Then he asked how serious I was about Skylar.

"Serious," I said. "In all of this, the one thing I have no doubt about is the way I feel about her."

Ken smiled. "Perfect. So let's bring her in here and talk about what she can do to help."

Feeling optimistic, I left his office building, putting up the collar of my coat against the cold. I was dying to run right to Skylar and apologize and tell her I was doing everything possible to get better fast, but I thought it might be better to spend some time doing some serious self-reflection, setting new goals for myself, and pondering the best way to show her that I wanted to make a life with her, if she'd give me another chance.

When I got back to the cabin, I texted her instead. **I miss you and I'm thinking of you every minute. If I'm silent for a while, it isn't to shut you out. It's to get well enough to let you in, and never let you go. I love you. I'll always love you.**

chapter thirty-six

Skylar

It nearly killed me not to call him the following week, but I knew he needed this time to work things out on his own. I answered his text with a simple I love you too and waited for him to come to me. I missed him terribly, but I was also glad he was taking this seriously. If he'd rushed right to my side, I might be tempted to think he wasn't taking enough time to think carefully about what he wanted for the future.

I knew what I wanted. Finally.

The days that Sebastian took for himself, I took for myself too, reflecting on what I'd accomplished this summer and where I was headed. I felt proud of the direction my life had taken: I had a job I loved and I was good at it; I had big-picture plans to save up the money to buy my own condo like my sisters had done; I made rent payments to my parents even though they said they didn't want them, I made a car payment each month *on time*, and I still had some left over for nice shoes. (Note to self: Do Not Wear Leopard Heels In Rain.)

Maybe I didn't have a wedding ring or kids like some people my age, but I had fallen madly in love…that was a good start, wasn't it? But the more days went by without hearing from him, the more I worried he'd changed his mind about me. His note had said I'll always love you, and in my mind I started to hear a sort of final, tragic ring to the words…like maybe we wouldn't get our happy ending but we'd always have last summer. Each night I went to sleep alone, I fretted and prayed and hoped and missed him. *Please don't let me miss him forever. Please don't let me regret anything. Please bring him back to me.*

And then one shivering cold evening in early December, I came home from work to find an envelope taped to the guest house door with my name on it. The writing was Sebastian's. Surprised, I looked around but saw no one around and heard only the wind gusting through the orchard. A few snow flurries were starting to fall from the inky sky as I pulled the envelope off the door and hustled inside, kicking it shut behind me.

Without even taking off my coat, I threw my gloves onto the counter and slid my finger under the flap. Inside were two sheets of notebook paper folded into thirds. Hands trembling, I opened them up. They had spiral fringe on the left as if he'd written them in his journal and ripped them out. The top one was a letter.

My sweet Skylar,

Sorry this letter isn't on nicer paper—you deserve beautiful things, and I promise to give them to you. But this paper suits me, I think. A little rough around the edges, but the words are heartfelt.

Thank you for giving me the time and space I needed to recover. I promise you, I have used it wisely. Not a day (and certainly not a night) went by that I didn't miss you, but the issues I had to work through meant focusing fully on myself, mind, soul, and body, something I never want to do when you're around.

(Your body is much more fun to focus on.)

I've learned a lot about myself during the last month, and feel stronger than I ever have. Strong enough to admit how wrong I was to close myself off from you. Strong enough to see how I let myself be the victim of my doubt and fear. Strong enough to realize what I need to do next.

Can I please have another chance?

This cabin, this heart, this life feels empty without you.

Love,
Sebastian

P.S. I wrote something for you.

The words blurred as my eyes filled, and I sniffed as I slipped the letter behind the second page.

Some Sort of Happy

Skylar
My mind is constantly ticking
with doubts
tick did I lock the door tick did I turn off the
stove tick did I check the outlets tick did I step on a
crack tick did I wash my hands enough times tick did
I turn off the lights tick did I walk a straight line tick
did I take the right number of steps tick did I turn off
the television on an even channel tick did I close the
book on an even page tick did I start the car on an
even minute tick
what if I didn't
what if I didn't
what if I didn't
I don't know.

But I know
you wore a gray sweater
and had a crumbling leaf in your hair
the day we had a chemistry test
before it started you turned and asked,
"Is sodium hydroxide an acid or a base?"

It was the first time you ever whispered to me.
(I liked that it was eight words.)

I don't know why eight
is better than seven or nine or twenty-one.
I don't know how many times I've told you
I love you
But I know that number is all wrong
because it isn't enough

Your love may never silence the ticking
but I would trade silence for your laughter,
calm for your storms,
tranquility for your madness,
the beautiful chaos of stars

The papers shook in my hands, and tears dripped off my lashes. I needed to see him. Tonight. Slipping the letter and poem back into the envelope, I tucked it into my purse and raced out the door, yanking it shut behind me.

• • •

The drive to the cabin had never seemed so endless, not even the first night we'd been together, Sebastian's hand sliding up my thigh. At the thought of his touch, every muscle in my lower body tightened. It had been so long. Had he missed my body as much as I'd missed his? The snow fell a little harder as I drove up the highway, and I forced myself to slow down and be safe.

As I pulled up at the cabin, my heart pounded furiously. Lights were on—that had to mean he was home, right? Sebastian would *never* leave home without turning the lights off. I almost laughed as I ran up the porch steps, careful not to slip in the dusting of snow.

He pulled the door open before I could knock, and my breath caught at the sight of him. He'd gotten a haircut, and he wore jeans and a light blue sweater. His scruff was short and neat, and he looked rested and healthy and gorgeous. Heart pounding, I threw my arms around him, and he laughed, squeezing me tight and lifting me right off the ground.

"Hi," he said, his voice muffled in my hair. "You got my letter."

"Yes. Thank you so much. I love your words. I love you." I inhaled the scent of him—there was smoke and wood on his skin, like he'd built a fire. "God, I missed you."

"I missed you too. I hoped you would come, but I didn't want to pressure you. Just because I was ready didn't mean you were." He pulled back just enough to kiss me, and the feel of his lips against mine was so thrilling I had no idea if my feet were on the ground or not. When the kiss grew deeper, he backed into the cabin, where I could hear a fire crackling in the fireplace, and pushed the door shut behind me.

"I'm ready. I'm so ready." Panting, I released him from my barnacle grip and started unbuttoning my coat. "Now take off your clothes."

He smiled. "I was going to say let's talk first, but—" His eyes widened and swept down my body after I threw my coat off, taking in the silk blouse, pencil skirt and heels. "Fuck talking."

One by one articles of clothing came off and were flung aside, and we tumbled naked onto the rug in front of the fireplace. I lay back as Sebastian knelt between my thighs.

"What do you want first?" he asked, his voice low and playful. "My tongue? My fingers? My cock?" He began stroking himself, sliding his erection through his fingers. "What did you miss the most?"

"Oh God, everything," I breathed. "I missed hearing you and seeing you and feeling you—every part of you."

"Which part first? You have to tell me or I won't let you have it." He rubbed the tip of his cock against one pale inner thigh.

Gahhhhhh, he was so hot! For the rest of our lives his quick mood switches might drive me batty outside the bedroom but inside it, they were like gasoline on the fire.

"Your cock," I managed, the fire hissing and sparking. "Give me your cock."

"Good girl. I'll be gentle," he said, giving me just the tip and then smearing my wetness up and down my pussy. He stopped and met my eyes. "At first."

My heart pounded hard as he slid inside me and then pulled out again, teasing me by giving me a little more each time but never enough. Between each tortuous thrust, he played with my nipples, licking and sucking and biting them, pinching them into hard little peaks that tingled with lust.

"Fuck. If I wasn't recovering from a broken wrist, I'd get rough with you right now," I panted, my good hand pounding the rug, the injured arm over my head. "Beat your ass for tormenting me."

He pushed in a little further. "Poor baby."

"Please," I begged, bringing my good hand to his ass. "I need you there. I need you inside me. All the way."

Finally, he slid all the way in, so deep I nearly cried with relief. "Like this?"

"Yes, yes..." I pulled him into me, widening my

knees. God, it was like he was *made* for my body. Every hot, thick inch of him filled me with such sublime perfection, I couldn't even breathe for how good it felt. His hips moved faster, thrusting hard and deep, and my core muscles started to contract. "I'm gonna come," I whimpered. "So hard, so hard. Come with me. Come inside me…" I moaned as my climax hit, and he growled low and long, grinding against me, his cock throbbing and thickening as my core pulsed around it.

He collapsed onto me, pressing his lips to my sweaty forehead.

"God, you feel so good," I whispered, closing my eyes. "Tell me you're OK."

"I'm OK." He lifted his head and looked down at me. "But I wasn't before. And I need to apologize for not being honest with you. It was a mistake."

"Apology accepted."

He smiled. "You're too easy on me."

"I love you. And I once told you I'd give you all the chances you needed." I took a breath. "Can you…tell me what happened?"

"Yes." He rolled to his side and propped his head in his hand. As he talked, he played with my hair, twining it through his fingers.

"When I first saw you again, I was doing pretty well, I thought. I'd convinced myself that a solitary life was the only way I'd know peace, and peace seemed like the right goal. But then there you were." He smiled. "Just as beautiful as ever, and those feelings I used to have for you came rushing back as if they'd never left."

I blushed. "You hid it well, at least at first."

"I had to. You terrified me. I felt strong for the first time in years, resigned to a life alone, and then here's this beautiful angel right in front of me— *kissing* me. Touching me. Accepting me." He shook his head. "I found myself wondering what if…"

"Me too," I said. "It wasn't only you."

"And the sex." He exhaled, closing his eyes. "The fucking sex."

"I know," I whispered, heat prickling across my skin. "It scared me too, how good it was."

"I was able to be myself with you, afraid of nothing. It was so incredible. After that, it was a constant battle between my heart and my head—my heart telling me I'd always been destined to be with you, and my head refusing to let me believe I was worthy of it. I'd never brought anything but pain to women, and I wasn't sure I was capable of letting you in."

"But you did," I said softly. "I felt it."

He nodded. "I did. But the more I loved you, the more I feared the loss of you—when had I ever been able to hold on to happiness? I didn't know how it would happen, but in my mind I always knew you'd leave, or something would happen to you, and it would be my fault."

"Oh, Sebastian. I wish you'd have said something."

"I couldn't. Especially not once you told me you loved me. Then I felt this need to protect you even more, but what you needed protecting from was me. I started engaging in all my old rituals, stopped going to therapy."

My heart ached for him. "I saw it happening. But

I didn't know what to do about it. And some days were so good."

"They were." He looked down at my hair twisting through his fingers. "And I should have talked to you on one of those days—I was just too scared. But the messed up thing is that you were right, you know."

"About what?"

"That subconsciously I knew I was driving you away with my behavior and continued to do it because then at least I'd be prepared. I wouldn't experience another sudden, shocking loss and feel blindsided and abandoned."

"*Another* loss?" It hit me. "Your mom."

"Maybe." He kept looking at his hand, and in the firelight his sea-glass green eyes were shiny. "I'm still working through that. I don't think it *caused* my OCD, but therapy is helping me to see how my fear of loss and abandonment has caused me a lot of anxiety and grief, and maybe that manifests as OCD related behaviors. Who knows?" He sighed. "For as much as science has taught us about the brain, some things are still a mystery. But I don't think a kid loses his mom suddenly and tragically and remains unaffected—and when I look at the way I chose isolation and emotional distance from people, it makes sense. And this probably sounds crazy, but I felt like I deserved the loneliness. Like a punishment. Whether it was penance for my mom's death, my violent thoughts, my cold treatment of women, my breakup with Diana...there was always something in my head I needed to atone for. But I don't want to be alone anymore. I want to be with you."

My throat closed up and I threw my arms around his neck, pressing my body against his. "You aren't," I sobbed. "I love you and I won't let you be alone. You deserve to be happy, Sebastian."

He gathered me in his arms, lying back and letting me weep against his chest. "Thank you. I can't say there won't be setbacks, and I'll tell you right now there will be good days and bad, but I promise to talk about it with you."

Nodding, I blubbered for a solid ten minutes as he stroked my hair and rubbed my back. I don't even know why I was crying so hard—relief? Sadness for the child he'd been? The man he was now? Laying my cheek on his chest, I listened to his heart beat and vowed he would never know loneliness again.

"Will you come to therapy with me?" Sebastian asked once my sobs had subsided.

"Of course," I said, picking my head up to smile at him. "I'd love that."

"Good." He wiped my tears from under one eye with his thumb. "Because this is it for me, Skylar. You're the love of my life."

"Really?"

"Yes. I've spent nearly all my days being dominated by doubt, unable to trust myself—tortured by what my mind says and what my heart knows. But for once, I feel—I *know*—this is right. You're the one." He smiled. "And that is the only time the number one will ever sound good to me."

I laughed. "I want to be the one."

"Do you?" He arched one brow. "Because you know what it means to be my one."

"Tell me."

"It means being the one I'll kiss good morning and good night—twice." He grinned. "It means being the one who'll have to hold my hand when we fly off to our villa in France." At my gasp, his smile widened. "It means the forever things, Skylar."

"I want them." I scooted up and pressed a kiss to his lips. "I want them all."

He flipped me onto my back again and looked down at me. "Then live with me."

My heart stopped. "What?"

"Stay here. Live with me."

"Are you serious?"

"Yes. I'm one hundred percent sure about this, and one hundred is a good number."

I laughed softly as tears filled my eyes again. "You keep making me cry tonight. What's with that?"

"I don't want you to cry. Ever again." He kissed my eyelids.

"They're happy tears, Sebastian. Of course I'll live with you."

"Good." He scooted down to rest his head on my chest and we lay together, the fire warming our skin, our breathing slow and deep. "Happy tears are good, I can handle those. And if there are sad tears, I'll handle those too. I'll take care of you, Skylar."

"And I'll take care of you." I closed my eyes and inhaled, loving the weight of his head on my chest, the warmth of his skin against mine, the promise of hope in the air. "Forever."

epilogue

Skylar

"Are you ready?"

"I think so." His face told me what a lie that was, but I'd budgeted plenty of time for his nerves into today's itinerary. After living with him for the past two months, I knew to allot extra time for pretty much anything we did outside the house. He was getting much better about checking, but today was new ground for him.

"Come on. You've got this." I tugged on his hand, but he didn't move. "It's not like we're getting on the plane yet, Sebastian. This is the airport entrance." As I talked, I took his elbow and ushered him gently through the automatic doors. "There are nice people in there who are going to look at our boarding passes and tell us what gate to sit at, and some other nice people are going to overcharge us for coffee and tell us to have a nice flight, and then some more nice people are going to show us how to use a seat belt and thank us for flying with them today."

By the time I'd finished my soothing little speech, we were inside the terminal.

"See? You're here, and you're fine," I said triumphantly.

"Now what?" he asked shakily.

"Now we'll check in and find our gate. We don't even have any luggage to check, so it will be nice and easy. OK?"

He took a deep breath. "OK."

"Good. Because this little Valentine's weekend jaunt was your idea and you paid for it, so it would be a damn shame if I had to give your ticket to someone else."

"Don't you dare." He caught me around the waist and squeezed. "How long is the flight again?"

I kissed his cheek. "One hour and ten minutes, and I will talk to you the entire time."

Some color returned to his face as he smiled. "I have no doubt."

I pulled out our boarding passes, which I'd printed at work, and we got in line to check in. Sebastian seemed more relaxed until we were told that the flight was leaving from gate three.

"Stop worrying," I told him, taking his hand again. "The gate number does not matter."

We located gate three, grabbed five dollar cups of coffee, and chose seats near the window. The weather was bleak and dreary, and I was *so* looking forward to getting away. Not that the Chicago weather would be any better, but it would be fun to stay in a luxury hotel together, shop the Magnificent Mile, have dinner in a gourmet French restaurant or maybe a cozy little Italian place. Honestly, I didn't care what we did—what mattered most was that we'd be there together. Our first vacation.

"Hey." I tipped my head onto his shoulder. "Thanks for this. I know you don't really want to do it."

"That plane looks small. Are you sure it's regulation size?" He squinted out the window, his right knee bouncing continuously.

I sighed. "Yes, dear."

"Let me see the boarding passes again."

"No," I said, lovingly but firmly. "You've looked at them a hundred times. You already know we're in an even row. Row two, first class."

His brow furrowed. "Are you sure?"

"You booked the tickets, Sebastian. Now let's talk about what we're going to do this weekend. How about massages?" I tried my best to distract him from his own thoughts, but he didn't make it easy.

When he tried to retrace his steps down the tarmac because it hadn't felt right the first time, I grabbed his hand and refused to let go.

When he took out the pamphlet explaining how a water landing works, I took it away from him and shoved it back in my seat pocket.

When he gingerly eyed the arm rest where our tray tables were tucked away, I brandished a package of antibacterial wipes. "Come at me, babe. I've already thought of everything."

He looked around. "There's eleven people sitting in this section. Someone needs to sit in that empty chair."

From my bag I pulled out a Barbie doll I'd dug out of a trunk in my mom's attic. "Now there's twelve in here. A nice even dozen." I stuck her legs in the seat back pocket in from of him.

"Oh for fuck's sake." He grabbed the doll and shoved her back in my bag. "I'm not that desperate." Cracking a smile, he leaned back in his seat, although he kept flexing and fisting his fingers in his lap.

"Hey. It's going to be fine." I stilled one of his hands by placing mine over it. "Say it."

"It's going to be fine," he repeated quietly, eyes closing.

I gave him a quick kiss on the cheek. "Now let's say it together eight times."

He opened his eyes and smiled at me for real. "God, you're adorable. We don't have to do that."

"You sure? I don't mind, if it will make you feel better. I know you're doing this for me."

"I'm doing this for us." He lifted my hand to his lips. "And the only thing I need to feel good is you next to me."

My stomach fluttered. "You'll always have me."

"Say it again, quick." He grinned sheepishly. "Two is still better than one."

"You'll always have me." I poked his leg. "Jeez, Sebastian, if we ever have kids, you're going to want twins every time," I teased.

"It's funny you say that." He took my hand in his, and suddenly I was very aware of him playing with my ring finger. "I've been thinking about it. About a family."

"Yeah?" I swallowed hard. "Me too." Being around the happy Fournier family had gotten to me over the last few months. I wanted that with Sebastian, and I thought I might be ready for the next step, but I didn't want to rush him.

"Maybe we can talk about the future a little bit this weekend?" he asked.

I nodded, awestruck by the turn this conversation had taken. "I'd like that."

He played with all my fingers. "You know, this is the first time in my life that thinking about the future doesn't mean dreading it. We're going to be happy together, aren't we?"

I smiled, squeezing his hand. "Say it again, quick."

Leaning toward me, he pressed his lips to mine before whispering softly against them. "Marry me."

the end

note from the author...

This book and the character of Sebastian were inspired by several things: the heartbreakingly raw and moving performance of "OCD" by poet/writer Neil Hilborn (please look him up, watch the live performance, like him on Facebook...I'm in awe of him), the song "Creep" by Radiohead (listen to the original and the cover by Hailey Reinhart of Scott Bradlee's Postmodern Jukebox), and my own life experience loving someone who struggles with anxiety. But how does a writer of romantic comedy take on something like Obsessive Compulsive Disorder, especially in the male love interest, do justice to its sufferers, and yet still write a lighthearted romance? I tried very hard to be true to the harsh realities of OCD, which is nothing like what I thought it was, and still write a compelling, sexy character, who is so much more than his anxiety. My heart goes out to anyone who suffers from OCD. Love cannot cure you, but I hope you find it with someone wonderful, and it brings you peace, hope, and happiness—you deserve it.

For more information on OCD, visit https://iocdf.org/

acknowledgments

To my family, I am so lucky to have the forever things with you. I love you so much.

To the team that makes it possible for me to put pretty books into the world: Tom Barnes, Cait Greer, Tamara Mataya, Angie Owens. I'm so grateful.

To Paula Erwin, for reading and sharing thoughts with me, especially for getting into Sebastian's head. This book is so much better because of you!

To Danielle, whose gorgeous poetry always inspires me. THANK YOU for letting me pilfer words and riff off your ideas.

To Linda Russell, for making me come out of the cave and talk about my books. You're awesome.

To Melissa Gaston, I don't know how I did anything without you! Never leave me.

To Kayti and Sierra and Laurelin, without whom there would be no Melanie Harlow, because you have talked me off the ledge so many times. Thank you for believing, even when I don't.

To the authors who have been so generous with their time and advice and experience, especially Laurelin Paige, Lauren Blakely, Geneva Lee, Corinne Michaels, M. Pierce, and Claire Contreras. I've learned so much from you, and I'm so lucky to call you my friends.

To the ladies of TWS, The NAturals, The Order, FYW and especially Melanie Harlow Books, thanks for never letting me feel alone in this endeavor! You make me smile every day.

Finally, thank you readers and bloggers for reading and talking about books you love, especially The Dirty Laundry girls, The Literary Gossip, Fiction Fangirls, The Rock Stars of Romance, True Story Book Blog, Vilma's Vixens, Schmexy Girls, Aestas Book Blog, Shameless Book Club, Shayna Renee's Spicy Reads, Short and Sassy Book Blurbs... None of this would be possible without you!

about the author

Melanie Harlow likes her heels high, her hair pink, and her history with the naughty bits left in. In addition to the HAPPY CRAZY LOVE series, she's the author of the FRENCHED series (contemporary romance) and the SPEAK EASY duet (historical romance). She writes from her home outside of Detroit, where she lives with her husband, two daughters, and one insane rabbit.

connect with melanie harlow

Website: www.melanieharlow.com

Facebook:
www.facebook.com/AuthorMelanieHarlow

Fan Group:
www.facebook.com/groups/351191341756563/

Twitter: @MelanieHarlow2

Email: melanieharlowwrites@gmail.com

Pinterest: www.pinterest.com/melanieharlow2/

Tumblr: melanieharlow.tumblr.com/

Goodreads: www.goodreads.com/melanieharlow

also by melanie harlow

The HAPPY CRAZY LOVE Series...
SOME SORT OF HAPPY
SOME SORT OF CRAZY
SOME SORT OF LOVE (coming Feb 2016)

The FRENCHED Series...
FRENCHED
YANKED
The Wedding Night (Mia and Lucas)
FORKED
FLOORED

The SPEAK EASY Duet

THE TANGO LESSON

Made in United States
Orlando, FL
25 January 2023

29046919R10192